FRIENDS IN FUNCHAL

FRIENDS IN FUNCHAL

KG Fleury

The Book Guild Ltd

First published in Great Britain in 2022 by
The Book Guild Ltd
Unit E2 Airfield Business Park,
Harrison Road, Market Harborough,
Leicestershire. LE16 7UL
Tel: 0116 2792299
www.bookguild.co.uk
Email: info@bookguild.co.uk
Twitter: @bookguild

Typeset in 11pt Adobe Jenson Pro

Printed and bound in the UK by TJ Books LTD, Padstow, Cornwall

ISBN 978 1915122 322

British Library Cataloguing in Publication Data.
A catalogue record for this book is available from the British Library.

Dedicated to Jenny Olney

ACKNOWLEDGEMENTS

Com os meus sinceros agradecimentos aos meus amigos no Funchal.

Tânia Andrade	Tânia Oliveira
Ricardo Arraiol	Diogo Ornelas
Luísa Clara	Kevin Ospina
Diogo Faria	Carlos Passos
Laura Freitas	Paulo Rodrigues
Pedro Freitas	Cláudio Sá
Gennadiy Goryachok	Jorge Sá
Edward Kassab	Joselino Santos
Carlos Macedo	Márcia Torres
Nuno Melo e Sousa	Nico Vieira

FOREWORD

The main subjects, locations and events of this book are real. They have been researched both here and overseas. Characteristics, conversations and some situations are, however, a combination of this research and educated imagination.

KG Fleury
Funchal

1

Doctor Robert Willan was scared. Scared like a child afraid of water as he lurched in the small rowed boat clutching his portmanteau as if it were a lifebuoy. Scared as an adult entering a new stage of his life in a new land.

As the clear water changed to a soup of debris, the boat shuddered towards the pebbles and sea-drift of the shoreline. Willan did not notice the panorama of the hills surrounding Funchal; he was focussed on the lone gentleman striding as if to meet the boat, hopefully his rescuer. The childish fear left him as, assisted by the two oarsmen, he stumbled ashore, declining their offer to carry his case.

Willan stood still on a large level plank, supported at each elbow by the oarsmen. They had correctly resisted his urge to continue forward; their strong grip prevented him falling as his legs wobbled and buckled. The lone gentleman approached. He stopped about two paces in front of Willan and bowed deferentially. At this, Willan broke free of his supporters, switched his case to his left hand and crossed to the man, his right hand extended in greeting. The man took his hand and shook it firmly but did not release his grip as Willan was still unsteady.

"Good morning," said the man. "I am Rodrigo Torres. I represent the Gordon family and the Quinta do Til where you will be staying." He continued his obviously prepared address. "I spoke to Captain Ashton of the *Alligator* yesterday, soon after you had anchored. He told me of the difficulties of your journey, but you have surmounted the bad weather and avoided Napoleon's fleet. I am here to welcome you to Madeira and to assist you throughout your stay".

Willan pulled back his hand and stood firm. Only then did he realise that the oarsmen were already rowing back to the ship, his home of the last fifty days.

"Ah, you have recovered your balance. Shall we proceed? Your effects are already at the Quinta," said Torres, and without awaiting a reply snatched Willan's case; they set off slowly along the planks towards what appeared to be a road. Only a few moments later and after crossing a small wall via an old wooden staircase of sorts, they reached what Willan considered to be land. "We must wait here for our carriage," said Torres.

Willan leant against the wall. He had recovered his case. He was wearing, as he always wore, a long black woollen coat, black woollen knee breeches and a black woollen waistcoat. He wore plain black shoes and white stockings. His high-necked white shirt was fastened with a bow at the neck. He never wore a hat, preferring to raise the collar of his coat if the weather demanded it, and his white hair was swept back and tied with a small black ribbon. His draining illness and the arduous sea voyage had shrunken him slightly within his clothes; he was pale, bony and one-dimensional. This sombre outlook was, however, outweighed by his genuine smile and keen eyes showing his true character: a kind, gentle man of even temperament.

Torres presented quite a different picture. He filled his clothes well without being fat. He shone from top to bottom; his highly polished brown and black riding boots met his mustard-coloured linen breeches at the knee. A finely tailored grey tail coat barely covered his green satin waistcoat which shimmered in the morning sunshine. A plain white shirt completed the outfit. Nothing adorned his short, thick, black hair.

"Here comes our transport now," said Torres as he turned to the left and looked directly at an approaching pair of oxen led by a small boy. The boy looked only eight or nine years old and wore dirty white linen clothes between his loose brown leather boots and leather cap. He carried a small stick. The oxen were yoked to a sledge. The heavy wooden runners contrasted with the lighter carriage upon it. Behind the sledge, hidden until now by the partially curtained canopy, came a man, possibly the boy's father. He was identically dressed but carrying a larger stick in his right hand and a bundle of rags in his left. Torres, who had known this arrival might disconcert Willan, began to explain.

"Sadly, our cobbled tracks and steep inclines do not always allow the use of horse-drawn carriages. The best way to travel is by horseback, but it is clear that, until you have prospered in our warm climate, it would not be safe for you to ride. Please climb aboard. I am sure you will enjoy our little pleasure trip." Willan stepped into the carriage, sat facing forwards and placed his case at his side, still gripping the handle. Torres sat opposite, framed by the rear quarters of the heavy animals. He spoke loudly in Portuguese to the man with the stick who, in turn, spoke loudly to the beasts. A short tap of the stick on the heavy wooden yoke and they were off. Willan's journey in search of health and recuperation was nearing its destination.

Willan relaxed a little and looked about him. His head filled with the sounds and smells of the small but busy waterfront. Men were pushing, towing, lifting and carrying cargoes, all of which seemed too large and heavy to be handled solely by manpower. Nobody was rushing but nor was anybody idling. Stamina, strength and persistence seemed to be the working ethic. Willan also noticed that the stocky men were shorter than he; in London his five feet three inches left him routinely looking upwards during conversations. He glanced across at Torres. They were of similar height.

The steady progress of the sledge was occasionally hiccuped by a greased cloth being passed under the runners to remove loose debris and maintain the smooth glide. Torres was the first to speak.

"I hope that you are comfortable, Doctor Willan. I feel sure our journey is smoother than that of the *Alligator*." Willan did not wish to remember any of his sea passage. Looking forward to recovering his health to be able to complete his research was his only goal and motivation. He replied that he was indeed comfortable and asked how soon they would reach the house. "It will be some time yet," said Torres. "We will shortly cross the bridge of Ribeira de Santa Luzia; apologies, I mean the Santa Luzia river. That marks the edge of the waterfront. We will pass by the offices, factories and commercial buildings and leave the centre. Then it is a steady climb through the dwelling houses. By then we shall be over halfway but the oxen will be unable to continue as the track becomes steep. Worry not, though. We shall have you at the Quinta do Til soon after with no difficulty." Willan was not worried. He was in no position to be worried. He had confidence in Torres.

Willan and Torres exchanged polite conversation, mainly about the weather and the purpose of some of the buildings. Even though Willan was hot under his high-collared coat the security it gave him outweighed his personal comfort; nor would it be correct for him to travel in shirt and waistcoat alone.

"You seem very concerned about the safety of your case," said Torres. "Is it brimming with golden guineas?" he added, a broad smile on his face.

"Indeed, it is not," replied Willan seriously. "It contains most important scientific papers which are vital to my studies. Without them I should not be able to continue my researches."

"I apologise, I was not being serious," said Torres, disappointed at Willan's obvious lack of a sense of humour. Willan too was disappointed; disappointed at, once more, failing to spot humour or japery. A short silence followed.

Seeking to end the silence and also to resolve a question, Willan asked, "If you do not mind my asking, are you from this island or are you British?"

Torres laughed and replied, "Of course I do not mind your question; it is an enquiry I have answered many times. If you will indulge me, I will provide you with a short summary of my existence, and perhaps you will do likewise before dinner this evening."

"I am keen to hear," said Willan. "Please proceed." Willan eased back. As a Quaker he had long known how to be an attentive listener.

His only concern was that he had agreed to give his history and background to a man he had met only minutes earlier. Nevertheless, he was a man of his word. He would honour his undertaking.

It was well that Willan was a keen listener as Torres began to speak immediately and the words came thick and fast. "I was born here on Madeira twenty-nine years ago. My father, Paulo, worked for the Gordon family. He taught himself English and thereby gained a good position of trust within the offices. When you are of improved health, I will bring my father to meet you. He has always been a man of agreeable conversation. I was taught English by my father from a young age; he knew it was essential if I were to succeed. I also spent two winters at the Quinta do Til being educated in all things British by Caroline, a niece of the Gordons, whose aim to be a teacher was thwarted by her poor health. Sadly, she died some years ago. I began working for the company on my fourteenth birthday, as I still do. Also, I now have my own business trading alongside and with the other British firms. I hope to re-name my business as 'Torres and Sons' but first I must meet a suitable young lady. So, as you can see, Doctor Willan, although I am of Madeiran descent and have never left the island, I have many British characteristics and attributes. I am, though, proud to be, as I always will be, a true Madeiran." Both men smiled. Willan was now more willing to summarise his own story.

There was no need for Willan to comment upon Torres' history as the sledge had stopped at the junction of their track out of Funchal and a smaller, rougher one heading upwards. At first glance it seemed that this track simply passed through a multitude of small, terraced vegetable plots hewn out of the hillside and only a few feet wide in places. Closer scrutiny showed small buildings, mainly thatched, which Willan took to be barns or sheds. They were, in fact, the dwelling houses of the peasants who scraped a living from this land. To the left of the track these terraces continued as far as the eye could see. On the right they only reached about halfway, above which was a long row of mixed trees forming a fence-like barrier. Beyond these trees was a large white house. This was the Quinta do Til.

Willan could not believe his own eyes. He was sitting in a sledge with a Portuguese Englishman. They had been towed by oxen looked after by a man and a boy, each with a stick. Awaiting them were two men holding upright what appeared to be the thick mast and some of the sails of an obviously stricken sailboat. Alongside the marine wreckage stood a young man, maybe sixteen years old, holding the reins of a very fine stallion. Adding to the uniqueness of this vista was the fact that they all appeared to be in the middle of an almost deserted land.

It was as if Torres could read Willan's mind. "Please take a moment or two, Doctor Willan, to acclimatise yourself. You are in the safest of hands. Grant me but a couple of moments and I will explain everything." Willan was incapable of speech. His only consideration was how he was to be transported uphill with the remains of a sailboat and a stallion. Torres, meanwhile, was in loud conversation with the others. There was much laughter and gesticulation. After what was clearly longer than a couple of moments, Torres returned.

"All is well," said Torres. "Please sit a while longer and I will explain how our journey is to be fulfilled. The oxen and drivers have completed their task and will now return to the waterfront. The men you can see nearby my horse are two of the strongest hammock-bearers on the island. They will easily transport you to the house. Do not be ashamed to be carried in this way; it is a common form of travel for both ladies and gentlemen. I have to leave you now as I have pressing affairs and will take my horse and return to my office. The young man will precede you to advise the house of your arrival. You will be welcomed to the Quinta do Til by Duarte. He is the house chief and speaks good English. You will be made most comfortable and can rest. I will join you later and we can enjoy a gentle evening of conversation and a good dinner. Are you ready to continue?"

Willan, realising he had no control over his immediate future, coughed and nodded his agreement. He climbed down from the carriage with his case. Remarkably, the sailboat had transformed into a sturdy hooded hammock slung underneath a thick bamboo pole of at least twelve feet in length. The men with the hammock were sturdier and darker than the ox-driver but of no greater height. They wore soil-coloured linen clothes and sported red, woollen, pointed hats. Their leather boots flapped loosely around their calves. The men lowered the hammock. Willan allowed Torres to hold his case as he slid backwards across the thick black canvas-like material. He fidgeted into a half-lying, half-seated position and reached out with his left arm for Torres to return his case. This slight, but fast, movement unbalanced Willan, who feared he might fall to the ground. Instantly the bearers raised and balanced the hammock, restoring Willan's stability and dignity. They were not laughing but had broad smiles, as did Torres.

"I bid you a safe journey," said Torres as he returned Willan's case. The young man assisted Torres onto his horse and set off up the track. Torres turned his horse, raised his right hand as if ordering a charge and trotted away. The sledge had departed previously. Willan remained, dangling from a pole, entrusted to the care of two strangers in an unknown land.

The lead bearer carried a long stick, not unlike a shepherd's crook, in his left hand and balanced the pole with his right hand on his right shoulder. The rear bearer had no stick and balanced the pole on his left shoulder. They set off, left feet first, at an exact and steady pace. Willan soon realised that he was, surprisingly, quite comfortable and, being only about eighteen inches from the ground, in no danger of injury from falling.

The only sound was an occasional creak from the bamboo pole; the men made no noise at all, not even their boots. The hammock swayed only slightly. Willan felt relaxed, so much so that he thought his daydreams might turn into actual sleep. Looking up at the hillside had reminded him of his birthplace, Sedbergh, in the dales of West Yorkshire. The topography was similar if you imagined Funchal without terraces or Sedbergh with them. Farming near Sedbergh was all animal husbandry; vegetables and grains were transported into the market from further afield. Willan surmised, correctly, that there could be no suitable flat arable land on Madeira and life for many people must be a matter of living from hand to mouth.

A slight jolt made Willan look up. The bearers were swapping the pole from one shoulder to the other. They did this without pause or change of pace, showing considerable strength and dexterity. Willan was fascinated and for the rest of the journey his eyes followed the lead bearer. His legs were like springs absorbing the mounds and hollows, ensuring that the pole remained steady at all times. Willan was so mesmerised he had not noticed that they had passed the line of trees and were nearing the Quinta. He was brought to life, though, when a shadow passed over him and he heard and saw the bearer's feet striding onto a mosaic of small round stones. The shadow had been cast by a stone arch which marked the entrance to the Quinta do Til.

2

The Quinta do Til was an impressive building. Exuding great strength and security with its thick walls and large rooms and windows, the almost Italianate style softened the structure and added well-designed sophistication. Never more than two storeys, its position on wide terracing gave an illusion of greater height. The grounds were immaculate and, although formal, seemed relaxing and welcoming. To the right of the main two-storey part of the building ran a colonnade-like walkway which looked as if it should join to another wing of the property. Perhaps the builder had overspent on decoration and sacrificed size for beauty?

Willan's journey was not quite completed. The bearers continued on the wide stone path, which ran for some distance uphill and towards the rear of the building. Tall trees sheltered the fern-edged path. Willan felt cooler immediately. Turning to the right they reached the main entrance, a heavy arched wooden door, to the left side of the property. To the side of this stood a small man dressed in dark brown breeches, waistcoat and frockcoat. He wore short, shiny, brown boots and nearly white stockings. His short, black, oily hair and wrinkled but fair complexion added to an overall appearance which was impossible to age. He might be anything from twenty-five to fifty-five.

The bearers lowered the hammock to the perfect height for Willan simply to swing out his legs and stand, all in one movement. He still carried his case, which he transferred to his left hand as the man approached. As Willan expected, the man stopped short of him and steadied himself. Willan pre-empted any bow or show of deference by almost knocking the man over as he secured his right hand. They shook hands enthusiastically. Willan was whole-heartedly egalitarian. Respect and politeness should always be shown, not humility or servitude.

"Bom Dia, Senhor Willan. Good morning and I welcome you to the Quinta do Til. I am Duarte, the chief of the Quinta. I am very pleased to meet you. Shall I carry your bag, sir?" said the man.

"Good morning to you, Duarte," replied Willan. "The pleasure is mine also. I shall willingly carry my own bag."

Duarte walked a few steps and opened one half of the large door. Turning to Willan, he said, "If it would please you to enter then follow me." Duarte disappeared from sight, leaving only darkness filling the opened door. Willan took a couple of paces inside the building and stopped to allow his eyes to adjust to the light. Slowly the hallway came into focus. Some distance away, framed by a large door with a fanlight above, stood Duarte, his left arm extended outwards. Between them the stone floor had a red and blue carpet providing the only colour; the stone walls were unadorned other than for a series of oil lamps. Willan joined Duarte. "Welcome to your new accommodations," said Duarte as he turned to his left and into a high, light room. Willan was awestruck as he finally caught up with Duarte.

The room was magnificent. Willan stood and stared. The ceiling was over fifteen feet high and beautifully and ornately plastered. This was clearly the main reception room. The door was in the corner and to Willan's left the long wall had a single, full-height, window with a writing desk and chair to the near side and a dining table with three chairs beyond it. The wall opposite him was splendidly opulent. Three wide, also full-height, windows filled the wall, their plaster surrounds smothered with delicate Italian designs. Two small decorative, bowlegged tables separated the windows. To Willan's right was a good-sized wooden bed with a chair beside and then another desk with a single chair. The remaining wall had a solid stone fireplace to the centre, no furniture and a closed door in the right corner. A vast green and red carpet filled the centre of the room, leaving a stone border of perhaps four feet. The windows had been un-shuttered and thin white muslin drapes gently swayed in the sunlight. Shadowing on the yellowed plaster walls showed where pictures had once hung. Oil lamps were the only fittings now. Every aspect of the room pleased Willan and his open-mouthed staring changed to a warm smile.

"Is the accommodations to your satisfaction?" said Duarte. Willan had not replied before Duarte continued. Perhaps his smile had answered the question. "Through the door is your dressing room and washing jug. I am to tell you that Dona Esmeralda has your clothes until later for cleaning. I leave you now for some minutes to rest and I will return for you shortly with further indications." He had no sooner finished talking than he left the room, closing the door behind him.

Willan placed his case on the table, removed his coat and placed it on the foot of his bed. He entered the dressing room seeking a chamber pot; he had noticed that there was nothing under the bed. The room was not as small as he had feared and contained not only a French-style commode with a patterned pot, but also a small table with a jug of water, a bowl and many clean towels, cloths and handkerchiefs. There was also a dresser and robe for his clothes. Willan needed a piss. In recent months he had ceased pissing from a standing position as his bowels had become prone to sudden evacuation. He lowered his breeches, un-buttoned his drawers and sat on the pot. As he started a piss of which Torres' stallion would have been proud, he felt stirrings in his bowels. A fart accompanied the rapid discharge. He suffered from diarrhoea most days. It drained him and added to the weakness he felt from his shortness of breath and rasping cough. After cleaning and dressing himself, he inspected his slurry – as usual, no solid matter at all. He returned to the room and sat at the table to regain his composure; gentle breaths with his eyes closed helped. He was not too downhearted. Hopefully this was now the start of his recovery.

Willan opened his eyes and looked around him. The room made him feel very small. He walked towards its centre and stood between the foot of his bed and the three large windows. He still felt small. A glance at the ceiling made him dizzy. After several deep breaths to restore his equilibrium, he crossed to the central window. Moving the drape to one side he pressed the handle down and was delighted when the window opened easily, notwithstanding its size. He stepped onto a wide stone-paved veranda edged by an elegant, again Italianate, balustrade. Motionless, he stared ahead. Funchal, in a panorama, was spread before him. Several large ships lay at anchor in the harbour with dozens of smaller vessels between them and the waterfront. He wondered which was the *Alligator*. His eyes re-traced his route of earlier and he was surprised at how high he had climbed. The sun was ahead of him and although low in the sky, warmed him to his core. Remembering that it was December and that he had come to Madeira solely for its health-giving climate comforted him. He continued to stare ahead as he vainly attempted to count the ships and boats in the harbour, an easy task were they to stop moving.

"There are no troubles in the world when you look at the scene," said Duarte, who had returned and was one step onto the veranda.

"I cannot disagree," replied Willan, turning to Duarte and forgetting why it mattered how many ships and boats were in the harbour.

"It is my duty to invite you to Dona Esmeralda and some soup," said Duarte before he disappeared back into the room. Willan was obliged to follow. It was like a child's game. Duarte was now by the door to the hall, clearly itching to proceed, and no sooner had Willan reached the carpet than he was gone. Leaving the room, Willan followed Duarte straight ahead; immediately left would have returned him to the front door. After passing a wide but modest staircase, he finally caught up with him in a large library. Or was it a dining room? There was a large window to the right and two smaller ones ahead of him. The other two walls held bookshelves. There was a single side-table and chair. Between the two windows was a modest wooden fireplace framed by two red leather armchairs. The centre of the room was filled by a dining table set for only one person but capable of accommodating at least twelve. Duarte stood in a doorway to the right of the fireplace.

Suddenly Duarte jumped forward as if pushed and from behind him entered a small, doll-like woman. She wore a full-length, broad, red skirt with a blue tunic. Her hair was black and tightly tied back. Her cheeks were red, her eyes sparkling and her lips smiling.

"Please to meet Dona Esmeralda, she does not speak English," said Duarte. Willan crossed to the woman and shook her hand. He was surprised that she reciprocated the handshake with both hands. She looked up at him with the warmest of looks and he liked her immediately. She spoke to Duarte at some length; he listened attentively then addressed Willan, obviously taking his lead from what she had said. "It is my duty to tell you that your crates of goods, which are not your clothes, will soon go to your chamber. They are heavy and I can help you place them. Some clothes are cleaned and will be back with you. The rest will follow. If you sit now for soup."

'It is clear who the chief of the Quinta is,' thought Willan as he sat, as instructed. Dona Esmeralda had left the room. Duarte hovered by the door, smiling at Willan. To the front of him, on the table, were a glass of water, an empty plate and a large spoon. He faced the window. The quiet did not concern Willan. He enjoyed silence.

The peace was broken by a call from beyond the room. Duarte left and returned almost immediately, carrying a wooden tray. He placed a large earthenware bowl of soup on the plate and a hunk of dark bread directly on the table. There was no further cutlery. He stepped back and spoke. It sounded as though he were addressing a group of people rather than just Willan. "Today we have sopa de trigo, which you call wheat soup. It is the finest of Madeira. It is made by Dona Esmeralda. The parts are wheat, potato, pompion, old pig with salt and other vegetables. It will fill you well." Speech over, he left the room. The rich smell of the soup whetted Willan's appetite; he dipped a piece of bread into the bowl and ate. It was delicious. Each ingredient retained its own flavour but combined to make a fresh, wholesome mouthful. He resisted the urge to eat like a hog and savoured each and every morsel. Finishing the last of the soup with the last of the bread, he felt revived. Willan had always known, through his work with the down-trodden poor of London, that diet was vital to health, but had never had the time to study the whys and wherefores. Hot soup such as this could, surely, only be beneficial. Willan stood, crossed to the fireplace and sat on an armchair. Within moments he was asleep.

*

"Please to awake sir," said Duarte, tapping Willan's shoulder. "Please to awake sir." Willan coughed into consciousness. He resembled a lunatic as he stared ahead, open-mouthed, hair dangling un-tied and his head to one side. There was a small dribble of saliva on his chin. Slowly he focussed his eyes and his brain, and realised and remembered where he was. He straightened himself and swept back his hair with his hand; he found the ribbon, loose, beneath his ear.

"My apologies," said Willan. "Have I been asleep for a long while?"

"Not even an hour," replied Duarte. Sensing that Willan was now aware of his own situation, Duarte continued. "A letter has arrived for you and I have it here. Dona Esmeralda and I invite you back to your room to read this letter and then to sleep. I will arise you after, when Senhor Torres visits for dinner." Duarte moved to the doorway. Willan rose unsteadily and followed.

Back in his room, Willan saw his two chests of belongings placed to the left of the room. He was pleased at their safe arrival. His case remained on the table. Duarte placed a small envelope on the first desk and left the room. Willan's bed had been turned down and one of his nightshirts, freshly laundered, lay at the foot. The letter would have to wait; Willan needed his chamber pot. He entered the dressing room and noticed that several of his clothes, clean as if new, were neatly in place. The pot had been emptied and washed out. He took a long piss. His bowels held their contents. He undressed to his shirt and returned to the main room and his letter. Ignoring his nightshirt, Willan picked up the letter and climbed into the bed. The freshness of the fine linen felt comforting. He studied the envelope; it had the words 'Doctor Willan Esq' in a fine hand. There was no address. He opened the letter.

Dear Sir,

Allow me humbly to introduce myself. I am William Gourlay MD, fellow of the Royal College of Physicians, Edinburgh, and physician to the British Factory at Madeira.

I have been advised of your arrival at Quinta do Til by Sir Roderick and write to offer my services. I have been on Madeira for over twenty years and have gained expertise in the treatment of itinerant patients from Britain who have been ordered here seeking relief from phthisis and consumption.

If it is to your agreement, I will call upon you tomorrow before noon to make your acquaintance. If it is not convenient, please pass word to Sir Roderick or Duarte.

Yours faithfully,
Wm Gourlay

Willan read the letter twice. A fellow graduate from Edinburgh with a knowledge of his illnesses was precisely what he needed. He was greatly cheered. After circling the room with his eyes a couple of times, and liking what he saw, he leaned back upon his pillows and returned to sleep.

3

Willan was disturbed from his sleep by a noise. Looking up, he saw Duarte closing the shutters to the central of the three windows. The left window was already shuttered. The lamps to the walls were lit. The effect was neither light nor dark, just gloomy. "I have illuminated the dressing room as it is needed," said Duarte. "Senhor Torres has just arrived but there is no hurry; he is with his horse at the stable. There is time before the dining room." By now Duarte had shuttered all the windows and, as always, he departed without warning.

Removing his shirt as he walked, Willan entered his dressing room. He washed and dried himself and did the best he could with his hair, in front of the looking glass. He looked satisfactory and felt comfortable in clean clothes. Returning to the main room, he vowed to unpack his chests of belongings tomorrow morning before his visit from Doctor Gourlay. He moved his case from the table to the bedside chair, for no good reason, and left for the dining room.

It was empty. For want of something to do he inspected the bookshelves. There was little to interest him; the books in English were mainly geographical. He sat next to the fireplace. Although it was December and now dark, the fire was not lit, nor did it need to be. This room could easily be in England; his living and bedroom would always be foreign. He wondered what hour of the day it was. He had dispensed with carrying his pocket watch aboard the *Alligator*; he would ask Torres the time and whether or not he would need a timepiece. He had many questions to be answered.

He heard Torres long before he saw him. From what he could hear, Willan surmised that he was in the kitchen talking with Dona Esmeralda. There was also another male voice which was not Duarte. Torres came through the door. Willan stood.

"Please sit," said Torres; "we have no formality here." As Torres sat opposite him, Willan noticed that a small, middle-aged man had followed him into the room. He was of the usual Madeiran short stature and black hair, but unusually the hair was long, reaching almost to his shoulders. He wore a very loose white shirt and Cossack-style, wide black trousers tucked into tight black leather boots. On a taller man the clothes would have seemed dashing. This man, however, appeared to have recently left the employ of a circus. He carried a tray bearing two small glasses of dark wine. Willan half-expected the man to perform a somersault without spilling a drop. He placed the glasses on the small table which separated Willan and Torres, bowed and left. "That was Jorge," said Torres. "He has been at the Quinta longer than anybody. Nobody is certain of his role but he is popular with all."

Torres lifted his glass. "A fine Madeira wine to wish you good health and an enjoyable, health-giving stay." He sipped his drink. Willan did likewise, although he normally abstained from alcohol. Long ago, especially when seeking funding for his people's dispensary, he had come to learn that politeness benefitted all. The drink was deliciously warming, so much so that he had to resist the urge to swallow it all in one mouthful.

"I understand you have received a note from Doctor Gourlay. I imagine he intends to call upon you," said Torres.

"He will visit tomorrow, before noon," replied Willan.

"And stay for soup, I have no doubt," added Torres with a smile.

"His letter was simple but leaves me with two questions you can help me with," said Willan. "Firstly, he writes that he was informed of my presence by Sir Roderick. Do you know of him? Also, he states he is physician to the British Factory at Madeira. Do you know of this place?"

Torres was laughing. "I am Sir Roderick. Gourlay is playing a joke. I am called Sir Roderick by Madeirans and British alike, because of my British characteristics, usually outwith my presence. I am flattered by this nickname. It does no harm to my business. The Factory is not a building; it refers, collectively to the British businesses on the island, whose owners meet regularly to their mutual benefit. I too am part of the factory. As our physician he receives a generous stipend and should not present you with any type of account. He will also drink as much of my wine and Dona Esmeralda's soup as he can manage." Willan was relaxed. He could assimilate any amount of information and the resolution of questions was always pleasing.

"Our dinner will shortly be with us. We are fortunate to have Dona Esmeralda as our cook. Some say her food lacks style and sophistication, but they are wrong. She cooks the finest foods perfectly and straightforwardly; she does not hide a lack of skill beneath unnecessary sauces and gravies. Tonight, we shall feast upon kid goat," continued Torres. Willan was of two minds. He liked his food plain and unadorned but was unsure of goat; he had never eaten it. However, 'nothing ventured, nothing gained,' he thought.

Torres stood, drained the last of his wine and headed to the table. The two place settings were at opposite ends. "If you will permit me, I think we shall converse better when not separated by the length of the table," said Torres. He then moved one setting alongside the other.

"You have pre-empted me. We are not a King and Queen dining in our castle," said Willan.

"In that case I shall cancel the minstrels," responded Torres.

Willan remained silent. After some moments it dawned upon him that Torres had been joking. "Oh, very amusing," he said, vowing to himself that he must be more watchful for these types of remark. Torres, on the other hand, was vowing not to make witticisms as they were all falling on stony ground.

Willan joined Torres at the table and, as if on cue, the door opened and Jorge entered carrying a large tray. He carried two plates of sliced meat, two bowls of potatoes and two small plates of green beans. He placed the food on the table and left, again without speaking. Torres lifted his knife and fork and sliced his cuts of meat into smaller pieces. He then added some potato and all of his beans. He ate heartily, mainly with his spoon. Willan was more cautious in his approach. Firstly, he cut a small sliver of the meat to try. It was sweet, juicy and had a fresh, pastural taste. No gravy had been added: it lay in its own juices. The potatoes and beans were of perfect texture, full of flavour and tasted as if they had left the garden only minutes earlier. Willan was soon eating at the same rate as Torres. They did not speak; idle conversation would have been an insult to the food. Both men ate all that had been placed before them. "That was truly splendid," said Willan, surprised at his choice of words. It was the largest meal he had eaten in several months. Torres smiled warmly in acknowledgement.

Jorge re-appeared. He spoke briefly to Torres, collected the empty plates and bowls, and left.

"He will bring us some tarts to complete our feast. They are a Portuguese speciality and Dona Esmeralda makes the finest in all Madeira," said Torres. Willan could not imagine any food eclipsing the meal he had eaten. Jorge and the tray returned. He gave each of them a small plate holding two small round tarts and another glass of Madeira wine.

"I believe I could eat a dozen," said Torres. Willan inspected his plate. The tarts contained a baked custard, were uneven and almost, but not quite, burned. There being no cutlery, he picked one up and bit. The pastry was sweet, flaky and delicious. The custard was rich, creamy and with a hint of spice. He soon finished the second tart, took a sip of wine, not out of politeness, and looked up. Torres was picking the crumbs from his plate. "I have dined well," said Willan.

Torres had moved to an armchair so Willan joined him. He had finished his second glass of Madeira. "You seem very tired," said Torres.

"I confess that I am," replied Willan. "It has probably been the strangest day of my entire life. I do not mean that as any form of criticism. I cannot thank you enough for your help and kindness. I feel I must retire early as I need to unpack my belongings in the morning before the doctor's visit."

"Of course," replied Torres. "I will not delay you for long but I need to inform you of a couple of matters. You will not be alone in the house overnight; one servant always sleeps in the room next to the kitchen. I do not normally sleep here, although I do have a small room at my disposal, should the need arise. My horses do sleep here. I retain rooms at Bachelor's Hall, a short step down the slope. There is a chamber stick for you" – he pointed to the side table – "but all the other lamps will be taken care of. Duarte will attend to your toilet in the morning. I will join you for dinner again tomorrow and look forward to hearing of your eminent career. I bid you goodnight." He left via the kitchen door.

Willan returned to his room, undressed, took a long piss, without any accompaniment, snuffed his candle and fell immediately to sleep.

4

It sounded as though a flock of birds were in his room as Willan woke. The half-light was enough to guide him to the three windows which he un-shuttered. It was just before dawn; the sun would rise from his left. He could not see a single bird but still they sounded close. Each morning, a few minutes after he rose, Willan would feel an urge for his pot. He had always thought this was the natural reaction to his body shifting from horizontal to vertical; today was no exception. He lifted his nightshirt and emptied himself. Inspection showed some solid matter within the otherwise liquid diarrhoea. 'Hurrah,' thought Willan, 'perhaps I shall soon recover my health and strength.' He was feeling positive and itched to get on with his day, but God came first.

At approximately this time every day Willan opened his conscience to God. He would reflect on the previous day, assess his sins and errors, seek forgiveness for his past and advice for his future. He had a personal relationship with God, as did all Quakers. It was inconceivable to start any day without God's guidance; it was his duty to God to live his life in a truly Christian way for the benefit of all humanity, as well as himself.

His itch to progress took him, still undressed, to his chests. He opened both and began to unload all the contents. He had soon covered both desks, half of the table and two chairs. Books, papers, quills and inks flew about the room. The papers from his portmanteau were emptied onto his bed. The sooner he was organised, the sooner he could start back on his work.

He did not hear Duarte enter the room. "Bom Dia, Doctor Willan. Are we preparing for a schoolroom of children?" he asked.

"No, indeed not. These are…" said Willan, stopping mid-sentence. "I believe you are jesting with me, are you not?" he continued.

"Forgive me, shall I help you with your toilet?" said Duarte, wondering how his opening frivolity could have been taken any other way.

"I can manage well except for shaving," replied Willan. "If you are proficient with a blade, I shall be most grateful; I can ill afford blood loss." Willan was proud of his witticism.

Duarte was at a loss for a reply, not knowing if Willan was joking, but suspecting that he wasn't. He left the room to collect his thoughts and a keen blade.

Willan washed and dressed then prowled the room with a chair, seeking the most suitable situation for his shave. He never shaved himself, preferring to use a barber in Holborn, near his home in Bloomsbury Square. He had never seen the irony that he, a master with a surgical fleam, could not shave himself without blood loss. He located a suitable position for his chair, near to the table and, not knowing how long it would be until Duarte's return, sat and waited.

He did not have to wait long. Duarte returned with a pan of hot water, a blade, some soaps and lotions, and two towels, one large, one small. Placing the tray on the table, he covered Willan's shoulders with the larger towel, applied soap and shaved him expertly. Willan was soon rinsed, dried and smelling of a summer garden. Neither man had attempted idle small talk.

"For breakfast here or in the dining room?" asked Duarte. Keen to continue sorting his possessions, Willan opted for breakfast in his room. "We have tea and coffee," said Duarte proudly. Sensing that Duarte was asking a question rather than making a statement, Willan requested tea. Duarte gathered up the shaving paraphernalia and left the room. Willan immediately set about his papers.

Willan knew he had a good memory; he had been told this by many people as far back as his days at Sedbergh School. It served him well now as he did not need to open any file to know the contents. He was soon restoring order, logic and neatness to his papers. His inks, pens, blotters and the like were lined up in perfect military fashion, as were the spares and extra spares. To the average eye, all looked correct and in place. For Willan, though, there still remained the double- and treble-checking to complete. Willan and complacency were not bedfellows.

Again, Duarte had entered the room unheard by Willan. He had nearly completed setting the breakfast before he was noticed. There was a pot of tea, bread, butter, preserves and jellies together with a further two custard tarts, presumably from the same batch as the previous evening. Willan had given no thought as to what breakfast would comprise, but was pleased with what lay before him; in London he usually had bread and tea. The custard tarts were a welcome addition. Duarte left the room; Willan ate his food and drank his tea at a steady pace. The tarts elevated the meal from a routine to a pleasure.

Feeling short of breath, Willan decided to rest a while in order to gather himself together. He opened the middle window and took a chair to the veranda. The air was clean and fresh and not yet too warm. He sat to enjoy the scene and soon recovered his breath but did not return to his papers; he had resumed the futile task of counting the ships and boats in the bay. Finally admitting defeat, he returned inside. He was totally unaware of the hour of the day, a situation that he would never previously have allowed. His mood and attitude were changing for the better, he hoped nervously.

Resuming the organisation of his papers Willan thought long and hard not about the contents of the files, but as to which desk or table would be the most percipient location. Eventually, he decided to write at the desk nearest his bed and to file papers on the other desk and half of the table. The other side would be retained for occasional dining. Chairs were to be utilised for pending and overflow. Pens, inks and other stationery could be stored in readiness on the two small tables between the windows. The task completed, Willan relaxed slightly. He was satisfied with his solution and especially proud that he had remembered to allocate spaces and positions for correspondence and oil lamps.

His hard breathing was now accompanied by a rhythmic rasp. This could often lead to coughing and the production of phlegm. Rest usually helped, so Willan returned to his chair on the veranda. Certain that there were more ships and boats in the bay, he resumed his personal census but could not reach a definitive answer so resolved to keep his head steadier on his next attempt. That attempt would have to wait as, hearing noises from the room, he returned inside.

Duarte was just leaving, carrying the breakfast tray. On hearing Willan he stopped, turned and, to Willan's surprise, spoke loudly in Portuguese. The surprise was compounded as Willan watched a young girl dressed in a black skirt and tunic leave his dressing room carrying his pot and a handful of dirty cloths and towels. She was probably no more than twelve years old. She left the room with Duarte and he heard their animated but friendly conversation fade along the hallway. Willan immediately went to his dressing room and checked that a replacement sat in his commode. A new pot was indeed in place, as were fresh cloths and towels. He felt safe and secure knowing the whereabouts of the nearest clean pot and with a laundered handkerchief in his pocket.

Willan's stomach gurgled, not as warning of an impending evacuation but because he was hungry. He could not remember when he had last enjoyed a healthy appetite – certainly not in the last year or so – until yesterday, eating had merely been a chore to be accomplished. Despite having no indication as to the time, he headed to the dining room and sat at the side table to await Doctor Gourlay. Maybe it was the dust from the old books on the shelves or possibly just tiredness, but Willan began to cough. His chest was tight and his throat felt blocked. The pain of the coughing forced his head to between his knees where the last violent cough pained his ribs but cleared the blockage. His eyes were red with tears. The phlegm in his handkerchief showed a slight veining of blood. He sat upright, desperately gasping for air. Gradually his equilibrium was restored. Willan went to his room, collected a new handkerchief and checked his appearance in the looking glass. He then returned to the dining room and resumed his seat as if nothing had occurred.

Willan sat impatiently; he was a busy man with work ahead of him. He was eager to meet Doctor Gourlay, hungry for his luncheon and keen to return to his papers. He could ill afford to let minutes and hours pass un-utilised. Fortunately, his wait was not a long one. He looked hard as a white-haired man of similar age and height to himself and wearing identical black clothing entered the room carrying a small volume. Willan stood and looked again. The only differences between the two men were Gourlay's curled hair, his fuller girth and ruddy complexion; his face was that of an ever-thirsty country squire.

"Good morning, Gourlay of Kincraig at your service sir," he boomed. Willan shook his hand and both men sat near the fireplace. Gourlay continued, "I am sorry that you are here as a result of your malady, but selfishly, I am greatly pleased to meet with a fellow physician. I hope that we can be of mutual benefit." Willan agreed.

The men conversed well as they had much in common; both had trained at Edinburgh Medical College, only five years apart. They reminisced a little about their teachers and professors. Their careers had, of course, taken totally different paths. At a lull in the conversation Gourlay turned to the matter in hand. "If I may be so bold as to give medical advice to such a learned physician as yourself, I have some knowledge that may be of use."

"Please proceed," said Willan.

Gourlay proceeded. "The clean air and warm temperatures here are great healers, as you know, and almost all patients see an immediate improvement. To quote Omar Khayyam, this is a false dawn and I urge you to resist any desires to resume normal activities. I minister to many sufferers of endemic complaints of the chest. Too often their folly in undertaking strenuous activities in the belief that they have been miraculously cured leads to their inevitable relapse. Please forgive my bluntness but I cannot stress this strongly enough. I urge you to rest for some time and regain your health slowly; a short walk in the gardens should be exercise enough. I will call upon you regularly, if it is your wish, and you will be attended to by Dona Esmeralda, who is a finer healer of the sick than you and I can ever hope to be. We have studied and learned our profession; she has an innate gift to treat sickness and malady, not through magic or superstition but through sensible remedies and, of course, the finest of fresh foods. You are fortunate indeed to be under her roof." He paused before adding, "And if I am not mistaken, it will shortly be time for your medicine – the finest soup on Madeira. I will join you, if that is agreeable."

"It is more than agreeable," replied Willan. "You speak with great understanding, and I am keen to continue our words. It would be a great service to me if you were able to call. Please come at any time of your choosing."

"Gourlay of Kincraig at your service, sir. Before we enjoy our medicine, I have an item for you. It is a small volume of mine which has just been re-printed and I humbly hope it may be of some service. I have taken the liberty of marking the sections relating to consumption and phthisis. It also contains my observations on this health-giving island." He handed Willan the volume. It was entitled *Observations on the Natural History, Climate and Diseases of Madeira, during a period of eighteen years by William Gourlay, MD Fellow of The Royal College of Physicians, Edinburgh, and Physician to the British Factory at Madeira.* Willan recognised the description of Gourlay from his letter of introduction of the previous day. He also saw that it had been printed only that year, 1811.

Notwithstanding his hunger, Willan wanted to read the book from start to finish immediately. Coupled with Gourlay's words it offered, above all, hope. Hope that he could recover his health and hope that he could complete his researches. He would start reading after luncheon.

Meanwhile Gourlay had walked to the door which led to the kitchen and opened it a matter of inches. "There are two men here famished and faint with hunger," he said before returning to his seat. Willan thought this unnecessarily rude. Duarte came into the room with, Willan thought, an angry disposition.

"I can only apologise, gentlemen," said Duarte, "there are poor eatings today. We have only tomato and onion soup. Shall I order Dona Esmeralda to prepare something more to your likings?"

"What do you think, Willan?" said Gourlay. "Shall we eat like poor peasants or risk asking Dona Esmeralda to treat us as gentlemen?"

Willan stared blankly. He could not think, let alone speak. Gourlay and Duarte burst into laughter. They both looked at Willan and tried unsuccessfully to stop. Eventually Gourlay spoke. "Forgive our japery, Doctor Willan. Duarte and I are friends of many years. He knows full well that tomato and onion soup is my favourite and neither of us would dare give Dona Esmeralda an order for any purpose." Willan was silent. He was still trying to work out what was so amusing, when a female voice shouted from the kitchen. This caused another burst of schoolboy-like laughter from Gourlay and Duarte. Duarte then left the room. Gourlay sat at the table and beckoned Willan to join him. They sat together in an awkward silence until Gourlay said, "I am sure that you will enjoy this soup; it is just the thing for a man seeking health and recovery."

"Thank you," replied Willan, "I must apologise; I am sometimes a little slow to detect jokes and witticisms." Willan was pleased with his candour.

"Not at all," replied Gourlay.

The door opened and Duarte returned with their meal. He placed in front of each man a bowl of soup and some bread. He put a plate of four shelled, boiled eggs between them. He left the room. Gourlay spooned soup with his right hand and dipped bread with his left, his head positioned only inches above the bowl. Halfway through he paused and ate two boiled eggs, half an egg per bite. Willan was eating faster than he normally did but seemed slow in comparison. Following Gourlay's example he ate his eggs at the halfway point. In a short space of time both men were finished.

"I confess," said Willan, "that to be the finest soup I have tasted. I hope it is served often."

"Not often enough," replied Gourlay, before returning to his fireside chair. Willan joined him.

"I have a further enquiry to make of you, if you can spare me a few minutes," said Willan.

"Gourlay of Kincraig at your service, sir."

Willan began, "In London I was advised, on account of my illness, by many people, medical and otherwise, to seek a warmer climate. Many places were proposed to me. I decided on Madeira following the advice of a respected acquaintance and fellow Quaker, Thomas Bennett Smith. Not only did I know him to be a truly honourable man, he had sent his own son here for recuperation only a few weeks earlier. I doubt that his son, Thomas Bennett Smith junior, accompanied by his brother Ashby, had such a tortuous journey as I, and may well have been here some time now or even returned. I wonder, with your knowledge of the British community here and your medical position, whether you know of their whereabouts and situation. Although I have met them only briefly in London, I am keen to be at their service, should I be required.

"This is a small island and I believe that I know every British person here. I can do more than advise you of their location; I can pass on your salutations this very afternoon. They are currently residing at Bachelor's Hall, but a stone's throw from here. Sir Roderick also stays there and knows them better than I. I am physician to Thomas who, I regret to say, is still very weak and consumptive and I am to call upon him shortly. I will relay this conversation to him. I will advise Ashby that you are not yet receiving visitors. Sir Roderick can easily act as your intermediary. I feel sure that I have satisfied your enquiry, Doctor Willan, and, having earned my soup, I shall bid you good afternoon and proceed to Bachelor's Hall." Gourlay stood and departed.

Willan gathered together his thoughts. Gourlay seemed a fine man, if a little too dramatic, but he had answered his queries and left his treatise. Willan returned to his room to read. The natural light was perfect for reading anywhere in the room so he undressed to his shirt and, after an uneventful trip to his pot, took to his bed clutching the volume.

He skipped through the sections on Natural History and Climate and resisted the temptation to read about Affections of the Skin, his own speciality. He read, carefully, the section on Phthisis Pulmonalis, omitting references to the native population. Gourlay had written:

Madeira, from its uniformity of temperature, and purity of atmosphere, has long been, and still continues to be, the favourite retreat of consumptive patients from the northern parts of Europe. Here the unhappy sufferers, under this formidable disease, cheat the winter of their own climate, and gain that cessation of suffering, which such a situation is fitted to produce...

...But it is chiefly from the itinerant patients, who have been ordered here from Britain, my ideas of this melancholy disease have been drawn, and my experience in its treatment founded. In these patients I have remarked, that the disorder is of that species, which either arises from tubercles, and is connected with scrofula, or else is accompanied with a faulty confirmation of the chest. Before such patients repair to this last haven of health, their malady is unfortunately, in too many cases, in its last stage, when neither change of climate nor any remedy whatever can be of service. From what cause this backwardness to an earlier trial of a southern climate proceeds, is not for me to determine, but it would be well if the physicians of such patients, were to recommend a change of temperature, in the first stage of the malady, where the tubercle is yet in the inflammatory state, or where, if suppuration has taken place, it is still in a slight degree, and the lungs have suffered little derangement in their structure and functions. It is then, and then only, a change of climate will be truly beneficial. Besides the advantage of the voyage itself can only be reaped by those who are able to bear its inconveniences, not by the worn-out victim of suffering, sinking under the last symptoms of emaciation and debility...

Willan paused reading at this point. He knew that many physicians prescribed sea voyages as a cure for consumptive disease; vomiting was thought beneficial to clearing the complaint. They could not have had his passage in mind; they had sheltered off the downs from inclement weather and Napoleon's navy for over a month and yet had still suffered high seas and storms during a voyage of fifty days in total. Only the last few days of the journey in the warmth, off the Moroccan coast, had been bearable to any degree. Willan resumed reading Gourlay's recommendations for treatment.

...In cases of phthisis the mode of treatment I have found most successful, has consisted in the cautious administration of digitalis, with the use of those means that are suited to palliate distressing symptoms. On the subject of digitalis, I have the greatest satisfaction in stating, that in almost every instance where I have administered this medicine in Madeira, I have experienced the most beneficial effects from it...

...One constant effect of it has been delaying for a time the fatal issue of the malady. Where the remedy therefore has proved unsuccessful, I attribute the failure more to the disease being allowed, from neglect and inattention, to proceed to that confirmed height when neither medicine nor climate could be of service, than to any inadequacy of its specific influence. This unusual success I ascribe, in a great measure, to the concomitant advantage in the benignity of the climate, and also to a constant attention on my part to palliate the uneasy symptoms. The most distressing symptoms in phthisis, are Cough, Dyspnoea and Pains of Chest, Hemoptoe, Anorexia, Hectic Sweats, Costiveness, and Diarrhoea.

Willan retained hope. Gourlay seemed more than able and Willan did not consider his condition to be in its last stages; treatment and climate should speed a recovery. He would follow his doctor's advice and not overly exert himself. The volume dropped onto his lap as he fell into a contented sleep.

5

Willan woke. It was still light. Nobody had entered the room. Nobody was knocking at the door. Feeling rested, he washed, dressed and tidied himself. He would finish reading Gourlay's treatise in the morning and make notes. To this end he placed the volume on the desk near his bed and selected the pens and paper in readiness. He drank a glass of water from the decanter which had been left on his table and returned to his chair on the veranda; there were many ships and boats to count, requiring considerable time and concentration.

"I knocked but received no answer. I hope I am not disturbing you," said Torres, approaching Willan's chair.

"No, not at all, I am pleased to see you once again. I hope you have had a satisfying day," replied Willan. In truth, Torres had disturbed Willan's count, close to its conclusion. Willan hurried back into his room to fetch a chair for Torres; he did not wish him possibly to select the wrong chair and thereby disarrange his system of paperwork.

Torres sat next to Willan. "It is a splendid view, is it not? I have a fine table telescope upstairs which I feel sure will add to your enjoyment. I can ask Duarte to set up an outdoor table and chairs for you. I would only ask that the telescope is not left outside unattended; it is a delicate instrument."

"I am most obliged to accept your kind offer," replied Willan, already giving consideration as to where he would store the telescope and how it might help with his maritime census.

Torres, who was in control of the conversation, continued. "I am keen to hear your history and background, as promised to me, but firstly I have some news for you. I have spoken with Doctor Gourlay, who told me of your acquaintance with Thomas Bennett Smith senior. As he told you, Thomas junior and Ashby are currently lodging with me at Bachelor's Hall. They are fine gentlemen of the highest order. Gourlay and I are, however, both of the opinion that Bachelor's Hall is not an assistance to Thomas' recovery. It is far from tranquil, with people coming and going at all hours. It is, after all, a residence without women. I have given this matter some thought and have a proposal for you to consider. On doctor's orders you are to rest for at least a week. I will not disturb you after this evening. Today is Tuesday. I propose to visit you next Tuesday with Ashby Smith; Thomas, like yourself, is resting. My proposal is that Thomas move here, there is a suitable room upstairs, so as to receive care from Dona Esmeralda and the staff. Knowing Thomas as I do, I feel sure you will both benefit from this arrangement and each other's company. There will be no financial implications for either of you. There is no obligation upon yourself. I only ask for you to consider this matter between now and next week. What do you say, Doctor Willan?"

Willan's brain and mind were calculating. As always, his thoughts, decisions and opinions were governed by logic, never emotion. "I have no immediate objection to your proposal," he responded. "Will you come for dinner next week or earlier in the day?"

"Dinner is preferable. I would, of course, inform you via Duarte of any change to the arrangements. I also meant to tell you that if you have any requirements whatsoever, be they large or small, to address them to Duarte, who can send a boy to me at any time. Now, I suggest that we go to the dining room for a medicinal glass of Madeira wine and I can learn a little of your history."

Passing through his room, Willan lagged behind a little in order to have a quick check that everything was in order and correctly positioned and, so satisfied, followed on. As they entered the dining room Jorge was there holding a tray of two glasses of Madeira wine. 'How did he know we were due?' thought Willan. They sat by the fireside. Willan took a larger than normal sip of his wine and began his life story.

"You will forgive me my stutters, I hope; I am not used to talking of myself. My talking is normally confined to medical matters for the ears of students," he began. "I will be brief. I was born near Sedbergh fifty-four years ago and raised as a Quaker. I have never wavered from my belief and thank my father for instilling it in me. Sedbergh School taught me classical studies, which I enjoyed greatly, and the Latin and Greek were essential for my medical studies which I undertook at Edinburgh, the same alma mater as Doctor Gourlay. After graduation I had a short spell studying the waters of Darlington, a northern town, whilst practising there. Then I shipped to London, where I have remained to this day. I am proud of two parts of my career. Firstly that, under the guidance of Doctor John Lettsom, I operated the Carey Street Dispensary. To treat, and hopefully cure, the down-trodden poor of the city was a greater privilege than pandering to the vainglorious requests of the soured, so-called cream of London society. My twenty years in Carey Street brought me into contact with every known and unknown skin complaint which took me to my life's work, the classification of all cutaneous diseases. My initial works were published in 1808 but are not complete to my satisfaction. I fully intend, God willing, to finish this task. I married Mary in 1800 and we have a son, who is very nearly nine years old, and named after my brother. Richard is very attached to his mother and both are well provided for."

Willan sat back. He hoped that he had not seemed boastful in any way, but was pleased that he had said his piece. He was comfortable in the company of Torres. There was an honest affinity between them.

"Thank you," said Torres. "You have enlightened me greatly. It is an honour to talk and dine with you. Your throat must be very dry. I suggest another glass of Madeira between friends before dinner."

"Please proceed," said Willan.

Torres opened the door to the kitchen and spoke, fairly softly, in Portuguese. 'Whoever he is talking to cannot be far from the door,' thought Willan. Torres returned to his chair, closely followed by Jorge, who delivered the wine and left.

"To health and friendship," said Torres, raising his glass.

"To health and friendship," replied Willan.

Both men sipped their wine and relaxed back into the chairs. The silence between them was not awkward.

Torres was the first to speak. "Tonight, we are to have espada for dinner. The flesh of the fish is fine and white with a gentle taste. The fish itself is a black, ugly, eel-like monster dragged from the depths by fishermen, mainly at night. Were you to see the fish, you would not think it esculent, let alone a splendid dinner. Dona Esmeralda bought the monster today from a fisherman she trusts so you have no fears about the freshness; the fish was probably delivered from the deep not long before the accompaniments were lifted from the soil."

As if on cue, Jorge arrived with the food. 'How does he do this?' thought Willan, again perplexed by Jorge's uncanny ability always to be where he was needed, when he was needed. The men sat at the table and Jorge placed a fish fillet in front of each of them. Butter was slipping from the fish to the plate. Ahead of the men Jorge positioned bowls of potatoes, carrots and, as the previous evening, green beans. Both men ate quickly but not so fast as to appear ill-mannered.

No sooner had Willan put down his knife and fork and wiped clean his lips than Jorge re-appeared. He cleared the plates and bowls and presented each man with a small slice of cake on a plate decorated with flowers.

"Ah, honey cake," said Torres. "It is very, very sweet, hence the meagre portion. I should explain that on Madeira, honey does not come from bees. Mel, as we call it, is derived from the sugar cane grown on the island. I believe that in England you call it treacle." Willan ate the cake in two bites. It was probably one of the sweetest things he had ever eaten yet still retained a spiced, almost burned flavour.

"What a delightful treat that mouthful was," declared Willan.

The conversation continued at the table. Neither man wished to resume their position by the fireside. They exchanged pleasantries about the food for a polite time, each wondering who would make the first move to depart. Willan, who was already planning the following day, rose first.

"If you will excuse me," said Willan, "I am in need of rest and must bring our evening to a finish. Thank you for your excellent company. I would like to thank Dona Esmeralda for the fine food; perhaps you could do this for me, at your convenience."

"Of course," replied Torres. "I will add your compliments to my own. I hope you rest well and I will see you again in a week. Remember that Duarte can act as a messenger between us."

Willan collected the chamber stick from the side table and returned to his room. He checked that the now-shuttered room was as he had left it and, after a long piss, undressed and took to his bed. He was unable to complete his recollection of the day before sleep overtook him.

6

Wednesday dawned slowly; there was some morning cloud over Funchal. The temperature was no more than sixty-two degrees, about average for December. Fewer birds were singing than the previous day. Willan had slept soundly and felt refreshed as he walked towards the shuttered windows. He opened all three and, disappointed at the cloudy outlook, drew back the drapes seeking improved light, which helped a little. It was time for his pot. His bowels did not discharge as violently as of late, and Willan believed that he detected some solidity within the outpourings. Inspection showed two small turds amongst his slurry; he felt this an auspicious start to the day and he cleaned himself, washed and dressed in good humour.

Willan glanced at the bedside desk as he passed back into the room. Gourlay's book was perfectly in position. Sitting at the table he closed his eyes and told God of the previous day's events, even though he was certain God already knew. He hoped he had not been boastful or unkind in any way; he must ensure that he did not take the servants for granted; they were to be respected and appreciated. He thanked God for Tuesday and his improvement in health, then promised to fulfil his duty to others in the best way he could. Finally, he sought God's advice regarding how to help Thomas junior; they agreed that his moving to the Quinta was certainly wise.

Willan was unsure of the hour, as he had been since his arrival on Madeira. He had a solution, though: he would ask Duarte if there was an accurate timepiece that could go on the mantel. He had no use for a pocket watch and since he now used his waistcoat pockets for the essential items he previously carried in his coat pockets, there was no space. Unlike London in the winter, he did not need to wear a coat indoors.

Willan did not have to wait long for Duarte to arrive; there was a gentle knock on the door and he entered without waiting for an answer. This, rudeness to some, was not a concern to Willan, who spoke his request immediately.

"There are several clocks about the Quinta," replied Duarte. "I will test them all and select the happiest for you. I will bring later. For shaving now, sir?"

"Please proceed," said Willan.

Duarte completed a thorough shave, as the previous day, in silence. Apart from his hunger, Willan felt in fine fettle; he was looking forward to his immediate future, and life as a whole. He was further cheered when Duarte asked him where he wished to breakfast. Willan answered that he would take his food in the dining room, believing this to be the quicker option. He followed Duarte from the room and sat at the dining table.

Soon, Duarte re-appeared with tea, bread and butter, and preserves, similar to the day before. The custard tarts had been replaced by a small slice of honey cake. Willan admired the good sense and economy in using foods for consecutive days or meals; he was, as always, comforted by routine and system. Having enjoyed his breakfast, he returned to his room, passing, on the way, the young girl in black carrying his pot. Bravely he decided not to check his dressing room for the presence of a new one; his confidence was growing.

Feeling a little breathless, which he often did after food, Willan decided to fill his lungs with fresh air. He opened the central window and stepped onto the veranda, leaving the window open to refresh the air in his room. He deliberately avoided looking at the ships in the harbour. Standing with his feet apart, his hands on his hips and with his body leaned forward, he breathed as hard and regularly as he could. Some coughing interrupted his breathing but he persevered until he felt his lungs were rejuvenated. Now tired, he sat for a moment on one of the two chairs which had been left out from the evening before, again shunning eye contact with the ships below. Willan reminded himself he should always tidy up; it was arrogant to leave a trail of debris in the expectation and knowledge that others would repair the mess. The chairs were duly returned to their correct positions inside.

After a glass of water Willan was completely ready to proceed. Gourlay's book lay waiting on the desk. Lifting the book as he sat, he commenced his thorough study of the contents. Part One dealt mainly with the history and discovery of the island and its vegetable and animal production. Although Willan read it all carefully and would retain all the information therein, it was of little interest. The last section of Part One, dealing with the Customs and Manners of the inhabitants, was treated similarly but was of no interest whatsoever; Willan found it to be patronising and offensive, even though it spoke well of the Madeiran people.

Part Two dealt with climate from a geographical position preceding a *Meteorological Register of Weather, State of the Thermometer, Barometer, winds, and Weather, from January, 1793, to December, 1802, according to Observations made in the City of FUNCHAL, Island of Madeira.* This section listed the high, low and average temperature and pressure readings for each month, together with notes on the wind and rains. Willan studied the charts in detail and concluded that temperature was the foremost natural factor affecting chest complaints, but more detailed numbers were required. He would obtain a thermometer and register at least daily records. Willan was in total agreement with the last paragraph of Part Two which had been inserted:

> ...*The editor has taken the liberty of terminating here, the series Meteorological Observations. Their continuation for so long a period as sixteen years, afford undoubted proofs of the persevering attention and unwearied diligence of the author; but it seems*

questionable whether the curiosity of any reader could overcome their monotonous sameness, which is augmented by the steady uniformity of a mild and temperate climate.

Willan gave some thought to the format and style of the temperature charts he intended to complete before moving on to Part Three. This was divided into two divisions, Endemic and Epidemic diseases. Starting the first division, he raced through the eight sections on skin disease, making notes and corrections to pass on to Doctor Gourlay. Then he quickly read of the Anomalous diseases: Arthritis, Colic, Dropsy and Haemorrhoids. This left only the section on Complaints of Chest which he had previously read and which required special attention. He focussed on the eight symptoms of phthisis detailed, of which he suffered, from time to time, with four. Detailed analysis was required and Willan decided that he needed to record all of his own symptoms alongside the temperature readings.

Possessing a uniquely logical mind, Willan itched to draw up his lists and charts but, being thorough, he would finish the book first. This did not take long as Division Two relating to Epidemic diseases was of little interest or relevance.

The day got better and better. A short rap on the door was followed by Duarte entering the room holding a clock. It was a plain, square, polished-wood block, possibly mahogany, with a gilt handle to the top and a plain white enamelled face. He placed it centrally on the mantel. It showed the time to be ten minutes before noon.

"Is that the correct time?" asked Willan.

"Yes," replied Duarte, "this is the second finest clock in the house. The first is with Dona Esmeralda in the kitchen. It is very close to being first. I will check it each morning when the key is used." He slipped a large metal key under the clock which was raised a little from the mantel by spherical wooden feet. "The table and telescope will come this afternoon with Jorge and me also."

Willan felt guilty as he then asked Duarte for a thermometer which could be sited outdoors.

"If you please write on paper your need, I will send the boy to Senhor Torres," said Duarte. "Please to write now and bring to luncheon."

Keen to obtain a thermometer as soon as possible, Willan sat at the desk and wrote a short but polite request to Torres. He placed it in an unsealed but titled envelope and looked up to give it to Duarte but he had left, unnoticed by Willan. The clock showed ten minutes past noon as Willan headed to the dining room, letter in hand. He sat at the table and drank a glass of water. Looking forward to meals was, until now, but a distant memory.

Duarte came in and Willan handed him the letter. "I will send the boy now," he said, and left the room. It was several minutes until Duarte returned but Willan was heartened that he had soup with him. He placed the bowl and bread in front of Willan and stepped back to make his announcement. "Today we have caldeirada de peixe which is fishes stewed. The parts are fishes, tomatoes, potatoes and onions and the other parts from Dona Esmeralda for spices and taste." Duarte left the room. Willan ate it all in disbelief at how good it tasted, and sat happily, sipping from his glass of water. He closed his eyes and had a few quick words with God, thanking him for his providence.

Willan, back in his room, felt tired but did not want to give in to sleep so he decided to rest on his bed for a while without undressing; maybe half an hour would restore some vigour. He never lacked motivation but was restrained, these days, by all-consuming tiredness and shortness of breath. He was soon deeply asleep.

7

Noises from the veranda disturbed Willan's sleep. He rose from his bed. Remembering that he now possessed a clock, he saw the time was a little after two; he had been at rest for about an hour. As he stepped onto the veranda, he immediately saw a round heavy, wooden table but nothing else nor any person. How had the table been delivered through his room without disturbing him? His question was answered by the vision of Duarte scrambling over the balustrade to his extreme right. It was not a dignified entrance. Willan surmised, correctly, that the balustrade lay between the veranda and the stoned area to the left of the main entrance hidden by shrubbery.

Duarte turned and collected a wooden chair from the balustrade. He put it down, turned again and collected another. Willan briefly spotted Jorge's head amongst the bushes. Duarte removed both chairs and positioned them at the table; they were almost sited to Willan's satisfaction, but not quite. "Telescope is for cleaning and will come tomorrow," said Duarte, before leaving through the room. His departure would have been more dignified than his entrance were it not for the soil and leaves decorating the back of his coat.

The table and chairs were soon lined up to Willan's design and he took the opportunity to try both chairs, seeking the optimum position to view the harbour. There was plenty of activity there to interest Willan but too much for an accurate survey; besides, tomorrow he would have the use of a telescope.

Willan went to his dressing room, where he washed and tidied himself. His confidence in not checking earlier that his pot had been replaced was compounded as he enjoyed a lengthy piss from a standing position. He decided to take a walk in the gardens; it would be pleasant to take the air and discover more of his surroundings. The sun was now shining from time to time through the clouds and this was the exercise recommended by Doctor Gourlay. Furthermore, he could find a suitable location for the thermometer he felt sure Torres would supply.

Leaving his room, Willan tried the handle of the fan-lighted door to the right of his own. It opened easily and he stepped outside. Ahead of him lay a colonnade leading to an abrupt end with a small doorway. The colonnade was walled to the left with a fine frieze of blue and white tiles, depicting pastoral scenes, to the lower half. The right side was open. A pair of strong pillars at the beginning of the colonnade was matched by a pair at the far end and two pairs to the middle formed a central outdoor room from which to enjoy the vista. Willan imagined ladies taking afternoon tea from this spot, enjoying the view and idle gossip. There was a staircase immediately in front of him and a corresponding one at the other end; both led to the gardens below.

Willan strode to the middle of the colonnade and paused to admire the view. For a change, after a brief glimpse at the harbour, he turned his eyes inland; he could see small figures, bent over, tending to small plots of land. He admired their fortitude but despaired at the amount of work required for what appeared to be such a meagre return. Fair climate was no compensation for such endless toil. Nevertheless, the scene was one Willan felt he could never tire of.

Reaching the far end of the colonnade, Willan turned and looked back towards his room and the building as a whole. He liked what he saw; the building was sturdy and comforting as well as of a fine appearance. At this point he noticed that all of the building and its paths and surroundings were in perfect condition; the building was clearly not new, yet showed no sign of wear and tear. He looked down to the gardens. Again, all was in good, if not perfect, order. Willan was pleased; he considered that fine buildings that had fallen into disrepair were not dissimilar from humans whose health had suffered from the lack of basic amenities; there was no need for either in the nineteenth century.

Thermometers needed to be located away from buildings, out of direct sunlight, and at about head height. Why Willan knew this he had no idea, but he also knew that he could always trust his retentive memory. He descended the eleven wide steps to the formal garden. Its Italian style suited the building well and did not look out of place against the agricultural surroundings in the distance. Turning back to the house Willan saw a spring eagerly exuding water immediately below the centre of the colonnade. The juxtaposition of the natural rock and water below and the formal building above worked well; nature and humanity combined seamlessly.

Turning towards the harbour, Willan's attention was drawn not to the ships and boats in the distance but to a large multi-trunked tree at the far boundary of the formal garden. As he walked along another mosaic path towards it, he became more and more convinced that this could be an ideal location to site a thermometer. Dark rough trunks sprouted from the base and from about ten feet above ground, a mass of green glossy leaves spread, untidily, outwards and upwards, perhaps to a height of seventy feet. It was not a thing of beauty and clearly had been in position years or centuries before the formal garden or even the building. Willan studied and touched the trunks to the northern side of the tree; he had found a home for his thermometer.

The land attached to the house dropped down from where Willan now stood. He walked to the left, on the level, for about fifty yards until he neared a rendered wall which appeared to mark the boundary of the property. This path had been bordered by a tall soft-leaved hedge preventing access and sight of the land behind. Some ten yards before the wall the hedge stopped and, looking to his right, Willan saw a forest of short palm-like trees with enormous fronds or leaves shading trunks of about six feet in height; each tree was nearly ten feet tall. They formed a green carpet rolling down the slope and although there were no gaps within the foliage they seemed to have been planted in straight rows. He crossed the dry brown soil between himself and the trees and stared at the plantation, for that is what he thought it must be. Close examination with his hands and eyes showed what initially appeared to be a tree trunk was, in fact, the spiralled bases of the leaves tightly twisted together to form a trunk-like support to the leaves themselves. The plant dried and turned brown from the base upwards.

Willan observed some of the plants had large pendulum-like appendages hanging below their canopy and he walked four plants along to look at one more closely. He stood next to a structure, the likes of which he had never seen before; he was afraid to touch it. A long stem sprouted from the heart of the plant and bent downwards towards the ground. At the tip of this hung a large, slightly ajar, red bud-like flower of perhaps a foot in length. Above this were six rows of green fruit-like growths forming circumferences to the stem. The fruits resembled the clasped green fingers of a congregation raised upwards, as if in prayer.

Unable to take his eyes away from the plant and still afraid to touch it, Willan remained motionless, completely spellbound. Although discomforted by the alien appendage, the warm, sweet and earthy atmosphere, canopied by dappled winter sun, welcomed him and kept him, as if swathed by nature itself.

Only after several minutes of trance-like staring was Willan able to recover his senses. He began to wander from plant to plant and even ventured one row inside the plantation, which he found to be a little unnerving due to the proximity of the hanging fruits on some of the plants. Quickly he withdrew to safety.

He was not alone. Walking towards him came a man carrying a garden tool in his right hand. He did not seem threatening and Willan was not alarmed. As the man neared, he spoke in Portuguese. "Sorry," replied Willan as he extended his hand in greeting. The man dropped the tool and bowed a little as they shook hands.

"Banana," said the man, pointing towards a hanging bunch of fruits. Perhaps ten years younger than Willan, he wore a brown shirt under a sleeveless, four-pocketed, leather jerkin, supported by brown linen trousers and soft leather boots. His dark face was topped by short black hair, the only part of him not brown in colour; he could easily merge unseen with the soil. For no logical reason, Willan knew him to be a kindly, gentle man.

"Aha," said Willan. He had heard of bananas but never seen one. His memory reminded him that, in England, they were a fruit only to be found on the tables of the rich seeking to impress. He pointed to the fruits with his left hand and mimicked an eating motion with his right near to his lips. The man understood Willan's enquiry and returned the gesticulation by criss-crossing his lower arms from side to side in unison with his turning head. Clearly, the fruits were not for eating.

Pointing at a small table and chairs at the end of the first row of bananas, the man picked up the tool and started to walk that way, indicating that Willan should accompany him. Willan did so, realising that he was re-tracing his initial walk from the house, but this time on the other side of the hedge. They reached the table and the man pulled a chair out, brushed the seat with his hand and invited Willan to sit. After he had done so, the man extended his right arm and hand with the palm upwards, towards Willan, as he began to walk off. Willan responded by lowering his hands onto the table. Both men knew that he was to stay and the man would return. The man soon disappeared from sight as he followed a narrow track downwards along the right side of the plantation.

Willan sat contentedly. He was warm but shaded from the direct sun, and the smell of earth and banana plants was both fragrant and comforting. There was also a fine view of the hills dropping down to the left side of the bay of Funchal. Ever curious, Willan was keen for the man to return and for this episode to play out. He closed his eyes, thanked God for caring for his body and soul, and, not wishing to sleep, sat upright and continued to enjoy the scene.

The man soon returned. He placed a plate on the table in front of Willan. It bore a single banana fruit, similar to those on the plants but yellow in colour. Sitting down, the man mimicked the earlier gesture of eating and pointed at Willan. Taking his cue, and eager to taste the fruit, Willan reached into his waistcoat pocket with his right hand and pulled out a slender, silver blade, intending to cut into the fruit. As Willan unfolded the knife the man, who was still standing, quickly took hold of Willan's right wrist and firmly prevented him from continuing. As Willan pulled back, not knowing what he had done wrong, the man released his grip and mimicked that Willan should return the now re-folded blade to his pocket. Willan did so, which clearly satisfied the man, who visibly relaxed.

He smiled an apology towards Willan, picked up the fruit and, holding it at the same angle as the green fruits still on the plants, peeled back the rind to about halfway. This revealed a very pale off-yellow interior, which the man broke in half. He then divided this section in two, placed one piece in his mouth and offered the other half to Willan, who did likewise, albeit nervously. The fruit tasted a little of how the plants smelled; it was not over sweet and had a creamy taste and texture. The man peeled the remainder of the banana and handed it to Willan, who ate it confidently. It was extraordinary in a very pleasant way.

The man sat on the other chair, an action that pleased Willan. They smiled at each other before the man shifted his chair so that he too faced the view; they were sitting alongside, rather than opposite each other. Despite the closeness of the other man, to whom he could not converse, Willan was not uncomfortable, nor, would it seem, was his companion. They sat in silence, each with his own thoughts, enjoying the late afternoon sun and, to Willan's mind, the beauty of God's creation. Time passed easily.

Rising, the man faced Willan and offered his hand. Willan also stood and they shook hands in the way of old acquaintances. The man walked directly to the hedge and beckoned Willan to follow. As they reached the hedge the man disappeared from view into the foliage. There was a path through the hedge, ingeniously cut obliquely backwards; Willan had not noticed it when initially walking the length of the hedge. Both men were now through it and Willan realised how near to the house they had been sitting. The man waved farewell and returned through the greenery. Willan walked back to the house.

8

It was nearly five as Willan reached his room. He was very tired but dared not rest for fear of falling asleep. Although he had been outside for some hours already, he considered more fresh outdoor air would help stave off sleep; also, there were always ships to be counted. The sun was going down so Willan decided to survey the harbour for maybe half an hour before washing and heading for the dining room. His chest was feeling tight and his breathing a little short but he considered that, nevertheless, he was starting to feel the benefit of Madeira's climate; his confidence was still high.

After a few minutes Willan conceded defeat; too many ships and failing light made his task impossible. He returned inside and carried out a tour of inspection. Everything was in order but Willan felt that you could never be too sure. After a short piss, which he did not really need, he washed and tidied himself. Checking his appearance in the looking glass he realised his hair was long and curling at the ends. His last cut, made on board the *Alligator* by the ship's barber, had been all too unfortunate an experience; the quickest, roughest and worst cut of his life. He would speak with Duarte, and with this in mind he set off for the dining room.

Once there Willan coughed deliberately to announce his arrival and after only a few moments Duarte appeared. As the question of his long hair was foremost in his thoughts, he enquired of Duarte, immediately, as to where and how he could find a barber. "I will ask Dona Esmeralda for tomorrow," replied Duarte. For the first time, Willan did not understand Duarte's fractured English.

"I am sorry," said Willan, "but I do not understand completely. Are you to ask Dona Esmeralda tomorrow, or is she to cut my hair tomorrow? Or who is to cut my hair?"

"It is I who is sorry for my English," replied Duarte. "Dona Esmeralda will cut your hair tomorrow after your toilet. I will also attend."

"Thank you. Do not be offended by our misunderstanding. Your English is excellent," replied Willan. Both men smiled.

"If you wait, please, I will collect for you," said Duarte. He left the room but went, unusually, not to the kitchen but to the main hallway. He returned almost immediately carrying a small, green, cloth package. Unwrapping it, he handed Willan a thermometer, not new but in perfect order. Willan could hardly contain his delight. It was a mercury-filled, Fahrenheit thermometer of about nine inches in length, calibrated on the left from zero to one hundred and fifty. On the right it was marked at thirty as 'Freezing', fifty-five as 'Temperate', seventy-five as 'Summer Heat' and ninety-eight as 'Blood Heat'. There was a hole in the top of the wooden casing to assist hanging.

Willan thanked Duarte for the thermometer and explained he wished to collect the air temperature reading daily and he knew where he thought it should be sited. He led Duarte through the door leading to the colonnade.

Pointing to the end of the formal garden, Willan said, "I believe the ideal position would be on this side of the large tree at about our eye level."

"You have made a wise and most clever selection," said Duarte, continuing, "that is the til tree after which the Quinta is so named. It is very old."

Willan had not considered, at any time, as to what the word 'til' meant; he had assumed it was simply the name of a place or person.

Good information like this was always welcome. The question of how the thermometer would be attached to the tree was pre-empted by Duarte, who said that he and Jorge would 'fix the nail for the hole' the following morning, after Willan's haircut.

The men returned to the dining room and, ever seeking to resolve misunderstandings, Willan related the afternoon's events and the man's reaction to the sight of his knife; he produced the folded blade from his pocket to show Duarte and sought his opinion.

"This will be a long explanation," replied Duarte. "Please excusing my English." He continued, "You have met Senhor Abobora. He is a very fine gentleman. I will explain his names. His real name is Carlos Abreu but no person calls him that. Not even his wife. Madeirans and people who speak Portuguese call him Senhor Abobora as a sign of great respect. An abobora is a very large round vegetable which we cook a lot for stews. He grows the finest aboboras in all Madeira and is also the island's greatest groundsperson. There is not a fruit or vegetable at which he does not excel. Other Quintas send their groundspeople to be educated by him. Persons who speak English call him Senhor Pompion, which is the word for the abobora. Are you aware of this vegetable, Doctor Willan?"

"I believe so," replied Willan, "but I am not certain."

"I will fetch," said Duarte, who left for the kitchen.

He returned shortly afterwards carrying an enormous vegetable. It was bright orange, thick-skinned and about the size of a man's head, although flatter. What remained of the central stalk was still green and the sides were vertically ribbed. Willan did recognise the pompion but had only ever seen a smaller one.

"I do know the vegetable," said Willan, "but I do not remember ever tasting it."

"We served soup on Monday with abobora, sorry, I mean pompion," said Duarte.

"In that case I like it very much," responded Willan. "I now know who the gentleman is and I shall refer to him as Senhor Pompion henceforth. All that remains to settle my curiosity is to understand his distaste for my knife."

"I can explain this," said Duarte. "Many years ago, when Madeira was young, the people were a little afraid of the banana plant and its large leaves, but they found the fruits splendid. They considered, as some such as Senhor Pompion still do, that to cut the fruit with knife was a sin. They believe that after cutting with knife, the pattern appears as a crucifix. I do not believe this, but many do."

Willan was grateful that his curiosity had been almost satisfied; all he needed to do now was to cut open a banana with his blade.

"Are you now ready for the dinner?" asked Duarte.

"Please proceed," replied Willan, and Duarte returned to the kitchen.

Willan could hear Duarte and Dona Esmeralda talking, and even though it was in Portuguese, he could tell that Dona Esmeralda was in control of the conversation; she was the decision-maker. Duarte soon returned without food, which slightly disappointed Willan, who was sitting at the table in anticipation; he now looked forward to meals. "I have indications from Dona Esmeralda," he announced. "Today our dinner will be a stew of fowl. She is pleased that you have met Senhor Pompion, who she greatly respects. We will place bananas on your table in your room, but you should not eat other fruits as they are acid to your stomach. Tomorrow Dona Esmeralda will make soup of pompion for you. It is very nice. I will go now for the dinner." Willan felt safe in Dona Esmeralda's hands.

Duarte soon returned with the food. He gave Willan a bowl of presumably chicken, stew and a plate of, obviously very hot, orange-brown cubes about an inch square. "We call this milho frito," he said. "It is cooked and fried cornmeal with taste." Willan ate his food wondering if he would ever be given a meal not to his taste; it was delicious and only a few chicken bones remained in his bowl. He looked up and saw Duarte returning with a small plate.

"We now have Bolo de Familia, which is family cake made with Madeira wine, syrup of sugar cane and spices of Dona Esmeralda," said Duarte, handing Willan a generous slice of cake. Willan ate every crumb.

Now he had a clock in his room, Willan asked Duarte at what specific times meals were served. "Another difficult question for me." Duarte smiled. "Breakfast is whenever you are ready, luncheon is normally about noon, if you are here, and dinner is usually soon after the sun goes. Dinner in the summer is sometimes very late."

'Perhaps I have no need of a clock after all,' thought Willan.

Willan bade Duarte goodnight, asked him to thank Dona Esmeralda for the food and returned to his room. He was soon ready for his bed and fell asleep still recalling the day's events and thinking fondly of the people with whom he had shared them.

9

Thursday the fifth of December had started normally, but now, at nine thirty, Willan was sitting at his table, very nervously awaiting a haircut; he had rinsed his hair earlier in preparation. In London his hair, which had never been this long before, was trimmed, as necessary, after his daily shave.

There was a knock on the door and Dona Esmeralda entered the room followed by Duarte carrying a tray, the contents of which were covered by a towel. She smiled at Willan as if to say, 'Do not be worried.' Duarte placed the towel over Willan's shoulders and the tray on the table. Two pairs of scissors, a comb, a brush and two round jars were under the towel.

"Good morning. I am here if needed," said Duarte before Dona Esmeralda started. She began by brushing and combing his hair forward; it covered his eyes. Soon, the larger pair of scissors were snipping away confidently; white hair covered the towel. Gently nudging Willan's head back she combed his hair backwards and stepped back a pace to inspect her work. Seemingly pleased with her actions, she re-cut the hair with the smaller scissors before speaking to Duarte.

"Dona Esmeralda has cut the hair. Now she will finish with the oils. You will soon smell of nature," said Duarte. She opened one jar and scooped out a small amount of the lotion which she massaged between her hands before rubbing it into Willan's hair and scalp quite vigorously. For the second time since arriving at the Quinta do Til, Willan resembled a lunatic, albeit this time, a sweet-smelling lunatic. Again, Dona Esmeralda spoke to Duarte.

"We must now wait for some minutes for actions," said Duarte as Dona Esmeralda left the room. After a short while, mainly to break the silence, Willan asked Duarte if he and Jorge still intended to site the thermometer that morning. Duarte replied that as soon as Jorge arrived with the nails and tools they would indeed do so. The second silence was broken by Dona Esmeralda's return and further conversation with Duarte.

"Dona Esmeralda tells me that Jorge is here, but not to go to the tree until I go with him. I will go soon. She will now finish your hair," said Duarte. After brushing and combing Willan's hair into order, Dona Esmeralda gently smoothed some lotion from the second jar onto it, rather than his scalp. She then combed it again and stepped back; the haircut was finished. Duarte removed the towel with as much of Willan's loose hair as he could.

"We hope that your hair is good. Shall you go to the looking glass?" asked Duarte. Willan rose and entered the dressing room. His hair was short, tidy and, to Willan's mind, pleasing to the eye; he was completely satisfied.

"I am very content," said Willan, re-entering the room. Duarte was sweeping hair from the floor. Dona Esmeralda had left. "Please thank Dona Esmeralda for me," he said.

"Jorge and I will go to the tree now," said Duarte as he left the room.

Willan's immediate intentions had been decided for him; he could not resist spectating upon Jorge, Duarte, the nail and the tree. This urge had been strengthened by Dona Esmeralda's apparent reluctance to allow Jorge to attempt the task alone. Selecting the chair from beside his bed as being the lightest, he swept it up and headed for the colonnade. The central area made for perfect viewing; Willan positioned his chair, settled himself, and awaited the players and the performance.

And what a performance it was. Jorge and Duarte entered stage right. Duarte carried a hammer and the green cloth package; Jorge swung along with a hessian sack. They stared at the tree for some time, occasionally pointing at or touching it in various places, obviously seeking the optimum site for the nail. There was constant, earnest conversation between them. Having selected the position, both men took hold of the hessian sack at the same time, spilling the contents to the earth surrounding the tree. They clashed heads only once as they collected up the nails. Duarte made the first, unsuccessful, attempt to secure the nail and Jorge the second. They alternated until each of them had failed three times before standing back to re-appraise the situation.

Now came the finale. Entering stage left strode Senhor Pompion. He reached the tree, picked a nail from the ground and struck it home with an easy swing of his grub-hoe. A quick glance told him the nail was secure and perfectly positioned, and he departed. Not a word had passed between Senhor Pompion and the two men.

Duarte and Jorge spent a little time testing the fastness of the nail and inspecting it from different angles before hanging the thermometer and departing the stage. Willan's personal performance by Madeira's Rude Mechanicals was over.

Stifling a laugh, Willan looked back towards the house. He caught the eye of Dona Esmeralda who had, obviously, also witnessed the theatricals. Nearly laughing, she looked at Willan, shaking her head in exasperation. Willan opened his arms and gestured disbelief in return. Dona Esmeralda returned to the house with her right hand covering her mouth. Willan returned to his room soon afterwards, carrying his chair.

Although keen to inspect his thermometer, Willan resisted the urge to do so immediately; he was unsure if Duarte was aware of his observation of the nailing and thought it better to bump into him later rather than sooner. Willan decided to spend a little time designing his charts and papers ready for his data, the collection of which he intended to commence the following day.

Nearing noon, he left his room and headed outside to inspect the thermometer before luncheon. It was securely fixed at an ideal height, well sheltered and exactly to Willan's wishes. He picked up a nail from the ground, smiled as he placed it in his pocket and headed for the dining room.

Duarte appeared as soon as Willan entered. "The thermometer is firmly nailed is it not?" he asked.

"Indeed, it is," replied Willan. "My thanks to you and Jorge."

"Telescope is coming to the room after soup, please sit," said Duarte, clearly changing the subject from the thermometer.

Willan enjoyed his soup of pompion very much and returned to his room in a good humour and with a contented stomach. He sat at the table on the veranda to await the telescope.

Duarte soon appeared, carrying the telescope with great dignity. It was not cased, which surprised Willan; in London all medical and optical instruments were always protected by cases. Made of brass and coated with lacquer it was nearly two feet long with a diameter of about three inches; it stood on a detachable tripod and was easily adjustable. It had recently been thoroughly cleaned. Willan, who was familiar with microscopes, soon established it was in perfect working order and spare, velvet-wrapped, extension eye pieces were transferred from Duarte's waistcoat to his own. It was as well they were wrapped, as a nail still lurked in Willan's pocket.

As soon as Duarte had left, Willan began a systematic survey of the Bay of Funchal and its environs. He continued for as long as possible, only stopping when his eyes and brain no longer seemed to be in harmony. Willan felt he was in a privileged position looking down on the city and its people, and reminded himself that he must be grateful for his good fortune and always seek to help his fellow man, no matter their circumstances. Knowing God's will could best be served if he were in possession of good health, Willan decided again to follow Gourlay's advice and go for a restorative walk. He returned the telescope to its allocated spot, on the desk nearest the door, and set off.

He walked along the colonnade as far as the centre where he paused, looked at the til tree with its thermometer and remembered the events of the morning. Reminding himself that Duarte and Jorge had been providing assistance and were deserving of his gratitude, he was annoyed that he had found the scene amusing; he must try harder to remain sober of thought.

Having apologised to God and his own conscience for his failings, he decided not to re-inspect the thermometer; tomorrow would be soon enough. Instead, following his walk of yesterday, he carefully scoured the hedge for the hidden passage, which he located only by looking backwards after he had passed it without noticing. As he walked through the gap it was as if he were entering a different land; the air was warmer and the smell both sweet and earthy. He breathed in both the scene and the fragrant air.

The banana plants drew him like a magnet. He was fascinated and, unlike yesterday, not afraid to touch. The contrast between the textures and colours of the stems, leaves and fruits was remarkable, as was the beauty of the whole scene. Willan was reminded of the first two lines of a William Cowper hymn:

'God moves in a mysterious way, his wonders to perform.'

Although, like all Quakers, he did not sing hymns, Willan found the words of many to be moving and heartfelt; he had learned many by rote. As when he was looking down on Funchal through his telescope, Willan felt privileged and grateful to God for his good fortune in being in such surroundings. Optimism took over him. Tomorrow he would work on his research in the morning and commence his data collection after luncheon. He would then be able to justify the indulgence of a restorative walk in an apparent paradise. His health recovered, the winter passed, he would be able to return to London, his work and his family.

Willan returned to the reality of the present; he was unsure as to which way to head. He opted for prevarication and decided to consider the possibilities whilst sitting down. He resumed his seat of the previous afternoon. The path downhill to the right of the banana plantation, from where Senhor Pompion had emerged with the banana fruit, was both enticing and daunting. Prevarication won the day, however, and he remained in his seat, idly designing data charts mentally.

Sensing he might drift into sleep, Willan started back to the house, where he could note down some of his plans. Proud that he now knew the exact location of the passage, he hurried that way and turned back into the entrance without a second glance. He hit Senhor Pompion full on and both men crashed leftwards into different sides of the hedge. "Sorry, sorry," said Willan as he stumbled back to the path. Senhor Pompion had already regained the path and steadied Willan, preventing him from entering the opposite hedge. The two men faced each other, both brushing leaves from their clothes. Senhor Pompion burst into real laughter and after a pause so did Willan.

The laughter stopped as the men drew breath; both were smiling. Senhor Pompion stood to one side, bowed flamboyantly like a courtier, and bade Willan to proceed. Willan bowed his thanks and both men continued their journeys. Willan turned back but the obliqueness of the pathway served its purpose and blocked the line of vision.

Back in his room Willan sat at the table, his favoured position. He needed to take stock of his situation; he had been amused by the antics of others, and shared laughter with an almost stranger. He had enjoyed great diversion which was now making him unhappy and confused. Had he let down both himself and, to some extent, God, or was this frivolity allowed? These decisions, he knew, were his and his alone, and deeper thought was required. None of this was helped by the notion God might be laughing as he looked down upon him. In the meantime, he pledged to himself to maintain a dignified and sober existence.

Unable to concentrate on his charts and plans, and too early for dinner, Willan took his telescope to the veranda and passed nearly an hour counting ships and following their movements. This distraction served to clear his mind of philosophical and religious quandaries; he would sleep on it and resolve them with God the following morning.

The sun was dipping beyond the furthest hill and Willan caught what he thought to be the smells of either roasting, baking or both. He wasted no time in returning the telescope to the desk and cleaning and smartening himself. A quick check of the room and its contents, a couple of deep breaths and he was ready.

Jorge was waiting for him in the dining room and immediately proffered a glass of Madeira wine. Although sorely tempted, Willan declined; his behaviour this day had been bad enough already. Alcohol would surely add to his progression downhill into becoming the worst sort of man about town. Jorge took the glass in the direction of the kitchen, although Willan suspected the contents might not complete the journey.

Dinner was delicious, as always, and was followed by a creamy almond dessert which, unusually, was not to Willan's taste, although he ate it out of politeness. Just as he was about to leave, Jorge returned and spoke to him. "I hope you enjoyed your meal, Doctor Willan. Is there anything else I can get you to eat or drink? I apologise for the delay in the supply of bananas, but I have selected a nice bunch for you and put them on the table in your room. Are you certain I cannot get you anything? Some more dessert, perhaps?"

Willan was distraught with himself. Why had he assumed that Jorge did not speak English? He stuttered an awkward, "No, thank you," collected his chamber stick and hurried away to his room. The sight of the bananas only served to heighten his distress. He knew he possessed a logical mind; why was he not using it? He was ashamed of himself and his arrogant pomposity: but how could he resolve the situation? He sat on his bed, deep in thought.

After several minutes he got up, returned to the dining room and knocked on the kitchen door. Jorge opened it and Willan spoke. "I have returned to apologise to you for my ill-mannered and hasty exit. I confess I had arrogantly assumed that you did not speak English and your perfect words startled me. I am very sorry, please forgive me my rudeness."

"Think nothing of it," replied Jorge with a smile, "and thank you for your honesty."

"And thank you for the bananas," said Willan, greatly relieved but at a loss for more pertinent words. They wished each other a good night and Willan returned to his room. He would be able to sleep now.

10

Willan's folded blade was now more of a fruit-knife than a pen-knife: more precisely a banana knife. Over the last four days he had sliced apart at least eight bananas in his quest for an image of the crucifixion. Although he had not found the image, he had greatly enjoyed the bananas. He was sitting at the table, idly playing with his knife. It was silver, nearly four inches long when unopened and the perfect comforter to be toyed with in an idle moment. The silver sides were ribbed and the edge opposite the blade formed of mother of pearl. Willan considered it one of his most prized possessions.

The knife had been given to him by Doctor John Fothergill in 1780, shortly before his death. Over thirty years later, Willan still remembered him as being probably the greatest influence on both his life and his career. Fothergill, like Willan, had schooled at Sedbergh and studied medicine at Edinburgh, albeit over forty years earlier. He too was a Quaker. Willan had spent his first year after graduation working with him and assisting his research in London. Not only had he been taught further medicine, Fothergill also introduced him to other practitioners, all of the highest calibre. More importantly, he had influenced Willan through example; he was the finest of men and worked tirelessly for the benefit of others. He was also a keen botanist and plant collector; Willan knew that the flora of Madeira would have given him a great interest.

Apart from slicing bananas, Willan had also spent the last four days working on his research, collecting his personal medical data and establishing his routine; he was never comfortable without routine.

Each day followed the same pattern. After his toilet and breakfast, which he took in his room, he would spend the morning at the desk nearest his bed working on his research into and classification of skin complaints. He had written to Doctor Thomas Bateman, his assistant researcher in London, advising him of this resumption and requesting further papers and information. This in turn had reminded him to write to his wife to inform her of his safe arrival and remind her that if she had any requirements to contact his lawyer or, if necessary, Bateman. Duarte had sent the boy to Torres with the letters.

Immediately before luncheon, Willan would visit the til tree and take an air temperature reading; the first five readings had shown an average temperature of sixty-four degrees. After his soup in the dining room, he would return to his room and the desk nearest the door to collate his medical data after first entering that day's temperature reading. In addition to noting any of the eight symptoms of consumptive illness outlined in Gourlay's book, he also recorded the details of his bowel evacuations and any other factors that may have arisen. His greatest concerns were still the liquidness of his slurry, the occasional blood in his phlegm and his tiredness. Overall, though, he considered his health to be improving.

Only when he was satisfied all of his information had been recorded would he relax. He would walk to the banana plantation, where he had twice waved to a distant Senhor Pompion, before returning to the veranda and his maritime survey. After dinner he would retire early; he was sleeping well enough but still always tired.

It had been a very quiet four days, which had suited Willan. He was now aware, over a week since his arrival on Madeira, of the quiet, or rather the lack of constant noise – unlike London. Work, study and contemplation were much easier undisturbed. His only conversations of any import were with God, with whom he had still not resolved the question of whether mankind was on earth for endeavour or pleasure or, as Willan now hoped, mainly endeavour with a modicum of pleasure. He intended to follow a path of diligent service and to avoid frivolity or situations that might lead to it, although as his routine was about to be disrupted, he would have to be watchful.

Nearing six, Willan decided to head to the dining room where Torres and Ashby Smith were due to join him. He had heard no unusual sounds, despite listening attentively, so presumed they had not yet arrived. Despite being more than content with his own company, Willan was looking forward to the evening and the conversation and information it would bring.

The dining room had been transformed. A third leather chair was now in front of the fireplace and a small drinks table placed between the chairs. The table was set for three with a large silver candelabra flickering in the centre. The scene was one of warmth and welcome. Jorge arrived with a glass of Madeira wine.

"I believe your guests have arrived. I just heard horses heading to the stables," he said.

"Thank you, Jorge," replied Willan. "I am quite looking forward to the evening. I wonder what delights Dona Esmeralda has planned for us?"

"It is not for me to say," said Jorge, with a mischievous smile.

Willan and Jorge continued to chat politely and amiably. They conversed well but Willan always sensed there was something more to Jorge than seemed apparent. Perhaps there was a secret, but he did not think it was a dark one.

The sound of the main door handle turning and boots crossing a stone floor heralded the arrival of Willan's guests. Warm introductions and handshakes were exchanged by all, including Jorge and Duarte, who had now arrived in the room with more wine. Torres assumed the role of host and suggested they enjoy their wine by the fireside. Willan was struck by the similarity of Torres and Ashby Smith; although Ashby Smith was a good head taller, they could easily be brothers. The conversation was very general and, after enquiries as to health, mainly consisted of Willan asking after Ashby Smith's father, whom he knew well. Willan also took the opportunity, as was normal in this type of genial talk, of telling Torres that he had first met Ashby Smith when he was still suckling at his mother's breast. Willan formed a good opinion of Ashby Smith.

Willan decided the formalities had been served and turned to the main purpose of the evening. He spoke to Ashby Smith but not to the exclusion of Torres.

"I have been made aware of your brother's health from Doctor Gourlay and Senhor Torres, who have asked if I would consider giving my approval to his continued treatment here at the Quinta do Til. Not only do I approve, I would welcome this move as being of benefit to all. That is, of course, if it is still your wish."

Clearly this had been the decision that Torres and Ashby Smith had desired, and the talk quickly turned to planning the move; Torres would arrange it all. Thomas Bennett Smith junior would transfer to the room directly above Willan on Thursday, the day after tomorrow. At great relief to all they arranged names; Ashby Smith would be referred to as Ashby, his brother as Bennett whilst Smith would remain their father's name. Torres remarked that Ashby had better inform his brother that not only was his address to be changed, so was his name. Ashby laughed. Willan missed the joke.

Dinner was excellent: roasted lamb, roasted potatoes and fresh beans. They all praised the food and Ashby said he would only visit his brother at mealtimes, which seemed wise to Willan, but Torres laughed. After a slice of very sweet cake, they resumed their armchairs with a second glass of Madeira wine; they had drunk water with dinner.

The conversation was difficult. All three men knew that the main business of the evening had been achieved and that the detail would be dealt with by Torres over the next two days. There was no point in thinking beyond this time. Willan was about to make the first move and explain that his tiredness was urging an early retirement, when Ashby spoke.

"Gentlemen. If you will excuse me, I feel it is only fair that I hasten to my brother and deliver the good news; it will lift his spirits no end." Then, directing his words to Torres, he continued, "Perhaps you could show me the path to the Hall, of which you spoke."

"I can improve upon that," replied Torres. "I will accompany you. Two lamps will be better than one and it is not the straightest path. Our horses are well taken care of here, and will be well rested for our return in the morning."

After handshakes all round, Torres and Ashby departed through the kitchen door. Willan collected his chamber stick, lit it from the candelabra and returned to his room. He sat on the edge of his bed and reflected. He was satisfied that he had done the right thing in welcoming Bennett to the Quinta and thanked God for his guidance. If his routine were interrupted, so be it; the benefit to others outweighed his own selfish needs.

Contented, he retired.

11

Wednesday was Willan's loudest day on Madeira so far. Long before Duarte came to shave him, he had heard all manner of noises seemingly from throughout the building. Duarte explained that he and Jorge were preparing the room above for Senhor Bennett, and much furniture was moving about. The noises, accompanied by loud conversations, continued beyond breakfast and distracted Willan from his research, although the thought of complaining never entered his mind. Eventually, after a particularly loud crash and, he thought, the sound of breaking glass, he decided to de-camp to the dining room. He filled his portmanteau with the papers he needed and left the room.

As he reached the foot of the staircase, Willan paused and looked up, seeking a sight of what was making the noise. Descending the stairs quickly, with a countenance of despair and frustration, was Dona Esmeralda. On seeing Willan and his case, she too paused and as their eyes met, both knew exactly what the other was thinking; no words of any language were necessary. The silence was broken by a further crash from above, to which Dona Esmeralda responded by theatrically covering her ears. They were both still laughing as she entered the kitchen, leaving the door ajar, and Willan sat at the dining table.

Before starting on his papers, Willan cleared his mind of any thoughts that could be misconstrued as making fun at the expense of Duarte and Jorge; they were two of the most obliging and genuine men he had ever had the good fortune to meet. Willan settled down to his papers but had no sooner started reading when he was the recipient of a great surprise. Dona Esmeralda came to the table with a tray of tea. There was a blue and white porcelain teapot, milk jug and sugar bowl, accompanied by two matching cups and saucers. She sat opposite Willan and gestured that he should serve himself first. He indicated he would follow her. The stalemate was broken as they both reached for the teapot at the same time. Dona Esmeralda laughed and took over as hostess, pouring both cups and offering the milk and sugar to Willan, which he declined. The hot tea acted as a relaxant to both of them and Willan realised that he had discovered Dona Esmeralda's safety valve: a cup of tea and a short reflection away from any anxiety or difficulty. They sat together, without embarrassment, each enjoying the quiet and peace. Dona Esmeralda sparkled the warmest of smiles to Willan as she departed the room with the tea tray. He resumed his work with a clear mind and strong motivation.

Willan concentrated on his paperwork until he thought it might be time to take his air temperature reading. He returned to his room and was pleased with his time prediction; it was indeed nearly noon. The papers he had been working on were returned to their correct positions on the correct desk; the now-emptied portmanteau was placed on the floor alongside the desk nearest the bed. He took a quick piss, washed his face and hands, and headed to the garden.

As he walked towards the til tree, Willan considered what the reading was likely to be; he was normally reasonably accurate. Feeling slightly cooler he estimated sixty-one degrees and was satisfied with his judgement as the thermometer showed sixty-two. About to return to the house, Willan caught sight of a movement out of the corner of his eye. On the tree at about waist height and to his right was a brown lizard of nearly three inches in length. It remained motionless and as Willan stared at the tree he noticed others, of differing lengths but none longer than the first he had espied; their colouring camouflaged them well against the bark of the tree. Many of the lizards darted here and there, seemingly in relation to their size; the smaller the lizard the greater the activity. Willan resisted, for now, the temptation to start counting.

Although he had never seen a lizard in his life, his memory brought back images of these creatures formed whilst a schoolboy studying Greek and Latin. Willan walked back a few paces and rested, half sitting, on a balustrade; his mind had returned to Sedbergh school. He fondly remembered studying Greek mythology under the headmaster Doctor Wynne Bateman, of whom he had the highest regard. His closest schoolfriend William White had also been a Hellenophile and they had swapped many a story, normally of war and battles rather than love and intrigue. Willan wondered what had become of him; only good, he hoped.

Seeing the lizards and remembering his Greek studies reminded Willan of one of the tales of Demeter and her searches for Persephone, her daughter. Demeter had come across a peasant cottage and, being thirsty, had sought refreshment. The owner, Misme, had provided drink and Demeter greedily quenched her thirst. Misme's son, Ascalabus, witnessed this scene and mocked Demeter for drinking so much. Demeter, who did not take readily to insult, responded by turning Ascalabus into a lizard. Was there a moral to this tale? Willan was not certain, other than perhaps to keep one's thoughts and opinions to oneself.

Willan headed to the dining room, his thoughts transferring from ancient Greece to the current question of which soup was to be served for luncheon. It was tomato and onion, with bread and boiled eggs; he completely understood why it was Gourlay's favourite. As he sat at the table to gather his thoughts before returning to his room, it occurred to him that he would have to make changes to his diet when back in London. Meals there were heavy and dark – the more meat the better. Here they were fresh and light and, apart from tasting delicious, clearly of greater nutritional value. He joked to himself that he must kidnap Senhor Pompion and Dona Esmeralda and abduct them to London and to employment in his service. Pleased at his own light-heartedness, he made a mental note that such behaviour was acceptable and not a sin against God; he did not need to be serious all of the time.

Back at his desk, Willan quickly updated his medical charts; his condition seemed to be stable. The question of diet was still to the front of his mind so he decided to re-read the sections of Gourlay's book relating to soil, vegetable production and animal production. It was of little assistance, other than listing Madeiran fruits and vegetables. Not knowing which, if any, would be available in England, Willan undertook to interview Duarte and Jorge on the subject.

The clock showed three as Willan set off for his walk. Unable to resist temptation he returned to the tree, seeking lizards. At first there were none to be seen, but one by one several appeared, either from cracks in the bark or from the foliage below. As if unable to move, Willan remained staring and counting, so engrossed, in fact, that he did not notice he had been joined by another.

"Lagartixas."

Willan jumped backwards in shock, turned and was relieved to see Senhor Pompion, not a miscreant or bringer of evil.

"Lagartixas," repeated Senhor Pompion, pointing at the lizards.

Eventually it dawned upon Willan that 'lagartixas' must be the Portuguese word for lizards; he had presumed it to be the plural because of the 'shash' pronunciation by Senhor Pompion at the end of the word. Willan's first alarmed, then wrinkled, expression smoothed into a smile. Senhor Pompion smiled back at him, pointed in the direction of the banana plantation and mimicked swallowing a drink. Willan's face wrinkled again in confusement. Senhor Pompion repeated the gesture as he began to walk that way, still looking at Willan and with his right arm curved outwards. Realising he was being invited to join Senhor Pompion, in all likelihood for a drink, Willan followed.

As they passed through the passage in the hedge, Senhor Pompion stopped and mimed their previous coming-together. Willan joined in the masquerade and both men were laughing as they exited the hedge. Senhor Pompion indicated Willan should wait for him at the table and departed down the path to the right of the bananas, the path Willan had still not had the courage to follow. He felt at ease awaiting Senhor Pompion's return; he was enjoying himself and would try not to cause any offence or misunderstanding. His knife would remain in his waistcoat pocket.

It was not long until Senhor Pompion returned. From a distance Willan could see he was carrying something and, as he neared, he saw he held a glass of orange-coloured liquid in each hand. Willan assumed that he was about to taste the juice of oranges for the first time; he had seen an orange before but never had the opportunity to try or taste one.

"Manga," said Senhor Pompion as he gave Willan a glass.

"Manga," replied Willan, politely returning the toast and taking his first sip. It was fresh and sweet, and above all aromatic. The texture was so smooth as to be almost like butter; he sipped, rather than swallowing large mouthfuls.

Both men faced the view, not each other, content with their own thoughts. As with Willan's earlier encounter with Dona Esmeralda, no words were needed of any language. Willan felt at peace and that he was in a place to which he belonged; he thanked God for all the kindnesses shown to him.

Willan was neither awake nor asleep but somewhere in-between; he was dozelling but still vaguely aware of where he was. As he regained full consciousness, he realised that Senhor Pompion was asleep; his mouth slightly open and snoring gently. Willan made no sound as he left the table and tip-toed away. He glanced back before entering the hedge; Senhor Pompion remained peacefully sleeping.

Back on his veranda, Willan sat happily enjoying the view without the need to count the ships. He was looking forward to dinner and, he hoped, the opportunity to discuss fruits and vegetables with Duarte or Jorge. In anticipation of this conversation, he prepared himself and set off for the dining room earlier than usual.

Dropping a book onto the table to announce his arrival, Willan was soon joined by Jorge. After they had both politely enquired as to the other's health and the success or otherwise of their days so far, Jorge suggested Willan might enjoy a glass of Madeira wine before dinner. Usually Willan only drank wine in company and out of politeness but was beginning to enjoy the taste and comfort it offered. 'Why not?' he thought, and told Jorge his suggestion was indeed a good one.

Willan was still standing as Jorge returned with the wine. Taking the glass from the tray he raised it upwards towards Jorge.

"Manga," he toasted. Jorge appeared stunned but remained silent.

Willan took the silence to be astonishment that he had learned some Portuguese.

"Manga," he repeated with a broad smile.

The crash of the wooden tray falling from Jorge's hand to the floor via the table broke the silence. The smile left Willan's face but Jorge retained his open-mouthed astonishment, or was it petrification? Jorge's open hand still showed whence the tray had departed.

"Is everything alright, sir?" stuttered Jorge, bending to retrieve the tray.

"Everything is fine with me," replied Willan, surprised at the question, "but what of yourself?"

"Please forgive my rudeness and clumsiness, sir, but I am at a loss as to why you addressed me as a fruit."

Slowly it dawned upon Willan.

"Am I to presume the word 'manga' is not a salutation to good health?" he enquired of Jorge.

By now, Jorge was bent double with laughter and, after placing the tray on the table for safety, reversed himself onto an armchair to prevent his sinking to the floor. Willan sat on the other chair, and when Jorge had taken sufficient deep breaths to control his laughter, they resumed a conversation.

Willan related to Jorge the events of earlier between himself and Senhor Pompion, all the time being aware that Jorge was struggling to retain a serious outlook. Jorge, between mopping his eyes with his handkerchief, explained to Willan that a manga was in fact a fruit and Willan had not been drinking the juice of an orange but that of a 'manga', or 'mango', as it was known in English. In order to show that he was not offended and did not consider he was being made a fool of, Willan repeated the toast. Jorge responded with a resounding 'manga' of his own and both men giggled like mischievous schoolboys.

The downside for Willan of this frivolity was that he did not think it a suitable time to initiate further talk on fruits and vegetables; he would leave his questions for a later time. He changed the subject by asking Jorge how the arrangements for Bennett's arrival were proceeding. Jorge replied that the room was ready, some of his effects were already here, and Bennett was expected before luncheon the following day; he was to be transported by hammock.

Sanity had been restored to the evening and Willan enjoyed an excellent meal, thinking only as to whether this might be his last dinner alone for some time. It was only as he said goodnight and Jorge responded by mimicking the raising of a glass as a toast, that the evening's events were recalled. Willan departed, knowing that he and God would have a lot to discuss in the morning.

12

In exactly one year's time the date would be the twelfth of the twelfth of the twelfth. Willan was obsessed by numbers, especially when they lined up or patterned themselves in this manner; it was releasing some of his inner turmoil following an unsatisfactory conversation with God. The problem had been laughter. Willan had related the previous day's events to God and, to some extent, his inner conscience, and had only then realised he had enjoyed laughter three times. Not only that, it had been with three different people: Dona Esmeralda, Senhor Pompion and Jorge. Laughter was acceptable; genuine laughter could not be stifled. But as to how much laughter – that was the difficulty. Willan's concern was that he might be turning towards hedonism and he did not need God's guidance to tell him that was wrong. But where was the boundary line? How many bouts of laughter were acceptable? He would have to rely on an answer all in good time; God had never previously failed him.

Willan, who had toileted and breakfasted without incident, tried to settle to his paperwork but was still restless. His mind was now occupied by the immediate future, not the past. Whilst he was looking forward to Bennett's arrival, he could not help but wonder how his presence would impact upon himself. Willan was not concerned about any possible inconveniences; as ever, it was uncertainty that dogged his thoughts.

Knowing that accuracy in his research required an uncluttered mind, Willan decided fresh air and a different outlook might help, so he carried the telescope to the veranda. Having a mind capable of storing unlimited images meant that Willan initially carried out a methodical survey of the scene in case of change. Satisfied nothing had altered or required his especial attention, he turned to the pleasure of studying and counting ships; his mind was closed to outside influences as he considered whether the wind direction, sea currents or a combination of both determined the angle the ships lay at anchor.

Unbeknown to Willan there was great activity behind the scenes in the Quinta. Dona Esmeralda was patiently guiding Duarte and Jorge in final preparations for Bennett's arrival; as long as she held both men within her vision at all times, nothing should go untoward. Finally satisfied all was in place, she returned to the kitchen and her teapot. Duarte loitered near the main door and Jorge disappeared to wherever Jorge disappeared to.

"Bom Dia. Good morning, Doctor Willan," came Duarte's voice. Willan turned back to face the room but nobody was there.

"Over here, Doctor Willan," said Duarte.

Willan finally located Duarte's head amongst the shrubs behind the balustrade at the right edge of the veranda.

"The boy has indicated Mister Bennett Smith's coming soon. Do you desire to greet with him?" asked Duarte.

"Grant me but a moment," replied Willan, stalling for time as he calculated his answer. As much as he was keen to meet Bennett, he felt it would not be a service to him to be greeted by an old acquaintance of his father's immediately upon his arrival. Also, the present state of his health was unknown.

"If you do not mind, I would be most grateful if you, as chief of the Quinta, greeted our guest. Perhaps you could tell him I will join him for luncheon if he is of sufficient strength," Willan replied.

"Of course," came the reply, and the head departed the shrubbery.

Not long after he had resumed his observations, Willan heard voices seemingly near the main door. Not wishing to eavesdrop, he returned to his room with the telescope and, after a short time inspecting his possessions, decided to remove himself to the colonnade prior to reading the day's air temperature. As he was a little too early to take the reading, which needed to be taken at, or near to, the same time each day for accuracy, he strolled the length of the colonnade several times whilst enjoying the view. Judging the time to be suitable, Willan headed for the tree, gauging that the reading would be about sixty-five degrees, which proved prescient. His pleasure at his accurate prediction was, however, dissipated a little by the lack of lizards on the tree. He climbed to the colonnade by the further flight of stairs which enabled him to count the number of tiles in the frieze on the rear wall as he returned.

Entering the dining room, he noticed the table was set for three persons, presumably Bennett, Ashby and himself. This pleased Willan as it indicated that Bennett must be well enough to dine as normal, and not as an invalid in his room. Duarte came in and Willan enquired as to the success or otherwise of Bennett's arrival.

"All is well," replied Duarte. "Mister Smiths are in the room for preparations. They will come soon for soup."

"I am very pleased to hear that. Thank you for all your assistance," replied Willan.

He followed the sound of footsteps and voices down the stairs and towards the dining room; the brothers entered. Bennett, who was by four years the senior of the two, appeared much older than his twenty-seven years. He was of a pallid complexion with dulled eyes and red-edged lips. His shoulders were hunched and there was no spring to his step, which combined with his loose shabby grey clothing to generate an overall picture of decay.

Pleasantries and greetings were exchanged, and Willan was lifted that Bennett, despite his decrepit semblance, spoke in a spirited and interesting manner; his mind was clearly not impinged by his obvious illness. Duarte announced the serving of sopa de trigo and Willan was able to explain the ingredients, remembering he had been served a similar soup for his first luncheon at the Quinta. Bennett ate all of his soup, albeit at a far slower pace than his companions, and declared it to be the finest he had tasted. Throughout the meal Willan observed that Ashby's eyes barely left Bennett; he behaved as a protective elder brother and was without doubt devoted to and focussed solely on his welfare and recuperation.

A polite time after they had finished eating, Ashby outlined his and Bennett's immediate plans: Bennett was to rest for the afternoon whilst he returned to Bachelor's Hall, where he had duties to oblige, and if Doctor Willan had no objections they would all return to the table for dinner. Willan, who was greatly impressed by the maturity and good sense being shown by Ashby, replied that indeed he had no objections of any kind. He was further heartened as, no sooner had he risen to leave, Ashby began gently assisting Bennett from his chair and steadying him in the most caring way; Willan was moved by Ashby's love for his brother.

13

The previous night's meal had been uneventful. Bennett had made every effort to be sociable at his first dinner at the Quinta do Til but was clearly greatly fatigued and needed all of his limited strength merely to eat. Willan and Ashby, whilst unfailingly polite, had exchanged talk of little import. Willan considered the subdued atmosphere at the table was the outcome of nobody wishing to raise the subject or treatment of consumptive illness.

Willan had related these events to God in their regular morning conversation and had pledged to himself and God that he would do all he could to assist Bennett's recovery; with a gentle hand, was their agreed way to proceed. He then resumed his research with an untroubled mind and was satisfied with his progress.

A firm knock with no immediate opening of the door surprised Willan.

"Please enter," he answered, wondering who it might be.

"Gourlay of Kincraig at your service, sir!" greeted him, as the doctor invaded the room in his usual bombastic way.

"Good morning, Doctor. I am very pleased to see you once again; how do you do?" said Willan, extending his hand in welcome.

"It is I who should be making that enquiry of you, sir," responded Gourlay.

"I believe my complaint to be stable at present," responded Willan, who produced his medical charts and proceeded to describe his symptoms, both now and previously, in great detail. Gourlay agreed the illness was indeed stable but complacency would surely lead to relapse; he must continue to avoid unnecessary exertion. No specific treatment needed prescribing, other than rest and gentle exercise within the gardens which, combined with Dona Esmeralda's restorative meals, should result in a good prognosis. Willan was pleased this medical opinion was in accord with his own.

Willan, mindful of the delicate relationship between doctor and patient, offered his own services if there was anything he could do to assist in Bennett's treatment. Gourlay, who had called upon him only minutes earlier, thanked him and explained the current situation of Bennett's illness.

"Regretfully, Bennett has shown no improvement in the last four weeks. If anything, he has declined somewhat. This is partly of his own making in that he did not heed my firm advice to continue to rest, having declared to me soon after his arrival that he had been almost miraculously healed. His contrition at the folly of enjoying excursions with his brother is genuine and I feel his cause is not a lost one. You have provided the finest aid to his recovery in permitting his removal here; there is no finer place for him to be. If he can only follow your example and restrict his hours to gentle walks, breathe clean, fresh air, rest and confine his food intake to Dona Esmeralda's prescription, we will soon have two gentlemen booking springtime passage to England."

After thanking Gourlay for his kind and eminently sensible words, Willan presented him with a small file of papers he had collated for him.

"Please do not think me a wiseacre or that I am expressing contempt at any part of your fine volume, but you may find these words on the treatment of skin disease of some use. They indicate the latest research of myself and other cutaneous complaint specialists. I am, of course, always at your disposal should the need arise."

Gourlay thanked him for the file and suggested that medical

matters might now be concluded in favour of the delights of Dona Esmeralda's kitchen. Willan agreed and followed Gourlay from the room, pausing for only the briefest survey of the positions of his belongings and travelling via the til tree where he put to memory that day's air temperature reading. The atmosphere at luncheon was dissimilar from the previous night's dinner. The addition of Gourlay to the table meant there was no place for subduement; the conversation was both constant and interesting, although never touched upon matters medical. Gourlay departed when he had finished his soup and Willan soon after, leaving Ashby to assist his brother without an audience.

The air temperature reading duly entered, there was little more medical recording to undertake, leaving Willan unsure how best to occupy the afternoon hours. Wandering aimlessly around the room and veranda whilst considering all his options produced no outcome; unusually the attraction of counting ships did not entice him to collect up the telescope. Nor did he take the opportunity to cut some more quills, a precise task he always enjoyed. Eventually, he gave himself a mental prod and decided to commence his restorative walk at an earlier hour. 'I am not entirely governed by routine,' he tried to convince himself.

Stepping onto the colonnade, he was surprised to see Jorge leaning against the balustrade at about half distance, seemingly taking in the scene. Willan announced his arrival alongside by commenting on the splendour of the view.

"When your health is restored, Doctor Willan, you will be able to climb the mountains and enter the valleys. Pleasant though this view is, it will not then seem so splendid. Even your glorious Scottish lakes – sorry, lochs – and mountains are secondary in beauty compared with Madeira's," said Jorge, his eyes remaining focussed ahead.

"Am I to understand that your excellent English is as a result of visiting Scotland?" enquired Willan.

"In part," replied Jorge, going on to explain that when he was a young man, he spent over two years in both London and Letterfourie in Scotland as a personal aide to the Gordon brothers, but that he had already learned some English whilst a boy, employed here at the Quinta.

The conversation had dispelled Willan's ennui and, sensing Jorge was content to continue his reminisce, asked him about Letterfourie, a place of which he was unaware. Jorge explained that Letterfourie House was magnificent, at least four times the size of the Quinta do Til and built by the Gordon brothers some forty years previously. Just inland from the coastal village of Buckie, equally distant from Aberdeen and Inverness, it was also the coldest place Jorge had ever experienced.

Willan said he hoped to visit all of Madeira before returning to London, a place which they both agreed had no beauty, and although he had trained as a doctor in Edinburgh he had not travelled to other areas of Scotland. He did remark that the magnificence of the landscape surrounding his birthplace in the dales of West Yorkshire was yet to be equalled in his eyes, an opinion he would be more than happy to concede should the time arise.

In order to prolong the conversation and to solve an outstanding problem, Willan asked Jorge about the fruits and vegetables of Madeira and which would be available in England. Jorge replied that it was difficult to explain by words alone and proposed a visit to Senhor Abobora. They could go the following day after luncheon and he would act as translator. Willan could hardly believe his good fortune and, after ensuring he was not putting Jorge to any inconvenience, readily agreed to his proposal.

"Time and tide wait for no man, I must return to my silver polish," said Jorge before leaving the colonnade.

'What an extraordinary man,' thought Willan.

Standing throughout his conversation with Jorge had tired Willan so, preferring not to return to his room too far ahead of his normal schedule, he walked across the garden, through the hedge and sat at the table near the banana plants. Ironically, as he was reflecting on how well his day was proceeding despite the alterations to his routine, he felt his chest tighten and began coughing. By breathing as calmly as he could and then standing using the back of the chair for balance, Willan eventually brought an end to it; his handkerchief was reddened slightly with blood. He was light-headed and his legs as unsteady as when he took his first steps on Madeira; sitting down, at the risk of further coughing, was his only option. Fortunately, the tightness in his chest eased, and apart from a gentle rasp to his breathing, he felt almost restored.

Willan fought hard against the sadness that followed an hemoptoe; it did not necessarily mean he was in decline. His records would show the frequency of his blood-expectorating episodes; pessimism would only hinder recovery. He stood up, paused to confirm his stability and returned to the house at a steady pace. Walking along the colonnade put an idea in his mind so, instead of returning directly to his room, he entered the dining room and rapped on the door to the kitchen.

After only a short time Duarte opened it and asked how he could be of service. Willan explained that a table and chairs placed at the centre of the colonnade would be of considerable benefit to both himself and Bennett. He added that were suitable furniture not available, that on his veranda could be utilised.

"There are a great number of wooden furnitures in the storing rooms. When Jorge has completed the polishing, we will bring to the place," responded Duarte before adding knowledgeably, "In the Portuguese language the word for wood is 'madeira.'"

Unable to conjure up any response to Duarte's last words, Willan thanked him, perhaps too effusively, and returned to his room.

Although tired and tempted to retreat to his bed, Willan needed first to update and analyse his medical records. There was, as yet, no pattern to his hemoptoes, although it remained vital they were accurately recorded. Of comfort was the lack of any evidence of decline; he considered his condition remained stable. Having satisfactorily re-checked his conclusion, Willan gave in to his tiredness and reclined on his bed, intending a short rest. Sleep soon followed.

Before resting, Willan had overlooked Duarte's words that he and Jorge were intending to move the furnitures to the place. Had he so remembered he could have avoided his brutal extraction from slumber; how could two small men make so much noise? Now feeling wearier than previously, Willan sought solution by pouring a jug of water over his head in order to shock himself back to normality. After drying and brushing his hair he sat on the veranda and enjoyed the scene, albeit accompanied by the off-stage clatterings of the Rude Mechanicals.

The noises abated before stopping entirely; only the sound of earnest conversation lingered a little longer. Willan was keen to test the telescope from a new position and, after several minutes of complete silence, ventured from his room. At the centre of the colonnade was a large wooden table and four chairs which, despite their clumsy removal, showed no signs of damage. The table was symmetrically placed, sparing Willan the chore of centring it, and he soon had the chairs sited to his satisfaction. He returned to his room and collected the telescope, which he placed in the optimal position.

Despite being only a short distance from Willan's veranda, the new location offered a contrasting outlook and the challenge of identifying all the differences. He was stimulated into action and immediately set about a methodical survey of the view, completely oblivious to the outside world. Having counted ships for longer than he had intended and after blinking repeatedly to restore the balance in vision between his eyes, he returned to his room, carefully carrying the telescope. Washed and tidied he headed for the dining room a little earlier than usual, partly out of curiosity as to who would be his companions at dinner.

Entering the room, he noted that the table was set for two; he could not be certain who would be joining him. He did not have to wait long for the answer as he was soon joined by Bennett, whom he greeted warmly. Bennett explained that he had slept throughout most of the afternoon until he had been woken by a disturbance on the colonnade. Ashby had returned to Bachelor's Hall after luncheon to fulfil obligations and would call on him tomorrow, probably in the morning. Willan apologised for the disturbance and explained about the table and chairs. At Bennett's suggestion they continued their conversation on the colonnade.

They watched as the sun lowered towards the furthest hill, their gentle words being mainly in praise of the surroundings and the kindnesses being shown to them. Both agreed it was distressing to be a patient but that to be in Funchal rather than London was a blessing for which they were most grateful.

Jorge came to the table and asked if they needed lamps as the light was fading, and could he get them a glass of Madeira wine with which to toast the sunset. Both agreed it to be a splendid idea. Jorge returned with the wine accompanied by Duarte, who carried two already lit oil lamps. As Jorge handed him his wine, Willan thought he detected a wider than usual smile, but no words passed between them. Bennett commented that sipping wine by lamplight, whilst watching the sunset, before eating a meal prepared by Dona Esmeralda was proof indeed that God was caring for them and that it was their duty to repay him his benevolence. Willan agreed, delighted that Bennett thought as he did.

14

Doctor Robert Willan was excited. Excited like a child commencing a long-awaited adventure. Excited as an adult about to discover new curiosities in this new land.

It was almost exactly twenty-four hours since Jorge had suggested visiting Senhor Pompion and Willan was now at the same position on the colonnade, albeit sitting down, awaiting his guide. The previous evening and today, thus far, had progressed smoothly, which had served to give Willan more time to anticipate this excursion. As a schoolboy, medical student and research doctor, he had always been at his happiest when assimilating knowledge; today was no different.

Jorge arrived and they set off towards the passage through the hedge. He explained that Senhor Pompion was expecting them and although it was December, there would be much to see and also to taste. Dona Esmeralda had, though, forbidden the tasting of the very acidic fruits; there was no question of disobedience.

Exiting the passage they saw Senhor Pompion sitting at the table, obviously awaiting their arrival. Greetings were exchanged and the happy threesome set off down the path to the right of the bananas.

Jorge was at the heart of the conversation in his role as translator and Willan correctly assessed that he had performed this role on many previous occasions.

After perhaps fifty yards they reached the far boundary of the banana plantation. Ahead of them lay a landscape, the like of which Willan had never seen before or even dreamed of. Immediately ahead of them on a wide terrace to the right side were two white-rendered cottages facing inwards, with an orchard beyond. Similarly, the left boundary was formed by what appeared to Willan to be more fruit trees. The central ground, extending to about a hundred and fifty yards, comprised descending terraces of various plants and bushes forming a colourful arable mosaic of breath-taking magnificence. The far boundary, although difficult to see precisely, seemed to be a tree-formed hedge.

Jorge and Senhor Pompion mistook Willan's bewildered look as a sign of fatigue and asked if he wished to sit at the table outside the first cottage. Willan accepted the offer and sat, still trying to comprehend the scene before him. The uniformity of the planting, the straight lines and the precision impressed him the most; he was anxious to explore. It also occurred to him that this was the fourth outdoor table at which he had sat. He could walk from his veranda, along the colonnade, through the passage and now to the Quinta's own farm, never far from a resting point with an inspiring outlook.

Willan stood, keen to continue, and the tour began. Senhor Pompion proudly led the way into the centre, describing each plant; Jorge translated. The only difficulties were Willan's lack of knowledge of many fruits and vegetables which Jorge said were cultivated both in England and Madeira, and also that some had no English translation. This did not, however, detract from the occasion, which all three men were enjoying to the fullest.

Starting with vegetables, Willan was introduced to tomatoes, potatoes, turnips, cabbages and onions, with which he was familiar, and sweet potatoes and all manner of pulses, pompions, marrows, cucumbers and melons which he had never seen before. There were so many varieties of berries and currants stretching Willan's power of memory that when they came to tree-fruits he thought that even his capacity to remember might fail him. There were apples, pears, oranges, lemons, limes, cherries, peaches, apricots and pomegranates, amongst others, many of which could not be grown successfully in England.

Deep in the orchard beyond the cottages Jorge announced they had saved Madeira's two finest fruits until last, at which point Senhor Pompion stretched up into a tree and plucked a large green shiny fruit, which he handed to Willan. It was heavy, filling his hand, and although cold to the touch had a warm, rich fragrance. Clearly rehearsed, Jorge and Senhor Pompion raised their right hands in unison and toasted 'Manga', before bursting into laughter. Willan joined in, genuinely enjoying one of the happiest moments of his life.

Jorge announced that they would try some manga shortly but this fruit was not yet fully ripened. Willan returned the manga and they moved to a different tree. Senhor Pompion pointed to a strange-looking dimpled green fruit.

"That is an anona," said Jorge, "the finest of all our fruits. In England it is known as a custard apple, but it will not grow outside. These will be picked early next year; Senhor Pompion knows the best time. He also knows how to store fruits and vegetables in perfect condition for longer than any other man."

The trio headed back towards the two cottages. Senhor Pompion walked into the left of the two and Jorge and Willan continued to the table. Jorge explained that Senhor Pompion dwelt in the cottage and he had gone to collect some fruits for them to taste. Willan asked who lived in the other cottage, which caused Jorge to laugh.

"Senhor Pompion has both cottages. The one on the right is used to store fruits and vegetables under exact conditions and also to propagate plants and seeds; his tools and equipment are stored behind." Laughing again, he continued, "Many people, including myself, say Senhor Pompion would prefer to spend every hour in a cottage of vegetables rather than in a cottage with Senhora Pompion."

Willan felt it wise not to comment.

Soon Senhor Pompion emerged carrying an enormous tray of whole and cut fruits of all colours. They tasted them in a systematic way. Senhor Pompion selected the fruit and spoke to Jorge, who translated to Willan; then they ate. The other two laughed as Willan's initial caution at tasting soon turned into impatient desire for more. Eventually only some rich orange-coloured pieces remained. Willan extended his palm to silence Senhor Pompion, swallowed the largest piece, stood and declared, "Manga." Jorge and Senhor Pompion stood and applauded before the three men embraced. Willan's previous happiest-ever time had been eclipsed.

A cough startled the men from their embrace. Turning, they saw Dona Esmeralda smiling but with a look of disbelief on her face; she carried a basket in the hook of her arm. Involuntarily the men straightened as if awaiting inspection. Dona Esmeralda joined them and spoke with Jorge and Senhor Pompion before waving goodbye to Willan and departing with Senhor Pompion.

Jorge explained that Dona Esmeralda was going to her herb and medicinal garden, which Senhor Pompion tended for her. It contained a great number of plants whose Portuguese name even he did not know. He asked Willan if he had heard of fennel, to which he replied that he was aware of the word but had certainly never tasted it.

"Fennel will be part of your dinner tonight. Also, the Portuguese word for fennel is 'funchal'," said Jorge.

Using his logical mind and considerable memory, Willan proudly replied, "The Portuguese word for wood is 'madeira.'"

Jorge praised Willan, saying he would soon be speaking Portuguese like a Madeiran. He also explained that when the island was discovered some four hundred years ago, things were named and titled literally. They walked back to the house talking in the friendliest manner.

Bennett was sitting at the table on the colonnade and greeted Jorge and Willan as they arrived. Jorge continued inside, but Willan stopped and enquired as to Bennett's health and disposition. He replied that he was feeling improved with each day since he had come to the Quinta. Willan agreed with this and told Bennett, quite truthfully, that he had more colour to his skin, a sure sign that his blood was cleaner of foul matter and circulating at a renovated rate. Bennett remarked at how fortunate he was to be in the care of two such eminent physicians.

Willan said if he had no objections, he would join him at the table and recount his adventures, but that first he must visit his pot. Bennett replied he was keen to hear his tale, but no man should be kept from his pot. Having returned to his room, Willan emptied his bladder, washed and dried himself, and re-joined Bennett on the colonnade. He told Bennett of Senhor Pompion, the reason for his title, and of all the fruits and vegetables he had seen and tasted; he explained they would be eating funchal that evening as part of their dinner. Bennett had listened in attentive silence, a trait of all Quakers.

Time drifted by as they sat appreciating their situation. They spoke only infrequently but the conversation, such as it was, was neither strained nor unnatural. Duarte visited, offering oil lamps and wine, but they decided to repair to the dining room as the weather was a little cooler than the previous evening. Willan commented that his noon-time air temperature reading had been three degrees lower.

They were joined in the dining room by Ashby and, over a pre-dinner glass of Madeira wine, he told them the history of his day. Stressing that Bennett's health was paramount to his being on Madeira, he was using any spare moments to investigate the wheat and grain trades on the island. He had been in discussions with several businesspeople to whom he had been introduced by Torres, and was preparing papers to forward to his and Bennett's father. Willan knew that Smith's grain business in Southwark was one of the largest in London and had been so for many a year; he was highly respected. Ashby added that until 'Boney' had been defeated once and for all, there was little opportunity to establish a regular trade. He proposed a toast to Sir Arthur Wellesley, who was leading the British Army on the Iberian Peninsula. Willan resisted the urge to exclaim, 'Manga!'

The main talking point over dinner was the taste of the fennel in their 'stew of chickens'; their opinions were divided. Bennett thought it toothsome. Ashby was unsure and Willan found it disagreeable. However, all three agreed that the lemon pastry which followed the chicken was truly delightful.

Willan, who was very tired, apologised for his early departure and returned to his room, leaving Ashby and Bennett comfortable in the armchairs.

15

The first of January 1812 was a day Willan had been looking forward to, not just for the optimism a new year brings but also because it required drawing up new charts and new records, a task he enjoyed; putting the first ink on fresh paper was always a pleasure. Willan was totally engrossed in his labour, so much so that he did not notice a stronger than usual breeze had taken hold of the papers he was temporarily storing on his bed. Fortuitously his assistant, who was working at the table, espied the problem, quickly closed the central window and alerted Willan to the melange of paperwork on the bed and now the surrounding floor. Together, they calmly restored order.

Ashby had asked Willan if he could be of service as an assistant some two weeks previously because he had the time, a logical mind and a keen interest in all things medical. Willan had found his help invaluable and was also enjoying teaching him the basics of human anatomy and general medical practice. Ashby made himself available for at least three mornings a week.

A routine of sorts had been established to everybody's satisfaction, with the proviso that Bennett's and Willan's health was of prime importance. Ashby would assist Willan only after he had ensured his brother had no need whatsoever of his services. Similarly, Willan was under no obligation to accommodate Ashby if it were any type of inconvenience.

Bennett always took breakfast in his room before taking a short walk in the gardens; he had yet to venture as far as Senhor Pompion's cottage. After reading until luncheon, either in his room or on the colonnade, he would rest in the afternoon before joining Willan for a congenial discussion before dinner. He retired to his room soon after his meal and read by oil lamp until sleepy. Ashby supplied his books from the British Library in Funchal.

Willan's days were still much as before. After breakfast, occasionally taken in the dining room, he would work on his research, often with Ashby's assistance. He would take the air temperature reading before joining Bennett for luncheon. The afternoon was spent initially on updating his personal medical charts before heading towards the vegetable plot, where he would often enjoy a glass of spring water or fruit juice with Senhor Pompion. Returning to the Quinta he would meet up with Bennett before dinner, when they were sometimes joined by either Ashby or Torres, not both as yet.

Ashby's days were less routine, as befitted a young man in perfect health. He visited his brother every morning, often remaining to assist Willan. He occupied the rest of his days and hours either by discovering the island or establishing business contacts; he was greatly helped by Torres, with whom he regularly dined at Bachelor's Hall. Additionally, Ashby placed himself entirely at Bennett's and Willan's disposal and would gladly run any errand, large or small. Willan considered him the epitome of gentlemanliness.

Nearing noon, Willan set forth to the til tree to collect the air temperature reading. Ashby, who was staying for luncheon, went off in search of his brother. As Willan arrived in the dining room to join the others Duarte, who had been awaiting his arrival, addressed them.

"Today for soup we have Jorge in the kitchen. Dona Esmeralda is at freedom with her sister. The soup is not made by Jorge but he is working the heat and spoon. It is of vegetables."

As Duarte left, presumably to collect Jorge's stirrings, the men light-heartedly discussed remedies for gastric distress. The soup was, of course, delicious, and compliments to Jorge were given by all. Duarte then delivered his second announcement.

"Tonight for dinner we have Senhora Pompion in the kitchen. Dona Esmeralda is not here still. The cooking of Senhora Pompion is very good. There will be no complaints."

Leaving for his room, Willan told the brothers he expected a full attendance for dinner without any complaints.

Resuming work on his medical charts highlighted Willan's concern for his own gastric distress; his slurry was still consistently more liquid than solid. He had been on Madeira for a month now and considered that his diet could not be improved; what was the best course of action? After updating his records, he consulted Gourlay's book and his suggested remedies. In the section for Phthisis, under the heading 'Diarrhoea', Gourlay had written:

> No symptom is so alarming in this malady, as the colliquative diarrhoea, which marks its advanced progress. It is distressing to the practitioner, and if not carefully attended to, it will soon carry off the patient.
>
> When it is slight, and shews a prevalence of acidity in the first passages, the chalk mixture with laudanum will be of service; or, where the laudanum disagrees, the extract of white poppy, or the compound spirit of vitriolic aether, given in the quantity of a dram, or two drams, twice or thrice a day, may be substituted. But in general, absorbent medicines are too insignificant to check this symptom, and astringents must be had recourse to in preference.

There followed a complicated recipe for an astringent that even Doctor Willan could not discern. It then continued:

> To this mixture, I occasionally add a little tincture of kino, and with it I find it useful to administer at times a dose of opium in a solid form.

Willan considered the information; the presence of some turds in his slurry, albeit small ones, meant he was not about to be 'carried off'. Although he did not desire opiate treatment, it may have to be considered. He determined to have a candid discussion with Gourlay and would pass a message via Ashby that very evening. In order to clear his mind of medical matters, Willan carried his telescope to the veranda and began a new survey of the ships and boats in the bay below; he was soon fully captivated.

Having completed a successful reckoning of the ships, Willan turned his attention to a man toiling on a plot of land. He was digging and pulling either weeds or vegetables. As Willan watched his unceasing labour he wondered as to the man's thoughts. Was he content as he worked or was every swing of his hoe an onerous task? Was his mind focussed, or was his effort natural? At the end of the day were his muscles strained, or was this an easy task? Willan would never know the answers but had nothing but admiration for the man; he hoped he had contentment in his life.

After returning the telescope to the room, Willan took his walk to the vegetable terraces. Men were working in the distance in a similar manner to the man whom he had espied earlier. He could not see Senhor Pompion amongst them. He remained at the table viewing the scene but left sooner than he would have liked, feeling guilty at relaxing whilst watching other men toil. Bennett was not on the colonnade as Willan returned to the Quinta, so he found himself back in his room earlier than intended.

Unsure how to pass the time, Willan paced his room and veranda for a while before straightening his requisite stationery items; he did not consider resuming any task outside of his normal routine. His temporary boredom was eased when he heard Bennett and Ashby talking, presumably on their way to the colonnade. Allowing a polite moment to pass he scuttled after them, trying to assume a casual manner.

Only Bennett was on the colonnade as Willan strolled to the table and chairs. Having declared that he thought he had heard Ashby's voice, Bennett informed him that his brother had briefly returned to Bachelor's Hall as he had some matters to attend to; he would, however, be joining them for dinner. Willan worried that Bennett might not be as well as he appeared or that there might be some difficulty; Ashby had been at the Quinta for the entire day, which was unusual. When gently probed as to his health, Bennett gave no indication that anything was not as it seemed. Still concerned, Willan took a more direct approach and detailed to Bennett, quite truthfully, that he was suffering with diarrhoea from time to time and he intended that Gourlay should visit to discuss treatment. He asked if Bennett needed to consult Gourlay, so as to optimise the doctor's visit. Bennett replied that he felt his strength was improving, he was sleeping well and he did not wish to tempt his fate by a consultation at this time. Willan was cheered by this, telling Bennett he would ask Ashby to pass his message alone to Gourlay.

Leaving medical matters aside, Bennett and Willan conversed amiably, each man relaxed in the other's company. They postponed Duarte's offer of wine, knowing that Ashby was due to re-join them soon. A time later they changed their minds and enjoyed a glass of Madeira's finest, despite Ashby's non-appearance. The glasses were almost drained as Ashby returned. He was slightly red in the face and breathing more heavily than usual; clearly, he had been hurrying. After regaining his composure, he apologised for his lateness and explained that he had been making arrangements with Torres for a planned excursion and had failed to notice the hour.

Duarte served Ashby a glass of wine and replenished the other two glasses. Both Bennett and Willan told Ashby they were keen to hear of his plans. Ashby explained that in four days from now he and Torres were to travel by horseback to the 'Nun's Valley', a place Torres had described as being the most scenic of the whole island. There were grazing lands to the floor of the steep-sided valley and its small population also cultivated grapes, cherries and chestnuts. Ashby added that he would bring them edible mementos of his trip. As they were to leave from the Quinta do Til early on Sunday morning, both he and Torres would stay overnight on the Saturday; they would be a foursome at dinner. Knowing Dona Esmeralda was currently with her sister, Willan asked if these arrangements had yet been made. Ashby replied that the delicacy of that situation was best entrusted to Torres.

As they entered the dining room, Duarte again told them that it was Senhora Pompion in the kitchen, not Dona Esmeralda. Had they never been told this they would not have noticed; the food was as delicious as usual and they caught no sight of her. After dinner, arrangements were made; Willan would lead Bennett on a tour to the vegetable terraces the following afternoon and Ashby would assist Willan on Friday morning. Ashby also undertook to send word to Gourlay on Willan's behalf. Everybody agreed that it had been a successful day.

16

As they headed towards the vegetable terraces, Willan allowed Bennett to walk slightly ahead and, as he passed by the oblique passage in the hedge, Willan stepped smartly through and continued alongside Bennett, albeit with a hedge between them. Calling for Bennett to slow down as he was tiring, Willan awaited a reaction.

After a gulp, Willan heard, "Where are you, sir? Are you vanished or have my eyes failed me?"

"I am here, not two yards away," replied Willan, truthfully.

"You did not warn me of the bewitchment of these fields; I fear that I cannot continue," said Bennett, enjoying the horseplay.

"If you stare ahead, I will re-appear," said Willan, returning through the hedge.

Now standing behind Bennett, he clapped his hands; Bennett turned and both men laughed. Willan was proud as he showed Bennett the passageway, proud not of his knowledge of the route, but of his light-heartedness.

Bennett had previously encountered the bananas, so they wandered through the vegetables and orchards observing, touching and smelling.

Willan remarked that this natural beauty was enhanced by man but was finer than any study in oils; surely this was how God intended man to tend the lands he had provided. They sat for some time at the table, not only enchanted by the scene but understanding something of the connection between heaven and earth.

As the previous day, when Ashby had remained, Willan sensed that there might be something amiss with Bennett. He asked him directly if anything was troubling him.

"I apologise for my low mood," replied Bennett, continuing. "I do not wish to burden others with my depression but if you would consider my problem, I should be most grateful."

"Please proceed, but first I must apologise for my levity on our journey," said Willan.

Bennett replied, "I fear sometimes we are both too polite for our own good; good friends such as we have no necessity for apologies; your cleverness at the hedge lifted my spirits no end." Willan nodded in empathy and Bennett continued. "Yesterday, Ashby and I received a letter from our father. All is well in Southwark with our family and the business. His concern is my health, which he asks after, and if he can do anything to assist Ashby and me. Ashby has replied recently, so he will soon know of my successful move here. As such this is all good news; however, I cannot but feel I am an encumbrance. I love my family as they love me. But what have I done to deserve such love? Are my brothers and sisters receiving less of my father's love and care because of me? Ashby assures me this is not the case and I have no cause to feel any self-pity, but my mind cannot move from these thoughts. I am sorry to burden you with this, Doctor Willan, but perhaps your sagacity can assist me with a solution."

A short silence followed before Willan replied.

"My dear Bennett, I can only hope that I may be of some comfort. Please rest assured that my words are true; I would never seek to re-assure you with falseness or platitudes. Ashby is correct in that you have nothing whatsoever to be ashamed of; you are well deserving of as much love as can be shown to you. Would you not provide unlimited love and care to any of your family? Exactly. You can best return this love by recovering your health as is wished for you.

Restored to fitness, the world and your future are yours to utilise and God will guide you. I too am humbled by the kindnesses shown to me and am resolved to repay them as soon as I am able. We must fight our wretched illness together, and this will be assisted by our sharing of confidences. Thank you for your candour and I hope I have helped in some way. I feel certain you will be able to reciprocate when your mood is lifted."

"It is lifted already," said Bennett. "I apologise for my self-pity."

"Did you not say that true friends need not apologise?" replied Willan.

They returned to the Quinta and arranged to meet on the colonnade before dinner.

Willan sat on the chair next to his bed and pondered the earlier conversation. He was sure the advice he had given was sound; more importantly, he needed to apply it to himself. If it seemed selfish to put his health before anything or anybody, so be it; his work, when finished, would assist in the treatment of illness, of benefit to all. Also, when recovered, he would be able to repay all the personal kindnesses shown to him. The proverbs 'Charity begins at home' and 'Near is my shirt, but nearer is my skin' entered Willan's mind, and he vowed to consider himself as well as others.

Content with his conclusion, Willan lifted his telescope and sought relaxation on the veranda. It was not long before he was engrossed by the activity in the harbour. He had completely lost track of the hour and was only jolted back into his routine by the sound of voices from nearby the main door. Having no desire to eavesdrop, he returned inside to prepare himself for the evening. He was in good spirits and hoped that Bennett was similarly disposed.

Bennett was already on the colonnade as he arrived and although no mention was made of the earlier discussion, it was clear that both men were pleased with the outcome; their conversation was entertaining and light-hearted. They were soon visited by Duarte and Jorge with a decanter of wine and two glasses. Duarte appeared flustered; Jorge looked as Jorge always did.

"If it would please yourselves to serve the wine," said Duarte before departing the colonnade.

Jorge pre-empted their question by explaining that Duarte was agitated because Torres had informed him of his and Ashby's proposed stay on Saturday, Dona Esmeralda was due back shortly and there would be far too much to achieve in far too little time. Jorge added that he would assist Duarte and there was nothing to be concerned about. After Jorge had left, Willan and Bennett discussed the likely events of the following day; they agreed that whatever occurred it was certain to be ear-splitting.

*

The next day certainly did prove to be ear-splitting as well as disordered. Willan's shave left him more scabrous than smooth and he only just had time to finish his breakfast before his table was cleared. The clattering and chattering began almost immediately afterwards. Willan's initial amusement at the good-natured but clumsy efforts of Duarte and Jorge soon waned; it was not possible to concentrate through the noise, and any silence only gave a brief respite before the clamour resumed. Of equal concern was that it was Friday morning; Ashby and Torres were to stay on Saturday. Surely the noise would not last for two days?

Willan answered a knock on his door and was joined by Ashby and Bennett. They went onto the veranda, as being furthest from the noise, and planned their campaign for quiet. It was decided to take the telescope to the colonnade, where Willan would show the others the sights of Funchal he had discovered. The colonnade was a good strategic position from where to listen and watch for signs of progress in the removals; they might also espy Jorge and be able to get an update. Research or paperwork was not even considered.

Their plan proved to be a good one as the telescope provided great entertainment, each of them vying to get their eye on the scene below for as long as possible; it was a good distraction from the continuing hue and cry. So keenly were they concentrating on the view, they did not notice they had been joined by Dona Esmeralda. She had brought a pot of tea and, as Willan immediately noticed, three cups and saucers. He gestured by pointing and counting the fingers on his hand that she should fetch another cup and join them. Blushing a smile, she soon returned with a fourth cup and saucer, and, correctly interpreting the men's gestures, she poured tea for them all.

Bennett was proving himself to be a master of mime and soon after they had finished their tea, he invited Dona Esmeralda to take her turn at the telescope. He carefully positioned her and she nervously lowered her eye; her squeal at whatever she had seen nearly eclipsed the noise from inside the Quinta. She straightened up with her hand to her mouth. Bennett's excellent miming eventually convinced her that all was well, witchcraft was not present on the colonnade and it was safe to proceed. She looked like a young girl playing with her favourite toy as she resumed looking, and her happiness added smiles to the faces of the three men; their observation of Dona Esmeralda's enchantment bettered any view through the telescope.

Despite the men's gestured entreaties to continue her obvious pleasure, Dona Esmeralda soon withdrew her eye from the telescope and, after clearing up the crockery, returned to the house. Soon afterwards they heard her firm voice and slow words; clearly Duarte and Jorge were being returned to a straight and narrow path.

In order to occupy the remaining time until lunchtime, the men strolled the gardens and were warmed by the now higher sun. Willan mentally recorded the air temperature reading, and Ashby was shown the ingenious passageway through the hedge. It was a convivial time and none of the men considered the morning wasted. They entered the dining room for luncheon in good spirits, despite all that Duarte and Jorge had set against them.

Duarte was awaiting their arrival and answered their enquiries as to progress.

"Jorge and I have the new bed for Mister Ashby near to the floor but not up yet. That will be soon." He continued to speak as if Ashby were not present. "We will put Mister Ashby at the rear, near to Senhor Torres but not under the same ceiling. The room has most things and we will do the others. Doctor Willan and Mister Bennett will not be disturbed."

As soon as Duarte had left for the soup, Ashby remarked he was pleased that Willan and Bennett were not to be disturbed, but where did that leave him? The men laughed but only briefly; they did not want Duarte to think they were amused at his expense. After they had enjoyed their soup, they remained at the table making arrangements. Ashby would return to Bachelor's Hall to prepare for the excursion and visit his brother the following morning. Bennett hoped to rest prior to meeting Willan on the colonnade before dinner. Willan intended to update his medical records, take his walk to the vegetable terraces and then meet up with Bennett.

There was little disturbance in the afternoon and Bennett rested well. Willan attended to his records and enjoyed his walk. After a pleasant evening and dinner, both men retired early.

17

Saturday contrasted with the previous day; Willan enjoyed a smooth shave and a relaxed breakfast. Duarte seemed at ease with himself and remarked that the preparations were complete other than 'tying up the missing ends'. The day boded well; Willan opened his window to change the air and settled down to his papers. He worked efficiently and was pleased with his achievements. Adding to the success of the day was the presence of many lizards on the til tree when he checked the thermometer. Having counted the tiles on the back wall of the colonnade, he arrived at the dining room in a fine disposition.

"Good morning, Doctor Willan, Gourlay of Kincraig at your service," greeted him as he entered the room. "Ashby advised me that you wished to see me. I have only just arrived so might I suggest that I join you for a bowl of Dona Esmeralda's patent medicine and then we can talk at leisure?"

Willan, although surprised at Gourlay's presence, was pleased to see him and readily agreed. They were soon joined by Bennett, who, along with Willan, watched as Gourlay drained a bowl of chicken and vegetable soup in a matter of moments. When the meal was over,

Bennett left promptly for his room 'to avoid any medical consultation', thought Willan. Although Gourlay suggested they remain in the dining room to talk, at Willan's insistence they went to his room in order that his medical records be consulted.

The men talked un-hurriedly about all of Willan's symptoms and both reached the same conclusion; the condition was stable but the continuing diarrhoea needed intervention. Gourlay recommended that laudanum be taken because, as well as being proven to cause a ceasing of diarrhoea, its relaxant properties would ease cough. Willan agreed to the proposed treatment as although he did not have a great knowledge of the healing properties of laudanum, his medical memory reminded him that its use often resulted in costiveness; at present he would consider constipation a blessing rather than a hindrance.

Gourlay informed Willan that he had some laudanum with him. He explained he had prepared the tincture himself but it had no additions; it was simply opium and alcohol and would be too bitter to ingest until sweetened. He left to collect it from his case which he had left by the main door and said he would return via the kitchen where he was certain to find a suitable sweetener.

He soon returned with a brown, corked bottle (which was larger than Willan expected), a silver teaspoon and a medium-sized earthenware lidded pot. The instructions were to half-fill the spoon with sugar from the pot before adding the laudanum from the bottle to almost fill the spoon. This should be swallowed twice a day and improvement would be achieved in no more than two days. Gourlay also advised that when a satisfaction had been reached the treatment should on no account be ceased for at least a further week, or preferably until after another consultation with him. Willan readily agreed to the regime and thanked Gourlay for his time and expertise. After shaking hands, Gourlay departed.

Consideration now needed to be given as to where to store his medicine and when he should take it. He decided to place the bottle, spoon and pot on the table next to the decanter so he could take a glass of water after his laudanum and it would be noticeable when taking breakfast in his room. Whether to have his first dose before or after breakfast was yet to be decided: probably before. The timing of the second dose was straightforward; he would take this just before departing his room for dinner or to meet Bennett.

Content that his medicine was correctly positioned, Willan set off for his walk. As he passed along the colonnade he smelt cooking aromas, even though dinner was still a long time off. Perhaps Dona Esmeralda was preparing a special meal as there were four dining that evening. Thoughts of what might be served occupied his mind, so much so that he passed by the passageway through the hedge, completely unaware of how far he had walked. Amused at his own oversight he focussed his mind, returned to the passageway and crossed through to the first table. He sat for a while contemplating whether to continue to the vegetable terraces. The decision was made for him as he was joined by Senhor Pompion, who, after they had shaken hands and smiled greetings, sat alongside him enjoying the same outlook. Both men contentedly appreciated the tranquillity of the location. Senhor Pompion was the first to leave. He rose, replaced his chair, nodded and left. Willan remained, his mind grappling with the question of why Senhor Pompion should choose to sit alongside a stranger with whom he could not converse. Finally, logic won the day, and he accepted that they were not strangers to each other and they both appreciated the earth upon which they were fortunate to sit; words were redundant.

Willan walked back to the Quinta in a relaxed frame of mind, a mood which remained with him as he washed and tidied himself. It was time for his first spoonful of laudanum which, despite the sugar, was still one of the most bitter substances he had ever tasted. A glass of water helped his distaste and he set off for the colonnade, still in high spirits.

"Here comes a happy man," said Ashby as Willan joined him and Bennett. "You have the countenance of one with not a single difficulty to consider."

"Thank you," replied Willan. "I have been appreciating the beauty of our situation and it has placed in me great peace and comfort. Also, I am looking forward to a pleasant evening in good company." He did not mention the laudanum as he considered it neither the time nor the place for medical talk.

The conversation continued happily amongst the three for a short time until Ashby declared that he would search for Duarte or Jorge and the wine decanter. He was away longer than seemed necessary and when he returned was alone and without wine. Apologising for his delay he said that he had been engaged in idle tittle-tattle with Jorge, who would be along shortly with the drinks. Willan considered this a little out of character but thought no more of it. Jorge arrived soon afterwards and, as well as serving their wine, informed them that Torres would shortly make up the party as he had heard his voice from the direction of the stables. The wine had been drunk before Torres arrived, presumably because he had preparations to make for his excursion with Ashby the following day. Upon his arrival, Ashby suggested they repair to the dining room, and politely the others followed.

The dining room looked magnificent. A lit candelabra and a glass bowl piled high with fruits adorned the table which was laid with silver cutlery. Only Ashby's face did not look amazed. The kitchen door opened and Duarte, Jorge and Dona Esmeralda entered, Duarte carrying a tray of seven glasses of Madeira wine, which he passed around. Ashby, who had placed himself slightly apart from everybody, straightened himself and spoke.

"Good evening, lady and gentlemen," he started, directing his eyes towards Dona Esmeralda, who was being whispered a translation by Jorge. "I will not take too much of your time but I have a few words to say. I believe we are all friends and I wish to thank everybody for the kindnesses shown to me and especially my dear brother, Thomas. I would like to propose that we raise a glass to ourselves and to Thomas, who will be embarrassed when I tell you all that it is his birthday and he has attained twenty-eight years. The toast is ourselves and Thomas."

"Ourselves and Thomas," came the cheering response from everybody except Dona Esmeralda, whose smiling face afforded the benevolent look usually reserved by a proud mother for her sons. The gaiety continued for some minutes before Dona Esmeralda walked across to Bennett, pulled him down by the arm, kissed his cheek and left for the kitchen. Duarte and Jorge followed.

The dinner was splendid, the fine quality of the food matched by the friendliest of conversation. Torres said he and Ashby would be leaving early the next morning and that in all likelihood would be late returning. Ashby promised a full account of the excursion to Bennett and Willan on Monday morning and was reminded that he had undertaken to bring back edible mementos. Torres, having noticed the tiredness on Bennett's face and the slouch in his shoulders, brought the evening to a close by saying that he and Ashby needed all the sleep they could muster for such an intrepid adventure.

Willan, back in his room, took to his bed with the happiest of hearts.

18

Dawn was reluctant to appear, despite Willan staring from his bed to the nearside window urging the sun upwards. He always left this window un-shuttered in order that the first light of the morning did not pass unnoticed. Today he was keener than ever to proceed with his day; his sleep had been troubled by constant self-reminders that he must not forget to take his laudanum. The fact that he had an outstanding memory and was never forgetful carried no weight; he must never allow complacency into his life. He also intended to make more detailed inspections of his slurry than previously, in order to monitor the effect of the medicine. Sitting upright to prevent any possibility of returning to sleep, he continued mentally re-designing his medical record papers, a thought process of which he would never tire.

After what seemed to Willan to be over an hour, but was probably only twenty minutes or so, the room began to lighten. This cheered him immensely and lifted his impatience as he waited the further few minutes until there was sufficient light to allow him to depart his bed and start the day.

As usual, by the time Willan had crossed the room and un-shuttered the three opposite windows, his bowels had sensed his upright stance and begun their grumbling dawn chorus. He sat on his pot and not a minute later was closely inspecting his first slurry of the post-laudanum regime. There were three small thin turds of between one and one and a half inches in length, and seven solids of about little finger-nail size within the liquid outpourings; an auspicious start. He hurriedly washed and dressed, keen to enter his findings in the records, all the time needlessly reminding himself that he had yet to take his morning laudanum.

Admonishing himself for prevaricating over whether to update his records or take his medicine first, he entered the details of his morning slurry, adding comments about the total amount, colour, speed of evacuation and consistency. He then carefully dispensed and swallowed a dose of laudanum which he considered to be less bitter than the previous day; perhaps he had taken more sugar or perhaps his good mood had sweetened the medicine.

Duarte arrived soon afterwards and Willan's shave and breakfast were soon completed. However, outside the normal routine, Duarte then returned carrying a folded material package of about a foot by six inches, which he placed upon the table before speaking.

"I have for you a gift from Dona Esmeralda which she has fashioned herself from old dresses of ladies. It will be fitting perfectly, we think. Dona Esmeralda has made many for several gentlemen and she is always desired for this. I have one also to wear on feast days."

Willan was still assimilating the words as Duarte unfolded the material. He held aloft a satin waistcoat as blue as an unclouded sky. It was double-breasted with satin-covered buttons, had two pockets and a high collar folded at the front into a smaller collar above the top buttons. It was bright but not gaudy and styled to display good taste, not wealth.

"Please to see the backside," said Duarte as he turned the garment.

The reverse was tailored from a darker blue woollen material in a tapered style with two small tails which contrasted with the squared hem to the front of the waistcoat. Duarte handed it to Willan, who held it as if it were the most delicate object he had ever carried. Only then did he realise it was intended that he should wear the waistcoat; he had never worn anything other than black wool clothing. As his mind came to terms with the situation, he began to concede that the beautifully tailored waistcoat was not ostentatious but simply the finest garment he had touched or viewed. Not only that, it had been made for him by Dona Esmeralda and presented as a gift. Tears formed in his eyes.

"Now we must see the clothings on," said Duarte, and, confused as to Willan's sad demeanour, added, "but only if you are pleased with the waistcoat and its appearance."

"Please forgive my tears," said Willan. "I am truly pleased. I have never seen a finer garment or received such a splendid gift. I am humbled by the kindnesses and generosity shown to me."

Duarte un-buttoned the waistcoat as Willan removed his loose black woollen one and stood with his arms stretched behind him. Duarte placed the waistcoat over Willan's shoulders and soon had it securely buttoned. It fitted perfectly, as both men knew that it would. Duarte stepped back and, after a polite period of consideration, declared it to be a fine garment befitting a fine gentleman. Willan hurried to his dressing room and the looking glass. After his initial appreciation of the colour of the waistcoat and its fine tailoring, he realised that its perfect fit gave him a healthier appearance; the high collar un-slouched his shoulders and the double line of buttons lessened his small paunch.

Willan returned to Duarte, failing in his attempt to adopt a casual manner and with his tears replaced by a boyish grin.

"Is Dona Esmeralda in the kitchen?" he asked. "I must thank her immediately."

"Unfortunately, Dona Esmeralda is away from the house. She is with Senhora Pompion delivering foods for other people. They are of great kindness. She will be returned by soup time for your thanks."

Appreciation of the women's charitable endeavours combined with Willan's happiness and, after telling a departing Duarte that he would indeed thank Dona Esmeralda at soup time, he sat down, composed himself and opened his conscience to God. He was not ashamed of his new plan to consider himself as well as others, nor was he willing to reject the kindness of others even if it did mean that he was now proud of his appearance; pride was not always a sin. He must, however, show gratitude, support and respect whenever they were due. These calm thoughts confirmed to Willan that God was in accord with his sentiments and still his true guide.

The first problem for Willan was whether to continue the day in his fine new blue satin waistcoat – or should he return to black wool? He strode the room undecided before collecting up the old waistcoat and heading for his dressing room. He stood before the looking glass then covered and un-covered the new blue waistcoat with the old black one. Although it was clear which was the finer garment, Willan struggled with thoughts of vanity and ostentation. Eventually, blue won the day as he remembered that Ashby and Torres routinely wore finely tailored bright waistcoats and neither man could be considered in any way vain or a braggart.

Turning to his research papers in an attempt to restore routine to the day resulted in a second problem: Willan's mind was not on his work but on his new waistcoat. He constantly fidgeted with the pockets and brushed his hands on the satin, as well as checking on the neatness of his undershirt at the junction of his breeches and the hem of the waistcoat. He chuckled at the ironic thought that he might be turning into a stuffed shirt and resolved to forget his work for a few moments in order that he might learn how to return to his previous relaxed comfort, despite his new finery.

Not unhappy at the brief delay to his paperwork, Willan took his telescope to the veranda and began a complete survey of the scene before him. His logical mind had correctly deduced it was only the unfamiliarity of the new material that was occupying him and the passage of time would transfer the familiarity of old black wool to new blue satin. Willan's pleasure at solving a problem and enjoyment of his surroundings eliminated his earlier discomfort; he considered himself a fortunate man.

Having returned to the room and realised there was little time left for paperwork, Willan rehearsed a nonchalant walk, in readiness for his pre-luncheon trip to the thermometer. This practice, however, counted for nothing as he tripped on the sill of the door to the colonnade. Still upright and in good humour, he apologised to God for his conceitedness, continued his journey and, realising that his gait was entirely natural, knew that God was laughing at him from on high.

With the air temperature reading memorised, Willan headed to the dining room. As he entered, he was astonished to see Bennett, resplendent in a green satin waistcoat, standing next to the fireplace.

"I am pleased to see you have followed my example and dressed for luncheon," said Bennett, failing in his attempt to adopt a serious disposition.

"What kind of gentleman would not so dress?" replied Willan, adding, "I apologise for my appearance, but my finest clothes are away for cleaning; I am compelled to make do with this old jerkin."

Each man inspected the other's waistcoat: they were identical in style; only the colour differed. Willan thought that Bennett appeared healthier but retained his opinion. Both men complimented the other's appearance and declared their extreme happiness at their gifts.

"I have yet to thank Dona Esmeralda," said Bennett.

"And I," replied Willan.

Bennett then seized the initiative, rapped on the kitchen door and as soon as Duarte opened it declared, "There are two finely dressed gentlemen here who cannot possibly eat soup without the largest of napkins for protection. Can you please request that Dona Esmeralda deliver us such materials as soon as possible?"

The look on Duarte's face revealed that he understood the request and soon conversation could be heard from the kitchen side of the door. Duarte and Dona Esmeralda then entered the dining room. Each was carrying a very small piece of white linen cloth, no more than four inches square.

"Dona Esmeralda says that a real gentleman does not spill soup. It is a poor show. These napkins should be for wiping the lips in a correct way," said Duarte, as he and Dona Esmeralda handed over the small cloths. Everybody laughed. Following a close examination of the men, Dona Esmeralda declared her satisfaction at the fit and Duarte translated their gratitude. Both men kissed Dona Esmeralda on the cheek before she returned, blushing and smiling, to the kitchen.

Willan sensed that, unless the soup had been served in a larger than usual bowl, both he and Bennett had taken more time and care in their supping; it would be the ruin of everything were soup to fall from the spoon between bowl and mouth. Each man also noticed the downward checking glances of the other. As the bowls lay empty, both men relaxed back in their seats and praised the meal, although Willan felt that neither of them had actually tasted the soup, merely swallowed it.

Back in his room, Willan entered the air temperature reading and updated his records. As usual, Bennett intended to read and rest in his room during the afternoon. Willan would take a walk to the vegetable terraces and the men would meet on the colonnade before dinner. At this point Willan's confidence deserted him; convincing himself the temperature had dropped a degree or two, he decided to don a topcoat for his walk. His only concession was not to button it.

Adopting his usual quick walk, Willan soon passed through the hedge and arrived at the table nearby the bananas. He was hot and removed his coat, angry at himself for his meekness in wearing it unnecessarily. He realised that God was laughing at him and again apologised. Continuing his contrition whilst staring at nowhere in particular meant that Willan did not notice Senhor Pompion's arrival; he was almost sitting down before Willan looked up.

Using only gestures, Senhor Pompion praised Willan's waistcoat, miming distaste of his own jerkin and suggesting a swap; Willan mimed an arrogant air of dismissal in return. Senhor Pompion placed a chair alongside Willan and both men, still smiling, sat, simply enjoying the pleasure of their situation; neither man considered times such as this to be wasteful or non-productive.

A call from the distance plucked the men from their drowsery, and Senhor Pompion reacted by rising from his seat, gesturing an apologetic farewell and heading in the direction of his cottages. The person calling could not be seen but Willan assumed the owner of the voice to be Senhora Pompion; perhaps Senhor Pompion had lost track of the hour, an easy oversight given their blissful location. Content with his own company, Willan remained at the table for a further half-hour before returning to the house.

As soon as he entered his room, Willan removed his waistcoat and placed it carefully over the back of the chair at the desk nearest the dressing room. Only after he had washed and tidied himself and taken his laudanum would it be wise to re-adorn himself; his fear of spillage was so all-consuming that he had even given consideration as to what foodstuffs would comprise the safest dinner.

Resplendent once more in his waistcoat, he headed to the colonnade and sat next to a similarly dazzling Bennett. Greetings and compliments were exchanged. The pleasantries completed, Bennett asked if Willan would indulge him by listening to his concerns.

"Of course, please proceed," replied Willan.

"My concern is not really a problem; in fact, it is the opposite," began Bennett. "Since we spoke three days ago of my worries over the kindness being shown to me, and you convinced me of my entitlement to such benevolence, my doubts have returned. Everybody toasted my birthday yesterday evening and today I have received, as have you, the most wonderful gift from Dona Esmeralda. Am I wrong to hope that these kindnesses will cease? Surely I am not so deserving a cause?"

Willan, who had listened attentively as usual, was smiling as he replied.

"My dear Bennett, please forgive my happiness; I am not amused at your expense. I am pleased we think alike, for I too have been considering this situation. We are both fortunate to be surrounded by such tender-hearted people and we must show our gratitude for their bounteous actions the best we can. God will not forgive us ingratitude. I believe, as I said before, that the solution lies within us; we can only begin to repay our debts when we are recovered. I fully intend to complete my medical researches and to use my medical knowledge to serve those less privileged; I feel it to be my duty. If you will forgive my intrusion, may I ask of your plans and intentions?"

After a pause Bennett replied, "I am glad of your enquiry because I have given thought to this matter. My first intention was to return to the family business as my father wishes, but to use my personal time and any monies I might gain to the benefit of others. I confess I had not fully developed this plan and remain unsure if that course of action is enough or even suitable. Lately, I have come to a different opinion. I have a love of books and all things written so feel I can best help others through education. I plan to become a teacher, not of those adequately provided for but of those for whom education, no matter how basic, is but a forlorn hope. Do you consider this a wise intention, Doctor Willan?"

Willan replied, "It is both wise and generous. In fact, I salute your intentions and if I can assist in your achievement of this noble aim, I will happily do so. I am more than willing to sponsor these proposals and help with accommodation and the like, or just to offer an old man's words of advice. This plan sits hand in hand with mine, as I believe health and education to be crucial in the fight against poverty. Combined, they give opportunity, the single most important thing denied to the poor. You have pleased me greatly, and I am proud to be of your acquaintance."

"Thank you," said Bennett. "You speak with wisdom. Do you not think that perhaps you should consider parliamentary office to continue your good works and intentions?"

Willan stiffened at this proposal and, slightly angered in the face, replied, "I do not blame you for your kind suggestion, but were I to enter the immoral trade of politics I would surely drown under a sea of self-interest; these so-called leaders of the country have neither the knowledge of nor any interest in the wretched lives of the poor. They have never seen the puss-filled putridity of my patients, nor do they care about their suffering." His face redder, and after several racking coughs, he added, "It is government of the people for the good of the government, nothing more, nothing less."

Seeing Willan doubled over, coughing, Bennett placed his arm around his shoulder and tried gently to instil some relief to Willan's pain.

"We will make a formidable team to assist the poor and rail against parliament. We shall be known as the 'waistcoated workers for good,'" said Bennett.

The words caused both men to laugh and, after a period of careful breathing, Willan relaxed and his coughing ceased. He now spoke calmly. "We have both made our intentions clear and must now act upon them. I suggest a toast of Madeira's finest linctus to aid our recoveries and to fortify our resolves."

"Well said indeed," replied Bennett.

They did not have to wait long for Jorge to appear with the linctus and were soon sitting quietly, gathering their thoughts and immersed in the scene. Willan was smiling as he realised the paradoxical consequences of his intention to remark to Bennett that the silence enhanced the view.

19

Bennett and Willan were sitting at the dining table. As they looked towards Ashby, who was standing by the fireplace, the scene resembled that of a teacher addressing two boys on a school form.

So far Willan had enjoyed a successful morning; his thicker than usual slurry had contained two turds of nearly three inches in length, and he and Ashby had combined well in the battle against a wave of papers. Ashby had given Willan no details of his trip with Torres other than to suggest that he inform him and Bennett together before luncheon or, as they now called it, soup time.

Before Ashby started, Bennett feigned indignation at the lack of edible mementos to be seen, suggesting that Ashby had forgotten the two invalids imprisoned in their sanatorium. Ashby replied that such sentiments proved certain people were clearly not deserving of any gifts and would do well to listen attentively to their more learned betters. As the laughter ended, order was restored to the classroom and the teacher began the lesson.

Ashby detailed how he and Torres had set off on horseback soon after eight as the sun rose, Torres having looked up to the clouds above the hills and guaranteed the day would be fair. They had passed to the western side of Funchal to the rear of the waterfront and turned inland at the Quinta das Maravilhas, the site of an enormous green shiny forest of banana plants. Ashby surmised that all Madeirans must eat several each and every day. A short climb had taken them to Santo Antonio and its twin-towered church, which Ashby found difficult to describe other than as white and impressive.

As the climb continued, the air freshened and the temperature dropped a little, despite the rising winter sun. The terraces to the hillsides were called poios, according to Torres, and stretched upwards as far as the eye could see. The path was firm and they made good progress to a point with a fine view down to the river Soccorridos. The men dismounted and ate the bread and meats provided by Dona Esmeralda before joining the horses to drink from a fast-flowing man-made water course. The clear water was cold and reviving. All refreshed they continued the ascent, soon passing the last dwelling and a fine water cascade, the sound of which seemed out of place in the quiet of the hills.

It was just before eleven when Torres announced they had arrived at the Boca do Serrado, a flat area he said was over three thousand feet closer to God than Funchal. A small dark man of about twenty years greeted them and Torres explained it was his task to care for the horses whilst they proceeded on foot; he was from a good family and could be trusted.

Torres then led Ashby up a further hill, all the time promising that shortly they would witness the finest view in Madeira, that of the Grande Curral, or 'Nun's Valley'.

"It was breath-taking," said Ashby, adding, "I have never witnessed such magnificence. It resembled a bowl surrounded by rocky peaks on all sides with a small village way below. I was amazed when Torres told me that the village lay at half-height between us and the sea. He checked that I was feeling in good health as we were to descend via a zigzag path, take a tour of the village, have luncheon at a friend's house and then climb back to our current position. I could hardly wait to start; I felt privileged to view such beauty and have always enjoyed a physical challenge.

"Less than an hour later we were in the village. The walk down, although long, was without difficulty and the path well maintained. I wish I could give true justice to the grandeur of the panorama; it was wonderful. At first, we passed through laurel trees, but as we neared the village, the slopes were a forest of sweet chestnut, the main crop of the Curral according to Torres. He told me the villagers are self-sufficient as they have some flat land for crops and livestock, terraces for vegetables and trees laden with chestnuts, cherries and other fruits. The village is surrounded on all sides by high rocky peaks, yet the feeling there is one of tranquillity, not domination or foreboding.

"Our arrival was greeted by hugs and embraces from a large family group described by Torres as 'nearly cousins'. We crammed into a small stone-built cottage, ate pastries and fruits, and drank a small glass of homemade liqueur of cherries, confusingly called ginja. It was sweet and warming but I suspect likely to lead to befuddlement if taken in anything other than the smallest of measures. We bade our farewells and, after a brief turn around the village, began the return journey.

"Before we commenced the climb, I was advised by Torres to adopt the Madeiran style of walking. He suggested I should reduce my pace a little and also slightly shorten my stride. This would mean that I could complete the ascent without the need for rest and in greater comfort, and this indeed proved to be the case. In less than one hour and a half we were looking back down at the village from the Boca do Serrado. I was as happy as I can ever remember.

"We collected our horses and returned by the same route as our outward journey and arrived here just before sunset. We did not wish to disturb you both so, after stabling the horses, we returned to Bachelor's Hall where we sat after dinner recounting our adventure. I have only two more things to say. Firstly, as soon as you are both recovered, we shall all travel to the viewpoint, if not the village, so that you can share this wonder of nature. Secondly, by way of edible mementos, we carried back an amount of chestnuts which by now will have been transformed by Dona Esmeralda into today's soup. Torres says it is a delicacy of the island. I have my doubts, but we shall soon discover for ourselves."

Ashby bowed his head to indicate that he had completed his account and Bennett said that he felt that he had travelled with him, so good was his description. Willan and Bennett thanked Ashby for his words before the topic of conversation turned to soup, the consensus being that it might not be as bad as they feared.

Duarte must have felt insecure as he entered with the soup, such were the stares of the three men. How was he to know it was the bowls on the tray that were the subject of the inspection, not him?

"Today we have soup from the collection of Mister Ashby and Senhor Torres. It is of the main part chestnut and agreeable to most Madeirans. Please to enjoy," said Duarte before departing the room, quicker than usual, thought Willan.

The three men faced the bowls of sludgy brown matter, their silence and lack of expression giving away their fears of the taste to come. Willan, who had kept to himself his notion that the contents of the bowl before him resembled those of his chamber pot, was the first to dip his spoon. Closely scrutinised by the others he swallowed and delivered the verdict that it was not entirely to his taste but nothing to be afeared of. Three bowls were quickly drained.

20

The first of February 1812 was a good date for Willan. Written as one, two, twelve, a regular, balanced number was revealed and, being the first day of a new month, new charts and records could be drafted and commenced. This date, however, was not the main reason for Willan's good mood. A message from Torres had informed him that a large chest had arrived for him from London and would be delivered to the Quinta that morning. He had washed, dressed, breakfasted and updated his body waste records without delay. It had now been nearly two weeks since Willan had experienced diarrhoea and that had only been for one day as the laudanum had been temporarily withdrawn. He and Gourlay had now decided he should remain on laudanum indefinitely as it eased his cough in addition to corking his bowel; this was to be reviewed monthly, and Gourlay still believed a late springtime return to England was likely. Willan was content with his treatment and relaxed about his prospects. In fact, he was increasingly relaxed about most things.

Willan sat on his veranda without the telescope, hoping to hear any sounds of the impending delivery. Assuming the chest was from

Bateman, his research assistant in London, his mind was focussed on calculating the exact nature of the contents. Upon hearing voices in the distance, he moved to the right of the veranda, nearer to the entrance but concealed by a large shrub, the perfect place from which to watch and listen undetected. The voices neared and eventually came into view. Two men, with a pole on each shoulder, carried the chest which was slung beneath. Duarte joined the men as they lowered the chest to the ground, at which point Willan decided to return to his room and check the arrangements he had made for the chest's arrival were correct. So satisfied, he sat at the table and waited, clutching the key to the chest which had been transferred from the captain of the ship the previous day.

Loud voices outside his room alerted Willan to the fact that his chest was now in the care of Duarte and Jorge and the last few yards of its journey were proving troublesome; why had Duarte not had the strong bearers bring the chest to his room? Heavy scraping sounds indicated that, being too heavy for them to lift, Duarte and Jorge were dragging the chest down the hall; Willan dared not look. Finally, as a strong thump shook his door, Willan opened it and greeted the two red smiling faces looking up at him. The long conversation about the siting of the chest that followed was, thought Willan, a fine opportunity for the men to re-compose themselves and only a few minutes later the task was completed. Engrossed in opening the chest, Willan was unaware of Duarte and Jorge evaluating the damage to the hall in general and the skirtings in particular.

Unsealed and unlocked, Willan eagerly opened his chest and transferred the contents to the cleared table. It was completely full of medical papers other than for some quills and a package of Willan's preferred soap; any spare spaces had been cleverly filled with clean writing paper. There was no accompanying letter, nor had Willan expected one. Having moved the soap to the dressing room, the quills to their position nearby the three main windows and the clean paper to the first desk, Willan inspected the medical papers; they were all that he had hoped for. In the main they comprised illustrated case histories of skin complaints, which were Willan's central interest, but Bateman had also wisely forwarded copies of the statistical totals and records for the various other diseases encountered at the Carey Street Dispensary.

There being no time like the present, Willan set about his initial sort of the papers. Bateman had done a fine job; the papers were organised exactly as he would have done himself. He then positioned all of them under the table, carefully ensuring they were in the correct order for him to appraise and work upon. The items temporarily removed from the table were returned and everything was in order. Shocked that it was now nearing soup time, Willan vowed to re-check his arrangements that afternoon.

The air temperature was sixty-four degrees as Willan occupied several minutes watching the darting of the smaller lizards; what did they eat and what ate them, he wondered? Arriving at the dining room ahead of Bennett, Willan took the opportunity to find Duarte, thank him for delivering his chest, and ask him if, at his convenience, he could now remove it into storage. Duarte replied that he and Jorge would oblige him that very afternoon.

It was only when Willan was readying to leave the dining room that he came to his senses and realised his rudeness. Resuming his seat, he spoke to Bennett. "My dear Bennett, what patience you have. I have occupied the entire time of our meal speaking only of my work and chest of papers, and you have listened politely without complaint. I have not enquired as to your well-being and the progress of your day, nor given you any chance to utter even a single word. I apologise for my ill manners."

Bennett replied that he enjoyed hearing Willan's news and shared his happiness. He added that in order to even out the use of their ears and mouths, he would treat him to a poetry recital that very evening before dinner. Willan said he would accept his punishment and if anything were to correct a man's failings it was surely the verses of a lengthy poem.

Willan hurried back to his room and began re-checking his newly arrived papers. Only after a second audit, was he content nothing had been overlooked and everything was correctly positioned. Tomorrow morning he would be able to commence his analysis without delay; all preparations were complete; even the re-sharpened quills lay ready for his hand.

He decided to wait for Duarte and Jorge to arrive and collect his chest before heading out for his walk. Their anxious keenness to please could easily disrupt his methodically piled papers; he must leave nothing to chance. He re-positioned a chair on the veranda so that it was only inches from the open central window; he would easily hear their arrival and be only seconds away from forming a physical defence to his marshalled ranks of files. About twenty minutes later, Willan leapt into the room as he heard a knock on the door. He then watched as Duarte and Jorge entered, wished him good afternoon, easily lifted the empty chest and departed without a murmur or any incident. Nevertheless, Willan thought, you could never be too careful, and still found it necessary to have a quick inspection of his room and effects before leaving for his restorative walk.

It was a fine afternoon; there was nary a cloud in the sky as Willan passed through the hedge. He stood, enjoying the view, whilst he decided at which table to sit, eventually opting to proceed to Senhor Pompion's cottages and the vegetable terraces. He sat, pleased with his decision; the beauty of the scene before him never disappointed. There were three men toiling in the distance, one of whom might be Senhor Pompion but he was not sure, nor could he ascertain the nature of their toil; it was clearly a strenuous task. He continued to watch, fascinated by the activity from a great enough distance not to feel that he was interfering or idly witnessing the toil of others.

Occupied with attempting to calculate the passing of time from the shadows cast by the legs of the table, Willan did not notice the men had ceased their toil; the three men had become one, who was walking uphill in his direction. He was greatly pleased that it was Senhor Pompion heading to the table. They smiled and greeted one another warmly. Willan wished he could ask Senhor Pompion the nature of his afternoon's toil but knew his gesturing would not be sufficient; Bennett was the master of mime. The shadow of the table leg lengthened as they sat happily in their own thoughts, only interrupted by Senhor Pompion collecting two glasses of water from the cottage. Sipping his, Willan thought himself the richest man on earth.

As he washed and readied himself for dinner, Willan saw the package of soaps that Bateman had thoughtfully enclosed with the paperwork. Both men, as dermatologists, knew the benefit of the best soap in the care of skin. There were to be four at dinner so Willan decided to make the others a present. The package contained two dozen bars; he could easily spare half a dozen for his friends. He wrapped each pair of bars in writing paper which he secured with tape, and after adding the recipients' names was pleased with his efforts; sniffing at the parcels he could not discern the contents.

Delaying his departure in the hope that all the others would have arrived, Willan set off for the colonnade carrying his gifts. As he had hoped, the others were half a glass of Madeira wine ahead of him. They began to rise but discontinued the actions as Willan implored them to remain seated. He presented them with their gifts, adding that he would explain the contents in due time and after his dry throat had been eased. Torres immediately left in search of Jorge and the decanter. Bennett and Ashby toyed with their packages, making ever more fantastical suggestions as to the contents. Torres returned with the decanter and a glass and, as Willan sipped at his wine, the parcels were unwrapped.

"You consider your dining companions to be un-washed barbarians, do you, Willan?" said Ashby, in the most serious voice he could manage.

"Hear! Hear!" added Torres.

"I suggest you explain your ill manners. The ears of your jury are open," said Bennett.

Willan, whose more relaxed attitude to life meant he could now more often spot a whimsical chestnut, replied, "Members of the jury, please consider my words. For some time, through subtleties and nuances, I have tried to appraise you all of your malodour, but my tact has proved insufficient against the stubborn stenches. I am forced to take a direct approach and so prescribe two tablets of soap to be taken daily. One to be applied to the skin to remove dirt, the other to be applied to the mouth to remove such foul words as I am hearing. I close my argument and await the judgement of those I thought my betters."

The others closed their heads together as if debating the issue whilst Willan feigned indifference. Ashby then spoke. "We have made our conclusion and I, as elected foreman, am bound to so inform you. As a gesture of leniency, we are willing to grant you the opportunity to redeem your wrongdoing by re-addressing us in a more truthful manner. Do you accept our decision?"

After stroking his chin for some moments as if in deliberation, Willan replied, "Gentlemen, I am grateful for this undeserved opportunity. My words will be wholly truthful. I have known Mister Andrew Pears since soon after he opened his barber's shop in Gerard Street over twenty years ago. My interest in his business came about as he began to manufacture soaps of a purer nature than others available. I made his acquaintance and was shown the lengthy methods by which he refined and purified his soaps; that they are transparent is a result of this refinement. The addition of not too great a perfume of the garden means they are suitable for both gentlemen and ladies. He has achieved great success and no longer cuts hair but owns a soap factory near Oxford Street. I hope you can find space in your hearts to accept my humble gifts."

Willan's jury applauded his words and the evening continued with a more serious discussion of the uses and merits of soaps. Willan used the analogy of applying saddle soap to prevent leather drying out and the need to re-apply moisture to one's skin, especially the hands and face, which dried the most; he pointed out that as the oldest he was drier in the pores than the others. Bennett suggested that, given Willan's great age, they had best return the soap immediately. As Willan explained that soaps made from vegetable oils were superior to those made of cheaper animal fats, and that the oil of the laurel was particularly well suited for the purpose, he saw Torres' eyes light up at the thought of a business opportunity. Unfortunately, in reply to Torres' question, he did not know the method used to extract the oil.

The conversation was brought to an end by Jorge, who pointed out that Dona Esmeralda was keen they should eat soon; there was no question of disobedience or delay.

21

February had been a good month for Willan on two counts. His condition, according to his records, had not worsened; he felt increasingly well in himself, and his research work had progressed smoothly in the four weeks since the arrival of the chest of papers. Ashby was proving invaluable as an assistant, and a good friend. The work was a pleasure, not a drudge. There was an increasing camaraderie between the four men, a feeling Willan had never before experienced. His continuing conversations with God had confirmed it was not only acceptable to enjoy friendship and happiness, it was to be encouraged; mankind could only benefit as a result.

It was Friday evening and Willan had returned to his room after dinner. He was not as tired as usual so had begun to look at papers whilst sitting at the table. He soon gave up; he had never found it easy to read by lamplight. Still listless, he opened the central window and paced the veranda, his eyes drawn to the gentle lights of Funchal as a moth to a lamp. The evening was warm and the muslin drapes barely swayed in the soft breeze. His mind and body suitably soothed, Willan returned to the room to prepare for his bed.

He undressed, took a piss and reached for his nightshirt from its normal position next to the washstand. It had been removed and replaced with a neatly folded white garment. Willan inspected it and, finding no buttons or fixings, placed it over his head and arms. It slowly unravelled almost to his ankles. The hem, round collar and sleeves, which reached almost to his wrists, were edged in pale blue embroidery. This served not only to please the eye but also to weight the garment gently in position.

Willan's embarrassment at wearing what was surely a ladies' summer gown was immediately lessened by the comfort of the shift; he felt clean and secure. In any case, there was no witness to heighten his anxiety and no alternative nightwear. Still attracted by the distant glow of Funchal, he walked to the open veranda window and the soft breeze flowing through his outstretched arms added to his feeling of well-being. Any person looking up from the garden below would have imagined an angel readying to soar to the clouds, trumpeting the glory of heaven.

The peace was shattered by the simultaneous knocking on and opening of his door. He turned and saw Bennett about to speak. Willan reddened and spluttered but no words came forth. Bennett, correctly sensing Willan's embarrassment at his dress, quickly spun around and left.

Willan was confused. He sat at the table to collect his thoughts. Why had Bennett called upon him? And why did he not await an answer before entering? Was it so important? Why was he himself embarrassed at his dress? He was not naked and Bennett was a friend. What, if anything, should he do now? He could hardly change clothes and seek out Bennett. His logical mind searched for a solution.

'Whatever now?' he thought, as his door was knocked again. He remained in his chair and simply said, "Yes." The door opened and in strolled Bennett, dressed only in an identical nightgown. He walked over and took Willan's left hand in his right, eased him upwards and danced him across the floor as in a gavotte. Centred in the room he released Willan's hand, stepped back a pace and smiled. Willan's open-mouthed astonishment, after what seemed an eternity, gave way to a similar expression.

Affecting a girlish voice, Bennett spoke. "Shall I call for the carriage? Shall we go dancing? Oh, please say yes. We can be at the Palmerston's in Church Olney in less than an hour. There is to be music and dancing and fine wines and," lowering his voice, "eligible gentlemen from the county and officers returned from licking Boney. Please say you'll come."

Willan laughed aloud and bowed his head. "Of course, we must go. Now run along. We must look at our finest and I fear that I may need more time than you to prepare". They glanced directly at each other for several seconds and Bennett left.

Previously only confused, Willan now felt guilt, shame, happiness and more confused than ever. He should not have been embarrassed in front of a friend and his annoyance at the further knock on his door was unforgivable. Bennett had again shown that he was kind as well as humorous; a true friend. Willan realised that embarrassment was a failing he must correct and that there was never a place for anger or annoyance. He felt undeserving of his friends and vowed to mend his manners. It had been very funny, though, and he was smiling as he climbed into bed in his fine new nightgown.

22

Willan woke with the same smile that had accompanied him to his bed. Had he smiled all night? As he rose, his nightgown unfurled; he repeated the gavotte of the previous night and danced to the central window. As he drew back the shutters his first glance, albeit through the drapes, seemed to show a different outlook. He could not, however, remain at the window; he was urgently required at his pot. He was pleased with his droppings, as was now usual, and his happiness continued as he swallowed his laudanum. Washed, dressed and ready for his shave and breakfast, Willan carefully folded his nightgown and placed it near his washstand; it seemed un-worn.

Only after his shave and breakfast did Willan remember that earlier there had been something different in the view from his room. He opened the window. Funchal Bay appeared smaller, as it was filled by the recent arrival of five large ships. They comprised three merchant ships of the type regularly operated to Funchal by the East India Company, accompanied by two of His Majesty's ships of the line. These were easily distinguished by their high-sided hulls with row upon row of cannons; there was a menace to their appearance.

Having collected his telescope, Willan sat at the veranda table and studied the scene. There was a constant coming and going of small vessels between the ships and the shore, and also between the ships themselves. The Quinta's elevation above the bay afforded a good view, but the distance meant the precise nature of the activity could not be ascertained. Willan was not only fascinated at the picture before him, but concerned as to what was happening; Britain had no need to invade the already garrisoned island, but the presence of the two war ships surely indicated sinister intentions. His eyes remained glued to the telescope as he considered how best to establish the true reason for the maritime animation before him.

A rap in the distance alerted Willan to the presence of a person at his door. "Enter," he said as he hurried to meet his caller. It was Ashby, arriving to assist with the paperwork; Willan had let this arrangement slip from his mind. He led him to the veranda, pointed out the ships and sought his opinion as to their intent.

"I asked the same of Torres not an hour ago and he informed me the merchant vessels are laden with a battalion of redcoats to replace men whose service here is complete. The war ships are for their protection. Unfortunately, there is to be no change to the status quo," replied Ashby.

Willan, seizing on the word 'unfortunately', asked Ashby why he was dissatisfied with the situation.

"My personal opinion, which I have never before shared with any person, is that there is no military reason for the garrison of troops on this island. Are we really to assume that Bonaparte has his eyes on this spot? He is fully occupied in Europe and, I believe, foolish enough to chance his forces against Russia, where he will surely learn a terrible lesson. No, these redcoats serve to protect British interests of a commercial, not military nature," said Ashby passionately.

Replying that he too was uneasy with the presence of the British redcoats, and compounding Ashby's passion, Willan added, "With my knowledge of medicine, I am certain that this wretched body of men do more harm to this island with their spurting of disease into the whores of the waterfront than Bonaparte can ever hope to achieve."

Happy to postpone his paperwork for the time being, Willan asked Ashby how the British army were considered by the local population.

"That is not as straightforward a question as it might seem. As I cannot speak Portuguese, I can only seek the opinion of those Madeirans who speak English. But they, to a man, depend on the British for their incomes and livelihoods; they are not likely to bite the hands that feed them. From witnessing the contempt shown in the faces of the Madeirans as drunken assemblages of redcoats stumble through their streets, I can only conclude that the day these troops depart the island will be one of great celebration."

Clearly a subject on which he held strong views, Ashby continued. "My other concern is the shameful lack of leadership or control shown by the officers; they simply strut and stroll around the place as if on a Sunday promenade. Their unruly mob are never admonished, no matter how bad the behaviour. They have requisitioned fine houses for their use, want for nothing, and know their ornate tunics will never be stained by soil or blood. This garrison is, to my opinion, rotten from bottom to top, and top to bottom. I would happily wave the Portuguese flag at their departure."

"We are of like minds," replied Willan. "Although I have not witnessed, as you have, these atrocities, I too see no acceptable reason for this military base. We must be grateful for the peaceful good nature of the Madeiran people whose sufferings at British hands are a shame of which I am embarrassed. I hope that somehow I might be able to repay my already outstanding debt to this island and its admirable inhabitants."

A period of silence followed before Ashby spoke again. "I believe that we three can repay our dues to some small part. Simply to endow funds, which I will happily do, is not sufficient in itself. I know my dear brother has good and strong intentions to assist those that need help through education, and this intention includes Madeira as well as London. He will make an excellent teacher. I intend to help my fellow man through medicine, a calling I have discovered from your good example and words of instruction. Your continued help would be of great service and I know you well enough as a man to realise that you will assist any person in need of aid, here or in London."

"You understand me completely," said Willan. "I have pledged to support your brother and will do all in my gift to assist you; I promise to teach you medicine of the interior of the body, not merely skin conditions. You will have to study at Edinburgh, as Cambridge still follows the King's religion and is not accepting of us lowly Quakers. That is no matter, for Edinburgh is the better school and I still retain a little influence with the professors there. I will draw up a schedule and commence your instruction on Monday, alongside our research work. You should rest well tomorrow for I intend to be a strict teacher not afraid to use the cane on those who do not meet the highest standards."

Willan strode the veranda for a short while practising swishing actions; Ashby fled to the room effecting pained shrieks. Catching up with Ashby, Willan continued in a serious voice, "I do have one concern, though. What of your dear father? Will he be accepting of a teacher and a physician rather than sons who can continue his successful business?"

Ashby replied, "I have considered this matter. Our father has a business brain and business blood; he has built a successful company through honest dealings. Above all, as I am sure you know through your meetings with him, he is a charitable man who upholds all that is good in our faith. He will assist us gladly, I am sure, and be proud of our achievements. Besides, our father has no shortage of children to fill any vacancies within the works."

At these words, Willan remembered that Thomas Bennett Smith senior was indeed the father of at least ten children, if not more. He would not pursue the exact count with Ashby as the likelihood of all his brothers and sisters reaching maturity was slim; he did not wish to resurrect sad memories of loss.

Not having prepared a schedule for that morning's paperwork and forgetting Ashby had arranged to assist, Willan decided to cancel any thoughts of research. At all events there was now Ashby's instruction to include in his plans, an amendment of his objectives to be relished. He would draw up new outlines tomorrow, which fortuitously was the first of the month; Willan was always pleased when things fell into place in an orderly manner.

"All of this talk has given me a strong thirst," said Willan. "I propose to seek out Dona Esmeralda and her reviving teapot, and that we transfer to the colonnade. Might you enquire if Bennett wishes to join us?"

Ashby thought it a splendid idea and left to locate his brother. Willan headed for the kitchen, hoping he would find Duarte or Jorge rather than having to mime a teapot to Dona Esmeralda. Willan listened at the kitchen door and, hearing not the slightest sound, knocked loudly. There was still no sound. As he counted to twenty to leave a polite interval before knocking again, the door opened, which surprised him and caused him to greet Dona Esmeralda with the most startled of looks. Her smile changed to a look of concern, to which Willan responded by waving his arms up and down slowly, an action he thought would put Dona Esmeralda at ease. The silent stalemate that followed was, fortunately, interrupted by the arrival to the scene of Ashby and Bennett.

Willan explained the situation and Bennett, the acknowledged exponent of mime, took over. His smile alone was enough to re-assure Dona Esmeralda that disaster was not impending and, after she readily accepted his outstretched arm, they departed happily into the sanctum of her kitchen. Knowing that tea would soon be served, Willan and Ashby walked to the colonnade and leant on the balustrade as they viewed the ships in the bay, each man aware of the other's opinions of the scene before them.

Bennett soon arrived carrying the tea tray in far too casual a way, if the look on Dona Esmeralda's face was to be believed. Her smile returned as the tray was placed on the table without incident. Accompanying the tea were some plain biscuits which tasted better than they looked, having a subtle flavour of almond and cinnamon. Ashby and Willan talked of the ships in the bay; Bennett and Dona Esmeralda communicated about subjects that clearly amused them both. It was a fine tea party and something to be repeated, thought Willan.

After Dona Esmeralda had departed with the tray, having declined Bennett's offer of assistance, Ashby said he too must leave. He intended to meet with Torres in Funchal and to collect books for his brother, which he would deliver the next morning.

Ashby left and Bennett spoke. "As ever, Doctor Willan, I seek your advice on a small matter. Can you spare me a moment or two?"

"Please proceed," replied Willan.

"I have asked Jorge if he will teach me something of the Portuguese language and he has agreed to help me with some lessons in his free time. I believe he will prove to be a capable teacher and I am greatly looking forward to commencing; a good teacher, as I hope to be, must also be a good student. My concern is that of how to reward Jorge. Should I ask him to name a rate? Should I decide upon a figure? I am unsure as to how I should proceed. I would not like any awkwardness or embarrassment. What do you suggest, Doctor Willan?"

Willan stroked his chin, an action he was unaware of, as he considered the concern. Bennett stared at him as if willing a prompt response. He replied, "I believe that if you ask Jorge, he will set you a low rate out of politeness; he is deserving of a decent remuneration but we are unaware of local salaries. I suspect they are less than we think and this is an opportunity to improve a good man's lot. I suggest you ask Torres for his opinion. Although he is a businessman with an eye for profit, I think him to be honourable in his dealings. Torres will propose a sum which I believe you should increase by a half again. Therein lies, to my mind, a solution to accommodate all parties."

"If I only had a half of your wisdom, I would be one of the cleverest fellows in London. Thank you once more, Doctor Willan, for your help. I will act exactly as you suggest," said Bennett, before adding with a grin, "Is it not time for you to establish the temperature of the lizard tree?"

23

Willan paced his room. Ashby had never arrived late for any arrangement and there was no reason why today should be any different. Willan's apparent impatience was an indication of how keenly he awaited Ashby's appearance. He had spent all of Sunday re-arranging his furniture and papers; he intended to surprise Ashby by the thoroughness of the arrangements for his first lesson in human anatomy. The first desk had been cleared for the purpose, shifted ninety degrees and equipped with paper, quills and ink for the pupil, who would sit facing towards the three large windows. Willan proposed to teach from a standing position and his papers lay in readiness upon the bed. The schoolroom only lacked its first student.

Hearing a sound from the hallway, Willan opened his door and narrowly avoided a blow to the face from Ashby's knuckles as they rapped clear air, rather than the wood of the door. Explaining his plan for the morning and showing Ashby the desk, Willan was greatly pleased by the enthusiasm and gratitude shown by the pupil on his first day. Remembering his manners, Willan enquired of Ashby's and Bennett's health, and as soon as it had been established that everybody was as well as could be expected, the lesson began.

"Edinburgh Medical School will, primarily, teach you anatomy, which is exactly correct. A knowledge of how the human body is constructed is a prerequisite of all medicine and is not subject to any theory or conjecture, as is unfortunately the case with certain specialisms and practitioners. Opinions can be formed later; the bones and organs and their interdependence must be learnt first. I do not have all of my medical texts here in Madeira but my knowledge of the human skeleton has not faded since the day I was sitting as you are now."

Having given his introduction, Willan began by asking Ashby to draw, as best he could, the human skeleton, using simple straight lines as bones. He was pleased that Ashby, as well as taking time with his effort, showed initiative in removing his waistcoat and examining his own frame for assistance. The resultant drawing was then compared with an outline Willan had drawn the previous day and the differences noted. Notwithstanding the amusement of both at the lack of a pelvis to support the upper body, Willan praised the effort. He then handed Ashby another outline of a one-legged, one-armed man, and said that they would now identify the main bones, the names of which should be entered alongside; he suggested small lettering and, as left and right arms and legs both contained the same bones, describing the right arm and left leg would prevent a congestion of words.

Starting at the top of the page to avoid smudges from un-dried ink, Willan named the main bones of the skull as the cranium and the mandible and described their function as the protection of the brain, ears, eyes, nose and mouth; Ashby need only title the bones. The vertebrae of the spine, linking the skull with the pelvis, and the sternum, rib cage and coccyx were identified by Willan placing his hands onto Ashby's body and pressing on the relevant bones. Ashby duly entered the names of the bones carefully in his neatest, smallest writing.

The anatomical journey continued from the clavicle to the scapula and thence to the elbow via the humerus. Willan then indicated that two bones, the ulna and the radius, linked the elbow to the wrist. Holding Ashby's lower arm, he explained the radius was on the side of his thumb, the ulna on the side of his little finger. Next came the eight carpal bones that form the wrist, the five metacarpals of the palm and finally the fourteen phalanges that comprise three for each finger and two for the thumb. Ashby, at Willan's suggestion, spent some time examining his own arms and hands. He struggled to identify the carpal bones but easily located the individual metacarpals and phalanges. He was fascinated and completely unable to stop moving his arms and fingers in every direction possible. Willan asked him to cease his bagpipe rehearsals in order that they might consider his legs.

"By what means are all of these bones joined to one another?" asked Ashby, to which Willan replied that he would explain the intricacies of ligaments, cartilage and tendons in due time; the bones must be determined first. He hoped that Ashby's enthusiasm would not wane with the strict learning agenda required for medicine.

"Forgive my excitement to leap ahead," said Ashby. "Must I identify the bones in my legs so that I can stop trying to run before I can walk?"

Both men laughed as they attempted to untangle Ashby's words.

"A conundrum indeed," said Willan, adding, "I am seldom unable to answer a pupil's question, but you have me confounded. After we have added names to your leg bones, I will test your knowledge and memory, which will conclude today's lesson. Next time we can link your bones and move you from a standing position to a walk and then a run. We may even have time to wave your arms."

After inviting him to stand, Willan placed his hands just beneath Ashby's waist and explained the siting and purpose of the pelvis and hip bones. He then named the bones from the hip joint to the toes in a similar way to his previous description of Ashby's arm. The femur led to the kneecap or patella, which was linked to the ankle by two bones: the larger tibia or shinbone to the front of the leg and the smaller fibula to the rear. The ankle was linked to the foot by the seven tarsal bones which led to the five metatarsals, and finally the three phalanges to each toe except for the large toe which, like the thumb, had only two. Ashby expressed surprise at the similarity of the bone structure in the hands and feet.

Leaving the ink to dry on Ashby's, now-completed, diagram of a skeleton, Willan asked that he join him on the veranda for some clean air and his first test. Ashby sat at the table as Willan stood before him pointing to various parts of his own body for him to name. Satisfied that Ashby had learnt all that was required of him, Willan praised his efforts and declared the lesson finished. Ashby was to take his diagram with him, in the file Willan had set aside for the purpose, and commit the names of the bones to his memory; he was to be tested again on Wednesday, when his education was to be continued alongside Willan's research.

"I have only one further suggestion to assist your learning," said Willan. "I think that it would be quite appropriate for you to enquire of Doctor Gourlay if he would permit you to witness aspects of his practice; you could also offer him the temptation of your services as an unpaid assistant. I believe this could prove to be an arrangement suitable to both parties."

Ashby said he had also thought of offering his assistance to Doctor Gourlay, and he would ensure that any increase in his hours of occupation would not lead to a shortcoming in his primary duty, that of caring for his brother. Willan was heartened by this tender response.

Having taken his air temperature reading in the company of at least eight lizards, Willan joined the brothers for soup. Bennett and Willan had long finished their 'soup of the fishes', as Duarte had described it, whilst Ashby continued to neglect his own bowl in favour of staring at each movement of his spoon-bearing hand. Willan commented that at least the table concealed Ashby's legs from his eyes, otherwise soup would be spilled if supped whilst pacing the room. Having eventually finished his presumably cold soup, Ashby declared, quite honestly, that he had not tasted whether the bowlful had originated in the sea or on the land, so occupied was he with his bones and joints. Bennett remarked that, out of politeness, his brother should commence his dinner at least two hours ahead of any companions in order that he might be able to join the conversation of the table.

Willan was the first to leave the dining room, leaving Bennett in the care of his brother. Only Bennett would be dining with him tonight as Ashby had other arrangements. Returned to his room, Willan updated his personal medical records; satisfactorily stable, there was still no indication of improvement. He was initially disappointed but soon convinced himself that he must be regaining his health as he felt more recovered within himself. Having re-arranged his papers and ensured nothing was out of place, he set off for the vegetable terraces in good heart.

The trip was curtailed as Willan joined Senhor Pompion, who was sitting at the first table beyond the hedge. They exchanged handshakes and smiles, each man pleased to see the other. Although conversation was not possible, an affectionate fondness existed between the men, the silence adding to the poignancy of their relationship with both their surroundings and each other. Willan thanked God for his good fortune and happiness and imagined Senhor Pompion thought likewise. Clearly, they spoke to the same God in the same way; churches, priests or ecclesiastical doctrines were of no concern.

24

"Rain does not come much on the island, but can be very strong sometimes," said Duarte, as he and Willan watched dark clouds heading down the hills towards them. It was Friday afternoon and, having completed his schedule, Willan was early for pre-dinner wine on the colonnade. Bennett was to be his sole dining companion that evening; Ashby had left before soup time to accompany Gourlay on a visit to an ill-natured gout sufferer.

"This rain will not be long. It will only be wet on the top of the soil," continued Duarte, whose relaxed lean against the balustrade showed he was not needed elsewhere and was content to talk. "The worst rains were in October, over eight years ago, when many hundreds of houses and people were washed away to the sea and their ending. Two of my cousins and several whose names I knew were gone, too. Some hillside is still missing."

Willan did not have the chance to reply or offer sympathy as the rain swept in accompanied by a strong wind, and they hurried indoors. Duarte said the rain would be gone in ten minutes and then he would bring the wine to the colonnade. He departed through the kitchen door leaving Willan at the foot of the staircase pondering his next action or which direction to take. Having wasted several minutes with his deliberations, Willan opted to watch the rains from his room. As he pulled back the drape to view the veranda, the rain had almost ceased, only an occasional drop landing on the now-sunlit puddles.

Bennett was already on the colonnade as Willan returned. They discussed the brief storm and watched as the paths dried before their eyes; soon, only the few remaining puddles bore witness to the earlier rain. Duarte arrived with the Madeira wine and Willan kept his amusement tight-lipped as Bennett attempted to speak to him in Portuguese, presumably to thank him for the glasses and decanter. Waiting until Duarte had left, Willan asked Bennett how his lessons with Jorge were proceeding. Bennett replied that he was enjoying his instruction and that 'speaking is easier than writing'. Every hour with Jorge was adding to his understanding and vocabulary.

The relaxed conversation continued and covered many topics, none of great importance, and Willan was pleased by Bennett's sunny disposition.

"You seem to be in fine spirits of late," said Willan. "Am I correct in suggesting that there is an improvement in your health and well-being, and that you are hopeful of a full and speedy recovery?"

"As ever, Doctor Willan, you have assessed my feelings quite correctly. I have not been as happy as I am now, for some months. My happiness comes from many sources but mainly from witnessing the good cheer and hopefulness of others. Tiredness and fatigue are being replaced by optimism and a purpose to my future. I firmly believe that you, I and Ashby will continue our friendship in London in the not-too-distant future."

"Well said indeed," replied Willan. "We must all look forward; there is much to achieve. Am I right to believe that some years from now, when my work has been completed and published, that I will be visited in my retirement by a pair of brothers, one a professor of medicine and the other a headmaster of a fine school?"

"We will bring with us a bottle of the finest Madeira wine and reminisce of happy times spent at the Quinta do Til. Our toast to each other will be the same then as it is now." Bennett raised his glass towards Willan and both men exclaimed, "Manga!"

Duarte returned to the colonnade and announced, "The fowl is prepared," to indicate that dinner was about to be served; Bennett replied with some words of Portuguese. As the three men walked towards the dining room, Willan distanced himself from the other two and their painful attempt to converse, each in a second tongue. The fowl' was splendid and after the last crumbs of cake had been digested, Willan and Bennett sat contentedly at the fireside. Willan remarked he had yet to see the fire alight.

After a little silence, Bennett spoke. "Do you not think it strange that our friendship and realisation of the path in life we wish to take, are as a result of our illness? Is our happiness a reward for our suffering? If so, why are *we* so fortunate? Most poor souls suffer with no relief or reward. I am experiencing thoughts of guilt at my happiness, which I know to be wrong, as I wish nothing but happiness for others. I think that I must learn to accept my good fortune."

"You have answered your own questions well," said Willan. "I have the same thoughts and struggles myself. At first, I truly believed that any amusement, happy event or diversion to be a sin against both God and humankind; a pure, sensible, grave, approach to life was the only way to proceed. I now believe, without twist to my personal argument, that there is space enough, in a good life devoted to our fellow man, for us to enjoy ourselves and the fruits of God's benevolence. Happiness is contagious and we must share our joys and blessings with every person, no matter his or her disposition or belief. We do not need to deny our good fortune or cheerful frame of mind."

Bennett nodded his agreement with Willan's words; the silence was not a discomfort.

Willan was the first to speak. "My bed beckons me, but before I retire, I will leave you with some words on which to ponder. It is an oft-quoted proverb from the Greek dramatist Sophocles. It will make for an interesting conversation between us tomorrow. Sophocles said, 'Deem no man happy, until he passes the end of his life without suffering grief.'"

No further words were spoken; Willan indicated his farewell and headed to his room. Having prepared for his bed, he sat at the table and considered the evening's conversation. Bennett was a fine man and a good friend but, more importantly, he, Willan, was Bennett's friend. Friendship could not exist in isolation; true friendship must correspond in equal proportion. Willan had never before in his life given or received friendship; he thanked God for the gift. Willan's last thought, as his head came to rest on his pillow and before sleep overcame him, was also a proverb from Sophocles: 'One word frees us of all the weight and pain in life: that word is love'.

25

Staring into his pot, Willan was caught between two stools; his droppings could not be described as firm, yet the slurry was not entirely liquid. The problem was not a medical one; Willan put this change in the consistency of his outpourings as a reaction to his decision, two days previously, to increase the laudanum dosage. He had done this to counter an increase in his phlegm and episodes of cough which he considered to be his body becoming used to the treatment; he thought this to be both normal and acceptable. The problem was far more straightforward; how should he describe the contents of the pot in his medical records? He scoured his mind for the correct explication throughout his morning toilet. Only after he had eaten his breakfast did he settle upon the words for his record; 'three fingers of bread submerged in chestnut soup'.

His mind at ease, Willan set about his morning schedule. He completed some cross-referencing of his six identified species of herpes before commencing the far more enjoyable task of preparing Ashby's next lesson. The intention was to study the gastrointestinal system and Willan proposed to follow the path of a piece of food from mouth to anus. The drawings were difficult and it took until nearly soup time for Willan to be satisfied with his diagrams; he had never been happier in his work than now.

As he walked towards the til tree, Willan predicted a temperature of sixty-five degrees. Although in the three months of readings there had never been a variation of more than five degrees above or below the norm, Willan considered he should continue these records; a rise in temperature was imminent, if not now, certainly in April, and there was always the chance of an abnormal reading which might have medical consequences. The thermometer showed sixty-five degrees and there were many small lizards to follow; perhaps this was the time of year for their reproduction and birth.

Bennett was sitting at the table and rose as Willan entered.

"We need to discuss your wish to see me dead," said Bennett with a smile.

Willan knew immediately what Bennett was referring to and replied that he hoped he had not spent too much time wrestling with the words of Sophocles.

Bennett continued, "It took me some time to realise the true meaning of the words, but I understand the sagacity of this Sophocles fellow now; we cannot have a completely happy life until we are dead because misfortune or worse may strike tomorrow. The words sit well with me as I consider myself fortunate in my present happiness. I hope you are not too disappointed by my desire to remain alive."

"Of course not," said Willan. "Shall I commence our study of Greek legend, drama and philosophy immediately? We shall have to coordinate these sessions with Jorge's Portuguese lessons and I fear that you will be well occupied. Such is the life of a good student and a good teacher. I am certain you will be both."

"Do you think perhaps I should cancel my planned study of cookery with Dona Esmeralda, and farming with Senhor Pompion; surely there are twenty-five hours a day in this part of God's world?" replied Bennett.

Willan did not have the opportunity to continue the light-hearted conversation as Duarte arrived from the kitchen with the lunch.

"Today's soup is from the farm with Dona Esmeralda adding," said Duarte.

The vegetable soup was thick and delicious; Willan struggled to finish but eventually downed his spoon in victory, declaring that the bowls must be larger than normal. He left the dining room having made the now-usual arrangement to meet with Bennett on the colonnade before dinner.

Having quickly updated his medical and weather records, Willan decided to take a short rest upon his bed; he was feeling more tired than usual, which he put down to his morning endeavours and the filling soup. He soon dozelled into a half-sleep and dreamed of walking the hills and fields of Sedbergh and the English Dales. This most pleasant of strolls was ended as he slipped on a wet, grassy slope and was unable to prevent himself rolling into a cold, shallow stream. His anxious cries for help went unanswered until a shuddering scream returned him to consciousness and his bed. He lay, unable to move, in a confused condition and cold with sweat; sanity and a true knowledge of where he lay were only restored after a period of regular deep breathing. Returned to normality, Willan hoped his screams had not been heard throughout the house; the absence of any person rushing to his aid gave him the comfort that his anguish had gone unheard.

The clock on the mantle showed he had been asleep for less than thirty minutes, which he found hard to believe and only accepted after he had risen gently, drunk two glasses of water and checked the position of the afternoon sun from the veranda. His equilibrium was only completely balanced after he had spent longer counting the boats in Funchal Bay through his telescope than he had walking and tumbling the hills of his youth.

Despite his lengthy marine census there was still time for Willan to take his afternoon walk. He decided to take his evening dose of laudanum earlier than usual so as not to forget when he returned, and also because it would surely help to relax his thoughts a little following his traumas and uneasiness.

Suitably emboldened, Willan set off for the vegetable terraces. Every step of the journey calmed his mood and, by the time he had crossed through the hedge and by-passed the bananas, he was of a positively jaunty disposition. He ventured happily amongst the vegetables and fruit bushes much as a child might dance across a field of flowers. Simply being near the plants and inhaling their aromas was a joy; there was no need to touch or disturb. No other person was on the terraces, yet Willan did not feel alone; he was accompanied by his greatest friend and thanked Him for his love.

Smiling, and with emotional teardrops in his eyes, Willan crossed towards the cottages and the table. As he sat, his thoughts turned to Senhor Pompion and the situation; what a pleasure it must be to live and work here. Such a rich reward for craft and labour. Willan's almost prayer-like hope that Senhor Pompion might join him was granted as the door to the further cottage opened and he appeared, carrying a sack in one hand and a tray with two glasses and a bottle in the other. His progress to the table was not hindered by his load.

Senhor Pompion placed the tray on the table and the sack on one of the chairs. They shook hands, each man patting the other's right elbow with their spare left hands. Opening the top of the untied sack, Senhor Pompion showed Willan that it was full of vegetables. He pointed towards the house and said, "Dona Esmeralda." Willan confirmed it was intended that he deliver the produce to the kitchen by lifting the sack and making as if to return to the house. He then mimed the passing of the vegetables to Dona Esmeralda. Both men smiled at their communication success.

Sitting down, Senhor Pompion un-corked the bottle, poured two small drinks and handed one to Willan. They raised and chinked their glasses before sipping the light amber liquid. The liqueur was delectably fruity but had an obvious adult strength; it was a drink to savour, not to quench a thirst. Willan sat with a warm glow in his belly from the liqueur and a warm glow in his heart from the balmy atmosphere of the scene before him and the close companionship of his friend.

Willan declined the offer of a second glass; the single drink had been the perfect measure to enhance the afternoon; an excess of anything always lessens character and quality. Neither man felt the need to leave the table; instinct would be the arbiter of the time to depart. Instinct was, however, replaced by a not-quite-sharp call from Senhora Pompion, who was standing between the cottages. Her unwavering look, whilst not stern, and folded arms indicated her judgement that Senhor Pompion's time would be better spent within the cottages than idling with an Englishman. Jokingly shrugging his shoulders, Senhor Pompion walked towards his wife.

The journey back to the house took longer than usual as Willan needed to stop twice for a short rest and to transfer the sack of vegetables from one hand to the other. He was proud to be carrying out a task, no matter how trifling, that was of assistance in any way. Physical labour was not to be demeaned; the greatest minds in the land still required their vegetables to be transported.

"I have a delivery from Senhor Pompion for Dona Esmeralda," said Willan, as Duarte opened the kitchen door in response to the knock.

"Thank you," replied Duarte. "These are for tonight for tomorrow's soup. Dinner has been supplied this morning. But it is not your position to be lifting sacks."

"I am always happy to oblige," said Willan as he bowed his head with his feet close together and his arms by his side. He turned smartly and returned to his room. Although tired, Willan resisted the urge to rest for even a moment, fearful of a repeat of his earlier nightmare. He quickly washed and tidied himself, checked that everything in the room was correctly positioned and headed to the colonnade.

Willan sat at the table and waited for Bennett. Duarte arrived with the decanter of Madeira wine and offered to pour him a glass. He declined, thinking it polite to wait for his friend. At a loss as to how to best occupy his time and thoughts, Willan walked to the furthest end of the colonnade, turned around and returned to the table, counting the wall tiles as he travelled. Having completed the distance, he repeated the journey and was pleased when he attained the same result. Less fidgety than before, he resumed his seat and followed distant clouds across the sky.

Bennett soon arrived and, as they sipped at their wine, related to Willan the two successes of his afternoon; an instructive Portuguese lesson with Jorge and the delivery, from Ashby, of a new collection of books, some educational and some of a more distracting nature. Willan in turn gave an account of his journey from the nightmarish slopes of the English Dales to the sanctuary of the Elysian fields of Senhor Pompion.

Duarte arrived to advise them that, "Dinner is ready, and now Dona Esmeralda is with Doctor Willan's vegetables for tomorrow's soup."

Bennett's perplexion at this statement was lifted as Willan explained how, in a labour worthy of Hercules, he had single-handedly delivered an enormous cargo of produce uphill from the vegetable terraces to the house. Duarte mimed Willan struggling to maintain his balance whilst carrying a sack small enough to fit in the palms of his hands; Bennett said he hoped to be able to witness Willan's next display of strength. Perhaps he could carry Duarte and himself to the dining room?

After a fine meal, which Willan declared to be ambrosial, they sat at the table continuing their conversation; the words flowed easily. Bennett said that one of the things he was missing was music. In London he regularly visited the King's Theatre, often to listen to operas, and that his father occasionally employed small groups of musicians to entertain important guests. He wondered if musicians were available on Madeira – perhaps he should enquire of Torres. Willan said that he shunned musicians and musical events following an unfortunate occurrence some years ago, but he was not a killjoy; he would never seek to disparage another man's pleasure. Bennett asked after the nature of the 'unfortunate occurrence', to which Willan replied that it was too long a story to be told now, but he would willingly relate the events tomorrow. Bennett replied that he would give his ears an extra wash in readiness.

26

Unusually for a morning, Willan was sitting on the colonnade. He had risen as normal, the only change to his routine being the extra sip of laudanum as a treatment for his still unsatisfactory faecal consistency. It was a suitable time to pause his research for a day or two, and the preparations for Ashby's gastric lesson the following day were complete. Convincing himself that a morning away from his room and papers would enhance his well-being, he now found himself listless and unsure of how to utilise the extra hours. The distant toll of a church bell reminded him it was Sunday.

Unable to think of an alternative, Willan set off on his usual walk towards the terraces. His lack of energy and intent was reflected in his leaden tread. As he stopped at the til tree, he was aware of footsteps behind him and turned to see Bennett hurrying to join him. After exchanging polite greetings and enquiries, it emerged from the conversation that both men lacked a purpose for their morning. Each man enlivened by the other's company, they walked together at a steady rate; there was now an extra spring to Willan's paces, and no need for Bennett to hurry as before.

They passed by the bananas and gained sight of the cottages. Seeing two children, a boy and a girl, playing outside the further cottage caused Willan to stop with the intention of turning back; he considered it an intrusion to continue. Bennett, however, had increased his pace and soon, from what Willan could observe, joined in the game. Sitting at the table, Willan worried about the reaction to Bennett's boisterous horseplay with the boy and girl he presumed to be Senhor Pompion's grandchildren. The worry was unfounded as, only a few minutes later, Willan was joined at the table by a smiling, obviously proud Senhor Pompion. Together they watched the children, a couple who must be their parents, and Bennett continuing the fun.

The games were brought to an end by a rhythmic clanging sound; Senhora Pompion was standing in the doorway of the further cottage attempting to put dents into a cooking pan with a wooden spoon. The children ran gleefully indoors whilst Bennett and the couple, and Willan and Senhor Pompion said their farewells to each other. The occasion had proved to Willan that happiness was indeed contagious.

Bennett, tired from his exertions, replied to Willan's compliments on his rapport with the children by reminding him that he came from a large family and the only way to gain peace in the presence of children was by exhausting or over-feeding them. Willan commented that when Bennett was headmaster of his own school, he would do well to employ a sports master and a good cook.

Soon back at the colonnade, Bennett said that his ears were clean and receptive, and reminded Willan he had pledged to relate the details of the musical incident. The men were sitting opposite one another, both very slightly inclined inwards; it was the perfect distance apart for conversation, not so close as to be overly intimate.

"I must begin with a confession," started Willan. "I know nothing about music, it played no part in my childhood and only once interrupted my adult life, that time being the subject of these words. In fact, my only dance partner ever sits not a yard from me."

Bennett smiled at the memory.

Willan continued. "Some eight or nine years ago, as now in springtime, I was impelled to attend a musical concert at the Hanover Square rooms. I was the guest of a wealthy titled gentleman whose name is not relevant to the story; it was my hope that he might make an endowment to the Carey Street dispensary. He collected me from Bloomsbury Square in his private carriage and we were soon at the concert hall.

"My fears for the evening were confirmed by the melee of cabs and coaches at the entrance; even my esteemed host and I were compelled to enter through a secondary entrance in Hanover Street. Have you ever attended these rooms?"

Bennett confirmed that he had, and Willan continued. "In that event I will not bore you with details of the opulent, over-decorated rooms. We remained on the ground floor where the tea rooms seemed to serve anything but tea; wine in large glasses was clearly the order of the day. My host was known by all and I remained a wall-side witness to the comings and goings. The audience was made up almost entirely of what I term 'the worst of London's finest and the finest of London's worst'. They were clearly at the concert in order to be seen in their finery, not to listen with attention to musicians, for whom, before a note had even been played, I was feeling sympathy. I watched and overheard the artificial conversations, the illicit liaisons, the bitterness and the jealousies. I sometimes believe these falsities to be worse than the plain dishonesty of the common footpad or trespasser who perhaps has more justification for his crimes.

"After a while, footmen walked through the crowd advising that the concert was about to begin; very few people departed for the upper floor and the concert hall. My host, ever considerate, delivered me a further glass of wine, advised me that we would attend the superior music of the second half and returned to his ill-mannered cohorts. I spent the next half an hour or so politely listening to the ramblings of an elderly lady who seemed unsure of her location, to a background of distant music and idle gossip.

"The music stopped and after a further interval my host, who had been enthusiastically quenching his thirst for some time, collected me and we transferred upstairs into the concert hall. I was greatly impressed by the dimensions of the room and the size of the orchestra; there were forty-two identically dressed musicians. We were seated to the right-hand side near to the front. My host informed me we were to hear Haydn's one hundred and fourth symphony and that it was in four separate parts. He laughed when I asked him which of the musicians was Haydn and replied that he lived abroad, but the music would be conducted by the violinist standing to the fore of the other seated musicians.

"Then the music began. Large loud notes, 'der-der-de-up', then 'der-der-de-down'; I was both shaken and stirred in my seat. The violins then set off in unison on their musical journey, which I found both impressive and clever; how can a person write such a piece? Another memorable set of six notes then began to creep into the music, albeit played at different times on different instruments."

Willan attempted to repeat these notes in his 'der-der' fashion but Bennett conceded that he had not exactly picked up the tune, but understood about musical themes and repetitions.

Willan continued. "After, I suppose, nearly ten minutes, the music stopped, the musicians arranged their papers and a few people clapped tentatively. I had no sooner re-arranged myself in my seat than we were off again. It was a totally different piece of music, more like a genteel afternoon dance. I preferred the excitement and rhythm of the first part and allayed my boredom by imagining the disruption that could be caused by a single left-handed violinist. Most of the audience were also restless and at the end of this section nobody applauded.

"Part three was acceptable, a short masculine mix of a dance and a march. I imagined dress-uniformed soldiers parading their virility. This time the ending was received by generous claps and hurrahs.

"There seemed to be a feeling of anticipation as the last part started in a soft gentle manner; I did not know then that this was the lull before the storm. Most of the audience began to sing and shout in time to the music. 'Der-der hot cross buns, hot cross buns. Der-der hot cross buns, hot cross buns.' I confess the tune did match the street cry but I found the behaviour unseemly and rude beyond belief. To make matters worse, the people began to drift away with no regard to the musicians who, at the end of the performance, stood and bowed to the disappearing backsides of the 'so-called' gentle folk of London.

"My host was keen to continue the evening and suggested we seek out a party. Fortunately, his coach driver whispered to me that he would take me directly to Bloomsbury Square and that my host would, in all probability, be asleep by then. The driver was accurate in this prediction and fully deserving of his generous tip.

"And there we have it. My one and only experience of music. My concern is not the shameful behaviour of the audience, it is the fact that, even after all these years, I cannot dislodge the notes and tunes from my mind and memory. 'Der-der-de-up, Der-der-de-down' and 'Der-der hot cross buns, hot cross buns.' It is probably nearly Easter, I hope Dona Esmeralda does not make any of these wretched buns; I hope never to see one again in my lifetime, delicious though they are."

"So, am I to take it that my intention to hold an Easter-time musical evening accompanied by traditional foods is not entirely to your taste?" said Bennett, failing to hide a smile. "I had hoped to invite you as guest of honour."

"I wish you and your friends an enjoyable evening," replied Willan. "I will pass the time in my dressing room with my ears bandaged and a crust of stale bread for nourishment. I will gain comfort by utilising the time to muse upon the subject of the generosity and kindness of true friends." Both men laughed.

Bennett remained on the colonnade as Willan checked the reading on the thermometer before they strolled happily to the dining room, where Bennett immediately asked Jorge if he knew of hot cross buns and were they a part of Madeiran Easter celebrations. Willan was relieved that Jorge was unaware of the buns and glad that Bennett declined Jorge's offer to have Dona Esmeralda join the conversation with a view to learning the recipe. The subject was then dropped as Jorge gave Bennett an impromptu Portuguese lesson, apparently about the weather, interrupted only by Dona Esmeralda's call from the kitchen and the arrival of soup.

27

Willan was holding Ashby by the throat, albeit gently. The lesson on the gastrointestinal tract had commenced and an imaginary piece of food had entered the mouth, been subjected to saliva and chewing, and had been swallowed in the pharynx, where Willan's hand pressed. He explained that branching off the pharynx were the trachea or windpipe, which led to the lungs, and the oesophagus, which would carry the piece of food onwards to the stomach. The windpipe, lungs and breathing mechanism would be considered at another time.

Lowering his hands from the throat, Willan placed them onto Ashby's lowest rib bones; due to the difference in their heights, he was staring directly at Ashby's chin and neck.

"Behind my right hand is your spleen, behind my left your gall bladder and between the two lies the vastness of your liver, which can reach three pounds in weight. I must now pause the journey of our food whilst we consider a fundamental basis of medicine," said Willan. "Since ancient times, physicians have considered the human body to consist of four substances, known as the humours. These are blood, produced by the liver, yellow bile from the gall bladder, black bile from the spleen, and phlegm from the brain and lungs. The balance of these humours was thought to be the prime influence on health and well-being. Now, with the benefit of modern science, many physicians, including myself, believe this too simple a theory. You will receive the latest teachings from greater minds than mine when you attend medical school."

Drinking a glass of water, Willan paced the room as Ashby annotated the diagrams that had been prepared for him. He then checked that each marking and title was correct. More than satisfied with Ashby's work, Willan continued their medical journey. He explained how the food was moved downwards through the oesophagus by means of muscular contractions before entering the stomach via a sphincter muscle, which prevented its return upwards. Using his right hand, Willan indicated Ashby's stomach lying beneath his liver to the left side of his body. Ashby found it hard to believe his stomach was about a foot long, six inches wide at the centre and capable of containing a quart of food; by now he had removed his waistcoat and was constantly prodding at himself, much to Willan's amusement.

The imaginary piece of food was softened in the stomach before entering the small intestine, where, it was believed, the goodness was extracted. Willan had Ashby write down the names of the three parts of this intestine: the duodenum, jejunum and ileum, the workings of which would also be explored at medical school with the assistance of cadavers. Willan completed the journey by explaining how the waste matter travelled into the two yards or so of the large intestine or colon, the six inches of the rectum and finally the anus. He added that the intake of food by the mouth and egress of waste from the anus were the only parts of the journey the brain influenced; everything else was innate.

Ashby completed his diagrams and then asked many questions about bodily functions, which Willan enjoyed answering, before asking questions of his own to test Ashby's newly acquired knowledge. These questions continued as they walked to the til tree before soup time.

Arriving in the dining room, Willan noticed that the table was set for four people. Ashby explained that Gourlay was visiting Bennett that morning and was obviously staying for soup.

"My guess is that it will be tomato and onion with eggs," said Willan confidently.

Bennett and Gourlay soon arrived and Jorge came in to check that everybody was present. Not twenty seconds later there was a painful shriek from Jorge; he slumped to the floor next to Gourlay, who quickly knelt alongside and cradled his head.

"Quickly, Ashby! Fetch my new medical bag from the main door. Quickly!" shouted the doctor.

Ashby ran from the room and nobody moved or spoke. Willan did not know what to do to assist.

As Ashby ran back into the room with the bag, Gourlay shouted again, "Open the bag, man. Pass me the large bottle of medicine. Quickly!"

By the time Ashby had uncovered a bottle from low down in the cloth-filled bag and raised his eyes, Jorge had risen to his feet and, together with Bennett and Gourlay, was laughing. Duarte and Dona Esmeralda, who had witnessed the scene from the kitchen doorway, came in, Duarte carrying a tray of seven empty glasses. Only then did an open-mouthed Ashby realise that he was holding a bottle of Madeira wine.

"Some medicine to celebrate the start of your twenty-fifth year, dearest brother," said Bennett.

Ashby was now crying and laughing and still unable to speak. Willan's shocked expression had now transformed into the broadest of smiles. As everybody relaxed with a drink from the now un-corked bottle, the subterfuge was unravelled; it was Ashby's birthday and the new medical bag was his gift. Ashby finally recovered the ability to speak and said he would never forget the day or the kindness of his friends.

The soup was not tomato and onion, as Willan had predicted, but more of a stew of meat which, although delicious, proved to be a challenge for both himself and Bennett. Gourlay and Ashby, however, drained their bowls as if they had not eaten for days, not even slowed by their constant discussion of what should be carried in a doctor's medical bag. Gourlay suggested that, as earlier, a single bottle of Madeira wine was more than sufficient; if it were not suitable for the patient it was certainly beneficial to the physician. They departed the table as soon as all the bowls were drained, intending to stock Ashby's bag at Gourlay's consulting room before attending the flutters and vapours of two delicate sisters. Ashby could not conceal his pride as he followed Gourlay from the room carrying his soon-to-be-filled leather symbol of office.

Willan and Bennett relaxed by the fireside, warm from the glow of happiness the lunchtime episode had delivered to all. Bennett explained that the theatrical ruse had been concocted by Jorge; he had written the script, supplied the case and cast the leading roles for himself and Gourlay. Apparently, there had been a rehearsal in the kitchen some days ago which had alarmed Dona Esmeralda into spoiling some cakes and nearly caused the cancellation of the performance and injuries to the cast. Still smiling at this incident and the earlier dining-room drama, both men left for their rooms.

Shunning his bed for fear of bad dreams and over-sleeping, Willan splashed his face with water in the vain hope that it might dispel his feeling of bloatedness and debility. Fortunately, there was a lot to see in the bay and sitting at the table with the telescope focussed his mind away from his stomach and tired brain. Only after nearly an hour of complete diversion did Willan suddenly remember that he had not updated his temperature and medical records. What had caused this oversight? Was it the jollity at lunchtime or was he over-confident of his memory?

He completed his records, which allayed his self-annoyance a little, but it was not until he had planned a physical reminder for future days that he was completely at ease; his medical record file was now sitting alone on a chair in the centre of the room where it could not be missed. His relief at solving the problem was short-lived. What if he were to forget other important matters? What if he were to forget his twice-daily medicine? Worried, he swallowed a large dose of laudanum and placed the bottle on the chair next to the file of papers. His task for tomorrow would be to draw up new task sheets and re-arrange his room and contents. He took a second dose of laudanum for good measure and set off on his restorative walk, trying to close his mind to the next day's requirements.

It was a restless night. Willan had been planning the morning in his mind and was eager to commence the implementation of a new regime. He rose from his bed as soon as he thought there was sufficient light and hurried to un-shutter the windows. Remarkably, as he fell to the floor having crashed into the chair placed directly between his bed and the windows, the bottle of laudanum bounced off his prostrate body and rolled onto the carpet unbroken. He lay for some time surrounded by loose papers and clutching the bottle as he tried to come to terms with his situation. Realising the folly of his actions he hauled himself to a sitting position and remained quite still as tears of laughter ran from his eyes.

Rising to his feet to re-arrange his furniture to its original order, he was compelled to delay the task as his bowels were starting their morning movements. His discharge was satisfactory: mainly solid with only a small amount of slurry. Adopting a calm disposition, only occasionally interrupted by chuckles of laughter, he washed and dressed before carefully restoring the room as if nothing had ever moved. Realising the morning's calamity was entirely the result of a single moment of forgetfulness, he pledged not to over-react in the future. Sitting on the chair that he had returned to the table, he confessed his ill-judgement to God, whom he suspected may have been amused by his actions. Baring his soul and conscience to God was always an uplifting experience and, with a spring in his step and happiness returned to his heart, Willan began his day as if nothing eventful had happened, notwithstanding the large bruise forming on his left thigh and buttock.

28

Checking his appearance in the looking glass that evening, Willan was content with what he saw; his hair had been cut only two days previously and he enjoyed the feel and style of his blue waistcoat. As Ashby and Torres were soon to arrive for dinner, they would be a party of four, which augured well for the evening; an input of fresh news and conversation was always welcome. Smoothing his clothes for a final time and wincing as his hand travelled over his now mainly yellow bruise, Willan carried out a quick survey of his room and contents before leaving for the colonnade.

Being the first to arrive was normal for Willan; he was never late for appointments and, if anything, perhaps too early on occasion. The decanter and four glasses were already on the table and the lamps lit. He resisted the urge to pour himself a drink, although it might help ease the slight tickle in his throat which he thought to be the result of some crumbs of bread taking the route of his trachea rather than oesophagus at lunchtime.

Bennett and Ashby were the first to join Willan and the resulting conversation caused Bennett to cough a reminder that he too was at the table; perhaps gory medical details were best discussed after food, not before. Bennett also hoped that whatever beast or fowl was to be served for dinner had been filleted; he did not wish to see his dinner dissected and the original purpose of its parts explained. Willan suggested that if dinner were to be either a suckling pig or whole chicken, Bennett would be as well heading for his room immediately.

The last to arrive was Torres; he strolled to the table deep in conversation with Jorge, who carried an empty glass and, with the approval of all, pulled up an extra chair and joined the party. Torres explained that he and Jorge had been making arrangements all afternoon and were now in a position to reveal their intentions. The plan was to travel as a group, not tomorrow but the Saturday after, to the Quinta da Achada, a fine house not too far away.

"We are to be the guests of William Penfold and his wife at a musical afternoon, which promises to be a fine affair," said Torres, who, looking directly at Willan and smiling, continued. "For those whose ears are not suited to the charms of a string quartet I can advise that the house is large with many rooms well fitted for private conversation and quieter diversions; also, the house sits on perhaps the largest level site above Funchal and has the most delightful gardens."

Torres added that it was not to be a boisterous party even though the Penfolds' many children would be present, along with a few other British families and business acquaintances known to the hosts, whom he described as being 'good sorts.' They would easily be back in time for dinner as usual. Jorge, who was to accompany them, would make the travel arrangements and Willan and Bennett would journey by hammock. Jorge said that he would confirm all the details during the coming week and he knew the trip would be a great success to be enjoyed by all. He then left for the kitchen, having quickly drained his second glass of wine.

The conversation before dinner consisted, in the main, of Torres not answering the many questions about the proposed trip fired at him by the others.

"It will spoil the occasion if I reveal every detail of the property and the guests before we depart," he replied consistently, adding, "Am I not to be trusted to ensure that the trip is a satisfaction for all, and only the safest travel arrangements will be made?"

The interrogation eventually ceased, to be replaced by the normal banter and badinage of the table. At Bennett's insistence, Willan repeated his tale of the chair and the falling laudanum bottle which led to Ashby offering to treat the contusion and Torres expressing concern at how a stumbling elderly doctor might be thought of at a refined gathering; perhaps Willan might be happier remaining under the care of Duarte when the others travelled to the Quinta da Achada?

The happy talk continued throughout dinner and afterwards, when they returned to the colonnade to make the most of the higher-than-normal temperature. A warm but gentle breeze and the faint lights of the city added to the convivial atmosphere, which was further enhanced by an elegant glass of port, savoured by all.

Willan, beginning to tire and concerned that Bennett was also ready for his bed, was greatly impressed by the way Torres, in his role as host, tactfully brought the evening to a close by suggesting that he and Ashby needed a good night's rest as they had a busy day planned for tomorrow. They departed to collect lamps to illuminate their walk back to Bachelor's Hall; Bennett and Willan returned to the house and then their rooms.

Sitting at his table, Willan drank a glass of water as his throat was still not clear of its tickle; this drink and an untroubled sleep should resolve the problem. He reflected upon the evening; although he was excited at the news of the planned adventure, it was the pleasure of being amongst friends that gave him the most joy. Realising that there was little or any difference between true friendship and love in its purest sense, he retired to his bed with a deep feeling of thankfulness at the good fortune bestowed upon him.

29

Duarte, having been shown the working mechanisms of the telescope, was clearly enjoying the view of Funchal Bay from the veranda and excitedly identifying and naming buildings and landmarks. This pleased Willan; he was always keen to acquire new information and add detail to his existing knowledge. Duarte had asked if he might have a look through the telescope as he had only ever heard about the magical pictures; he had never seen them for himself. Willan had readily agreed and apologised for assuming that Duarte had used a telescope previously; any discomfort between the two men soon disappeared as the enlarged scenes focussed in Duarte's eyes.

Having lifted his head from the telescope for the last time, Duarte walked to the balustrade and surveyed the scene un-enhanced, as if to check that no trickery had taken place. Willan considered explaining the workings of lenses, light and magnification but thought better of it; he moved alongside and both men took in the sunlit view.

"I do not visit you to see the pictures, I come to talk of Easter and our plans," said Duarte, which surprised Willan as he thought the visit may have concerned the following day's trip to the Quinta da Achada.

"I confess," replied Willan, "that I am unsure of when Easter takes place this year, but I would be very pleased to hear about the plans."

"One week from now will be the holy Friday, so not this Sunday but the one that follows is Easter. We call it 'Pascoa'. It will not be normal here as only Jorge will be present on the Sunday. Dona Esmeralda and I will leave after dinner on the Saturday which is earlier. Jorge will attend to you and Mister Bennett in the morning for breakfast and toilet and also stir the soup. For the dinner, cooked fowl and pig and other things not hot, Jorge will bring to the table. On Monday everybody comes back before the soup."

Willan thanked Duarte for explaining the plans and the continued admirable service; he said he was only too happy to fit in with any arrangement. Duarte then left without warning or a further word, as was his normal practice. The visit had not disrupted Willan's afternoon; the timings remained the same, the only difference being that it had been Duarte's eye on the telescope, not his.

The afternoon was warm and by the time he reached the passageway through the hedge, Willan had removed his waistcoat; although only a small act for most people, for Willan the new experience was both bold and liberating. He arrived at the table nearby the bananas, hung his waistcoat over the back of a chair and entered the green plantation. The plants and fruits still fascinated him; the textures, smells and warmth were beguiling. His mind contrasted the lot of a Madeiran banana grower with that of an English farmer in winter; Willan had never before held any desire to travel to foreign climes but could now see the attraction and the opportunities to learn from other peoples and races; if only he were twenty-five years younger.

Transfixed by the obviously recently formed, small banana fruits on a particularly green and shiny plant, Willan failed to notice that he was not alone until he heard the crackle of a trodden-on leaf, about two feet behind him. He turned and embraced a smiling Senhor Pompion before stepping back a pace and shaking his hand; neither man seemed embarrassed at displaying their obvious pleasure at seeing one another. As they walked back towards the table, Willan could hardly hide his gladness at the sight of Senhor Pompion's jerkin draped over the chair next to his waistcoat, a perfect symbol of close friendship.

They sat together comfortably at the table for a short time before Senhor Pompion returned to his cottage, indicating that Willan should remain. He returned with a large jug and two glasses. It was clear, cold water and the jug was soon emptied; Willan declined Senhor Pompion's gestured offer of more and the two men remained, contentedly enjoying their surroundings. The sun lowered and the temperature dropped accordingly, waking Willan from his slumber; he was alone, and after donning his waistcoat he strolled back to his room in a good frame of mind.

The evening was to be a repeat of the previous Friday with four at the dinner table. Willan was looking forward to both the company at dinner and hearing the final plans for the next day's adventure; he was ashamed that he had not left the grounds of the Quinta, even once, since his arrival on Madeira nearly four months previously. His shame was lessened by his realisation that he had achieved significant progress in his research and also obeyed his doctor's advice to treat his frailty and illness through a gentle regime.

Still with a slight tickle in his throat, Willan drank a glass of water before taking two doses of laudanum which he felt should relax the throat and ease the tickle, half coughs and gargling having failed to clear the obstruction. He took the opportunity to measure how many doses of laudanum remained in the bottle half used and the spare; calculating that there was enough laudanum for about two weeks, he resolved to obtain a further supply from Gourlay. Realising he had drunk three full glasses of water that afternoon, he took a precautionary piss before departing for the colonnade; it avoided the embarrassment of having to be excused from the table.

Bennett was already on the colonnade in conversation with Jorge which, as Willan neared the table, he realised to be a light-hearted Portuguese lesson. Not wishing to interrupt he crossed to the balustrade and began a casual count of the ships at anchor in the bay. Bennett and Jorge, however, immediately reverted to English and welcomed him over.

"I am glad you are here," said Bennett, "because Jorge was about to point out approximately where tomorrow's destination lies."

"Excellent," replied Willan. "Please proceed, Jorge."

They all gathered at the balustrade and Jorge showed them where the Quinta da Achada was situated, explaining that if the group of trees to the right of the first hill were not there they would, in all probability, be able to see the Quinta's roof.

"The trip is not difficult at all. I have walked between the houses many many times, and, were we able to travel, as a bird flies, the journey would only take minutes. The fly in our ointment is the Santa Luzia River which crosses our route. It means we must descend towards the city, where we can cross, and climb back up again. Do not fear for your safety, though, gentlemen. Very few travellers are dropped into the foaming waters," said Jorge with a grin.

Jorge left to collect the decanter and glasses and readily accepted Bennett's suggestion that he bring a glass for himself. Torres and Ashby arrived, and soon after Jorge's return, they were standing with raised glasses. 'Manga' was the toast, which never failed to cheer. A quick discussion and confirmation of the next day's plans passed in a business-like way, which relaxed everybody, especially as Torres said that the weather was forecast to be fine and warm. The conversation then assumed a lighter tone, firstly with Bennett attempting to impress the table with his Portuguese fluency, which caused Jorge to cradle his head in his hands. Then Ashby gave amusing details, without being indiscreet, of his medical travels with Gourlay. Torres said that his week had been profitable in a small way, but that details of his trade in raw materials was far too dull a topic for the evening's assembly of fine minds. Willan said that with his dry pores and great age it was his position to be entertained by others and not vice-versa. All eyes then turned to Jorge, who stood, smiled and said that he was a gentleman and therefore not given to idle gossip. He left for the kitchen, leaving a happy group of four and their laughter behind him.

The gentle conversation continued throughout dinner and for a short time afterwards. Willan was the first to leave, stating that he needed more sleep than his young companions and that he wished to be at his best for their intrepid expedition. He also re-confirmed, without necessity, that soup would be at noon as normal and they would depart about one hour later. Willan entered his bed happy at the thought of the next day's trip; not only could he not remember ever having undertaken any journey purely for pleasure, he would be accompanied by friends, a situation that had never existed before. Sleep soon closed his eyes but his smile remained.

30

The weather on Saturday morning was as Torres had predicted: warm and sunny and only a gentle breeze. Willan was sitting on the veranda enjoying the view, anxious for the two hours until soup time to pass quickly. He was unsure of how best to occupy this period, and although lonely for company thought it best not to interfere with the, presumably extensive, preparations for the afternoon trip. After only a few minutes he decided to take a gentle walk, with the hope at the back of his mind that he might come across a situation or person with which or whom to pass the time.

His hopes were answered not twenty yards from his room; Bennett was sitting on the colonnade. There was a book unopened on the table, which indicated to Willan that he might not be disturbing his friend, as he joined him. This proved to be the case as Bennett said he was pleased to have some company to help pass the time until their trip. It seemed to Willan that their amiable conversation was indeed making the hands of time accelerate towards noon. Having strolled to the til tree to take the temperature reading, he was heartened to find that Duarte had arrived on the colonnade to announce that 'the soup of meats, for the strength to travel' was ready.

Having quickly drained their bowls and dispatched the bread, Willan and Bennett were soon back in their rooms; Ashby and Torres would take luncheon at Bachelor's Hall and Jorge would make his own arrangements.

Willan washed and tidied himself and swallowed a large dose of laudanum; he did not wish to forget his medicine when they returned. He then paced the veranda, partly to relax his nervousness but also to listen out for any sounds of activity from nearby the main door. Adopting a casual demeanour, he dallied nearest to the right of the veranda but stopped short of putting his head into the shrubbery for a clearer view of the entrance to the Quinta. After some minutes he heard a voice in the distance and quickly darted back into his room. He took a precautionary piss and then stared at the hands on the clock for five minutes before heading to the main door and the start of the adventure. His attempt to appear casual and his rushed eagerness combined to produce a gait similar to that of a child riding an imaginary hobby horse.

Jorge was just outside the door talking to six short, stocky men.

"Good day, Doctor Willan," he said. "These are your hammock-bearers; four are to carry yourself and Mister Bennett, and the other two are needed to rescue any fallers, either on land or from the foaming river." Seeing the aghast look on Willan's face at his words he quickly continued, "But fear not, you are in the safest of hands." His grin gave away the fact that he was jesting and the colour soon returned to Willan's cheeks.

It was not long until the travelling party was complete. Torres was to the fore astride his stallion, looking every part a Hussar, his apparent military air outweighing his lack of uniform. His groom, a young man of less than twenty years, walked alongside; it would be his task to care for the horse at the stables of the Quinta da Achada. Then came Willan, confidently sitting almost upright in his hammock ahead of Bennett, more nervously slouched and swaying slightly in his. Jorge would walk alongside Willan, whilst Ashby was detailed to accompany his brother. The two extra hammock-bearers completed the troop, their presence being merely a precaution in the unlikely event of any mishap or as a relief to the other bearers in the event of strain or exhaustion.

The gentle but precise clip-clop of Torres' stallion as they crossed the stone-laid entranceway provided a slow marching beat for the others to conform to; if Duarte were an army general he would have been proud of his men leaving the fort on a sortie or mission in such a regimented way. However, as they left the grounds of the Quinta and crossed onto the mixed soil and rock surface of the track, the precise military formation unwound into a far more relaxed ragtag army as they made their way down towards the city.

Not feeling embarrassed at being carried by bearers, Willan's broad smile was evidence of his enjoyment of the trip; he was warm, secure and comfortable, and Jorge was giving an amusing but still educational commentary on their surroundings. Four separate good-natured conversations were taking place, producing a combined sound of bubbly cheeriness. As they encountered other people either tending small plots or making journeys of their own, fresh greetings, laughter and playful exchanges sprang up. Everybody they met appeared to be known by at least some, if not all, of their party; Jorge knew every adult and every child.

Willan felt that the journey was slower than when he had previously travelled by hammock on his first day on Madeira. Jorge confirmed that it was slower to travel downhill as the bearers needed to place their feet carefully and brace themselves against moving too fast. As he studied the feet and legs of the bearers, Willan was impressed by their strength and agility; they made a far from straightforward task smooth and appear almost effortless.

Having passed the point where their route joined the main track to the city, they started down a steep, narrow, overgrown path; Torres had dismounted and walked alongside his horse with the groom. Jorge said they would soon reach the river and had completed almost half of the entire journey; once they had crossed the often-fierce waters, it would be nothing more than a gentle stroll to their destination.

Leaving the path, they were at the river. It was at least ten yards across and strewn with rocks and boulders. A small stream of water about a foot wide trickled through the centre. Willan looked at Jorge, who was laughing, and said his prayers had been answered in that the torrents had eased. In a very short time, the entire party had crossed the riverbed and were enjoying a drink of water from the flasks carried behind Torres' saddle. Jorge confessed he knew that there was no depth to the river at the present time, but after heavy rains the torrents could be very strong and dangerous. He repeated the story that Willan had heard from Duarte, of the great storm and flood of October 1803 when hundreds had perished, many dozens in this river alone; the rocks and boulders, which had been carried down from the hills were proof of the might of the river when in flood.

The journey continued and now they were moving uphill, the pace increased and Willan could see it was less of a strain on the calves and feet of the bearers. This, despite the path being, if anything, more corrugated on this side of the river. As they turned slightly to the left onto a small level plot of land, Torres pulled up his horse, waited for the others to reach him and announced that the large red-roofed house up ahead of them was the Quinta da Achada.

Arriving at the front of the Quinta, the party disassembled; the groom led Torres' horse around to the left of the building, followed by the six bearers carrying the un-shouldered hammocks. They all appeared to know where to go. Willan looked first at the view from the front of the house. He was faced by extensive and beautiful gardens, level for a long distance before dropping down the hillside. The view of the bay of Funchal beyond, being more central than that from the Quinta do Til, made for a wider panorama. Willan was captivated by the view and longed for his telescope; he readily agreed to Jorge's offer to guide him through the grounds later.

Willan walked away from the building before turning to look back. The Quinta da Achada was a fine house of three storeys, twelve green-shuttered windows wide at the middle level, with a third floor of six, also shuttered, windows centrally above. The top floor also had a large balcony which Willan thought must give a magnificent, unhindered view of all of Funchal; he hoped he might get the opportunity to see it for himself. The Quinta, despite its size and formality, had charm and the feel that a warm welcome awaited those who called.

A well-dressed man of about forty years, accompanied by two young children, had left the house and was talking with the others. Willan scuttled back and was introduced to William Penfold, the

English owner of the Quinta, who invited everybody into his home and led the group inside, holding one child by the hand whilst clutching the other around his waist.

Entering by the impressive main door, they immediately climbed a wide staircase to the main reception rooms which ran, as a corridor, the length of the building. The series of fine rooms impressed without conceited display; it was a family home, albeit a very large one. Penfold, who had released his children, explained that music, refinement and tea lay in the rooms to the left, conversation and stronger refreshment to the right. There were to be about thirty guests in total, most of whom were already present; the expectation of the afternoon was as a diversion away from business and formality, any surfacing of which would be frowned upon.

Torres, Ashby and Bennett headed to the left, with Bennett commenting that they were refined enough already but that if the riff-raff wished to join them later they might find that 'music has charms to soothe the savage breast'. Jorge replied, whilst shaking his fists, that he would fight to the death any man who suggested he was savage. Willan pretended to pull him back from the intended conflict and everybody, including a slightly bemused Penfold, enjoyed the jesting. Penfold excused himself from the party and Jorge suggested that he and Willan head into the next room to the right, where they could enjoy a drink and view the parade of guests before deciding upon their agenda.

Soon after they sat, a young girl approached them and asked in stuttering English if they required any food or drinks. She relaxed noticeably as Jorge replied in Portuguese and was nothing but smiles and laughter as she left.

"I knew her mother," said Jorge.

The girl soon re-appeared with a large tray carrying the wherewithal to pour a polite cup of tea. There was also a small glass of dark brown liquid which Jorge swallowed in a single swift movement.

"A restorative tonic for my heart," he declared.

People passed by, introductions were made and light conversations entered into. Jorge, who knew every person, gave Willan morsels of gossip about them when they were out of earshot. Only one person chose not to engage with Jorge, a fat, dark-haired, slobbery man of about forty years whose fine clothes ill-suited him; he pointedly looked away as he passed by. Jorge said nothing and Willan, ever curious, asked who the rude silent man was.

"I will not even do him the courtesy of speaking his name; he is a cruel man who mistreats his workers and swindles all with whom he deals. I am surprised he is here, but they do say that great wealth can open any door. He is not worthy of another second of our thoughts or words," said Jorge.

"They also say great wealth cannot buy gentility or style," replied Willan.

The next person to arrive was Torres, who fell, immediately, into deep conversation with Jorge. Unusually, they were speaking in Portuguese, which they would never normally do in the presence of Willan, who considered they must be talking of the un-named swindler. Reverting to English, Torres said that a small recital was about to begin which Bennett and Ashby were keen to hear; he, however, was intent on making re-acquaintance with some old friends. After he left, Jorge explained to Willan that Torres was not keen on music other than to dance to, and the 'old friends' were, in fact, potential business contacts. Jorge suggested that with music at one end of the building and business talk at the other, it might be a suitable time to take a tour of the gardens. Willan agreed.

The gardens were glorious; the initial view of lawns and trees gave the impression of an English garden, but closer inspection showed that the trees, many of which were in flower, were different to any Willan had ever seen before; he was in a wonderland of varied colours, scents and shapes. The lawn was not of grass but of a coarser plant with noticeable leaves; it was sponge-like underfoot. Although the central part of the garden was bathed in sunlight, areas to the right and left were denser with trees and shrubs and offered tranquil shade. Willan would have liked to sit and rest for a while away from the direct sun, but strangely no seats were to be found beyond the veranda to the building.

Some distance from the house, where the flat terrain ended, was a wall. Leaning on the stones, they looked down upon a few terraces of vegetables beyond which a rocky, steep wasteland separated the

Quinta from the edge of the city. Down to the right was a large brown-stone fortress perched against the hillside with the Union Flag fluttering above; a few redcoats could be seen on and about the walls. Jorge explained that Madeirans called it 'Pico Fortaleza', or 'Peak Fort' in English. Originally it was the Fort of Saint Joao but is now, officially, the Fort of Saint Filipe. He did not know why one saint had relinquished the fort to another. Neither Willan nor Jorge mentioned the presence of British soldiers at the fort or on the island.

On re-entering the main door of the house and climbing the staircase, violins could be heard from the left, so they headed to the right, Willan seeking sanctuary for his ears, Jorge refreshment for his thirst. The furthest room, with its comfortable leather armchairs and dark-wood atmosphere, was ideal and they were soon settled comfortably by the window. The only other occupants of the room were two elderly businessmen, who, after exchanging greetings with Jorge in Portuguese, returned to their earnest conversation. The young girl who had served them earlier arrived soon afterwards with two large glasses of rich red wine and a plate of small pastries.

"I took the liberty of requesting these earlier," said Jorge. "I hope they are to your liking. The pastries are of meat and vegetables and quite delicious. Some people consider them to be peasant food and not suited for a gentleman's table. I am keen to hear your verdict."

Willan adopted a serious attitude as he nibbled at the outer crust of the small, still-warm pastry, before swallowing the remainder in one overlarge mouthful. Wiping the crumbs from his lips with his fingers, he declared to Jorge that the pastry was 'adequate to sustain the un-refined hunger of the lower types but would be best reserved for distinguished palates such as his own'. The plate was soon cleared, the final pastry shared.

"We are soon to have Gourlay of Kincraig at our service," said Jorge. "I can hear his gentle voice above the soothing strings of the musicians." Gourlay burst into the room and joined Jorge and Willan. He was carrying a large glass of wine and although the crumbs down the front of his waistcoat showed he had managed a small bite, his eyes still focussed on the empty plate on the table. Jorge departed with his glass, 'to water the garden'.

The conversation, after polite greetings had been exchanged, turned to Willan's health. He disclosed that despite increasing his dosage of laudanum, his bowels were still a little loose and his cough persistent. Gourlay said they had stalled the advance of the condition but probably needed stronger measures to defeat the enemy; he suggested that he visit on Monday and they could discuss the options. Willan agreed with the proposal and Gourlay said he would probably arrive late morning.

A man came into the room carrying a large tray of bottles, accompanied by the young serving girl with a tray of glasses. They stationed themselves at a table to one side of the room and Gourlay walked over to receive the first glass. The room began to fill and the doctors were soon joined by Bennett and Ashby, the music which they had greatly enjoyed having finished. Among the drinkers in the room was the unnamed swindler, whose complexion was now flushed red and coordinated with his half-unbuttoned shiny waistcoat. He was accompanied by a man of about thirty years, whose distinguished good looks, striking red hair and powerful disposition contrasted with the sloven alongside him.

"I see that we have Quakers amongst us," spluttered the unnamed man loudly, staring at Willan's table. "What is all this quakery? Is the King's faith not good enough? Are we to shake in their presence?" His already reddened eyes stared ahead, as he grinned; his companion raised his arm only slightly but enough to stop the man moving forward.

Willan, who had been asked similar questions on countless occasions, rose from his seat and replied. His words were well rehearsed and delivered in a quiet, authoritative tone; he commanded respect and did not need to raise his voice to gain attention.

"I am a Quaker. The true title of our religion is the 'Society of Friends'. I am proud, as was my father and his father before him, to be called by either title. Jesus said, 'You are my friend if you do what I command you.' God is my friend and I am his. Our relationship with God is a personal one and we do not need the intercession or guidance of priests in their steeple-houses to live in a worthy manner; why should a poor man pay his pennies to bloat the stomach of the clergyman and gild the walls of his temple? Every man is equal in God's eyes and in mine, be they the King of England, the Archbishop in Canterbury, the Pope in Rome, the peasant in his cottage, the prisoner in his cell or any man in this room, no matter their beliefs or behaviour; we all contain God's goodness and are worthy of respect."

The red-haired man smiled at the words as Willan continued; the sloven maintained a surly silence.

"We alone are responsible for our conduct whilst on earth but God will lead us; conscience will judge our morality. We must serve God and our fellow man by truth, honesty and example. As to why we are called Quakers, I am aware of two accounts. One says that our founder, George Fox, at one of his appearances in court for the crime of his faith, told the magistrate to quake at the name of God. The other account suggests we physically shake at our religious experiences. I have never witnessed such trembling so am inclined to believe the first account."

Looking directly at the unnamed man, Willan added, "I hope that any curiosity is satisfied and that God can lead us all in his light and love."

Willan sat down as his questioner left the room. The silence was broken by the red-haired man, who spoke, for all to hear, as he crossed towards him.

"Well said. Well said indeed. It is a shame we do not all share the same moral conviction and honesty. I am humbled by your words and salute your character."

Standing before Willan, he continued, "I am Henry Veitch and honoured to make your acquaintance."

Introductions were made all around, although Gourlay and Veitch had long been known to each other, and the conversation flowed effortlessly. The atmosphere throughout the room was one of mutual enjoyment; humour was abundant yet not to the exclusion of well-mannered behaviour.

Veitch said he had one last question for Willan.

"How do you manage truly to find God's goodness in everybody, notwithstanding any immoral action or ill deed?"

"We must search deep within ourselves, as well as into the hearts of others," replied Willan without any trace of swagger or piety.

"I shall remember your words, always. I must leave now but sincerely hope we shall meet again soon." Veitch bowed directly to Willan before leaving the room.

Gourlay said that Veitch, the British Consul, was a fine, honest man, an asset to Madeira and certain to succeed in any way of life. He also added the caveat that he was best kept at a good distance from one's wives, daughters and maidservants lest the island be overflowing with redheads.

The afternoon concluded as Torres assembled the Quinta do Til party at the main door, where they expressed their gratitude to William Penfold for a splendid time and bade a fond farewell. Torres also extended an invitation to their host to dine at the Quinta do Til, to which he replied that he would be pleased to be a guest at Dona Esmeralda's table and they must arrange a convenient date.

Torres, now astride his stallion, gave his usual flamboyant military-style signal to move off and the group headed home in good spirits; it had been a fine and interesting afternoon enjoyed by all, each in their own way. Willan dozzled for part of the journey despite Jorge's constant chatter with the hammock-bearers, all of whom were redder-faced and more loquacious than on the outward journey.

The party were met at the Quinta do Til by Dona Esmeralda, who said she would serve a reviving cup of tea in the dining room; any hope of a further glass of wine at this time was clearly not subject to discussion. The cups emptied, Ashby and Torres headed back to Bachelor's Hall; Bennett and Willan went to their rooms to wash before dinner. Jorge had not joined them for tea.

Willan prepared for dinner, which, thankfully, was imminent; any wait would surely induce sleep. Fortified by a further spoonful of laudanum, he joined Bennett in the dining room. Dinner was taken quickly with a minimum of conversation but enough to be polite, before both men headed back to their rooms and the contented slumber that awaited.

31

Doctor Robert Willan was worried. Worried like a wayward child awaiting discovery and punishment. Worried as an adult whose un-improved health left his future uncertain.

He had spent all of the previous day assessing and analysing his personal medical records; his ill health had initially improved, then remained stable, but was now waning, although not to the wretchedness of his condition four months previously. His records, neatly arranged, covered the table in anticipation of Gourlay's arrival. Willan was sitting on the veranda with the telescope, although today not even the presence of new ships in the bay could distract him. Gourlay's book suggested digitalis as a treatment. Was this the answer?

On hearing a booming voice at the entrance, Willan removed himself and the telescope back into the room, and moments later opened his door to greet the swirl of coat, bag and riding crop that was Gourlay. Greetings and memories of Saturday's pleasant afternoon were exchanged before they turned to the pressing topic of Willan's condition and Gourlay's prognosis.

The records were scrutinised in detail by both men and Willan outlined the thought that his health might now be on a backward path. When pressed by Gourlay for his present symptoms he declared that his outpourings remained loose, his cough troublesome, there was occasionally blood in his phlegm and a general fatigue was wearing into his bones; he confirmed that he was not specifically suffering from excessive or regular shortness of breath or pains in the chest. Gourlay repeated his opinion of Saturday: they had improved and stalled the condition but not cured it; stronger treatments were necessary. He added that he considered 'the patient is doing extremely well,' and he was confident of an early and complete recovery.

Gourlay recommended digitalis, as Willan had anticipated, and said he had long been a disciple of Doctor William Withering, the initial proponent of the effectiveness of purple foxglove in the treatment of many diseases and complaints. Willan was aware of Withering and his work but, as a skin disease specialist, had never had occasion to learn about or prescribe this medicine. Gourlay outlined his own successes with digitalis and suggested that a tincture would be the most suitable way to administer the drug; tablets and pills were available but were either large and difficult to swallow or, in the case of the gilded pills, likely to leave one's system exactly as they had entered; infusions would not provide a consistent dose. He suggested taking one spoonful twice a day and this could be taken alongside the laudanum as there were no known contraindications between the two medicines; a noticeable improvement should occur within the week and he would call again next Monday to check up upon progress. Willan was pleased with the prognosis and asked if Gourlay had the tincture with him. He replied that he was meeting up with Ashby that afternoon at his consulting room, would prepare the medicine himself and forward it to Willan via the ever-amenable Ashby, together with a note of his recommended dosage and a small measuring spoon.

Before leaving for soup, Willan asked Gourlay if he were aware of the well-known witticism about William Withering's final illness and death, to which Gourlay replied in the negative.

"That being so, I shall relate the short tale if you have no objection," said Willan.

"Please proceed," replied Gourlay.

"As I am sure that you are aware," started Willan, "Withering, apart from being a fine physician, was known for his knowledge of all plants. As well as his famed *Account of the foxglove and its uses*, he also wrote *Botanical arrangements of all the vegetables naturally grown in Great Britain*. He was an authority on trees, plants, flowers, herbs and vegetables, as much a botanist as a physician. As he lay on his death-bed, a wit, I do not know whom, stated, 'The flower of physic is withering'. Bad form, perhaps, to speak humorously of the dying but, nevertheless, a clever play on words, do you not think?"

Gourlay agreed politely and said Willan's amusing story was the perfect appetiser to the soup they would enjoy shortly.

Willan journeyed to the til tree before joining Gourlay in the dining room; they had discussed the need to maintain the temperature records and agreed, especially as the weather was now warming, that it would be prudent to continue; the thermometer read sixty-nine degrees. Bennett arrived for soup and chatted with Willan, each of them occasionally glancing at the top of Gourlay's head as it hovered, lips apart, only inches above his bowl, receiving spoonful after spoonful of soup as if delivered by the sails of a windmill. The metal spoon chinked increasingly against the earthenware as the depth of soup lowered, before a final clang left the spoon adrift in an empty bowl.

The smiling head surfaced. "You can forget ambrosia and nectar; Dona Esmeralda's soup is the true food of the gods," said Gourlay.

After Gourlay had swiftly attacked and dispatched two round fruit cakes, he rose from the table, said he was a tad behind schedule and headed for the main door, juggling his belongings as he went; a shouted farewell came from the hallway. Bennett, whom Willan had thought to be a little tired or out of sorts, confirmed as much and said he was intending to rest for the afternoon but fully expected to be 'on parade' before dinner, along with his brother. Willan remained sitting at the table thinking about how best to occupy his afternoon.

His pondering continued as he moved from the table to a comfortable armchair by the fireside. He re-considered his meeting with Gourlay and remained satisfied with the outcome. There was a logic to all that had been recommended to him and Gourlay was, without doubt, the expert in the treatment of phthisis and consuming illness; he was in safe hands. After thanking God for his providence, he left the dining room with his shoulders un-slouching as their load lightened; there was almost a spring to his step. He had not given any thought as to how to occupy his afternoon but found himself marching towards the vegetable terraces in the same fashion as a twig being swept down a fast-flowing stream; his choice of route had been selected for him.

Passing through the hedge he realised he was tiring and reduced his pace; he admonished himself for behaving as if he were twenty years younger and vowed to adopt a more mature and sensible manner. He sat at the table nearby the bananas until the warm, earth-scented air restored his panting lungs and then continued his now more sedate walk to the vegetable terraces.

Willan had not been sitting for long when Senhor Pompion hurried to join him at the table. They shook hands briefly before Senhor Pompion left, having indicated that Willan should remain. He seemed anxious and rushed, which worried Willan; he had never seen his friend like this before and feared that something might be amiss.

His fear was allayed as Senhor Pompion returned at an unhurried pace and with the broadest of smiles. He was clutching proudly a piece of almost-white paper about ten inches square, which he handed to Willan. Turning it over revealed a child's painting, obviously of the two men who were now both staring at it, each with the happiest of faces. To the right of the picture was a round yellow sun above a green tree, to the left two men standing either side of a table. One man was differing shades of brown, the other black and white with a bright blue middle; their straight arms and legs splayed outwards without bend or angle. The round heads were large, as were the eyes, noses, and smiles. Underneath was written in an adult hand, 'avô e amigo'; Willan presumed the artist to be a grandchild of Senhor Pompion and probably one of the two children whom he had witnessed playing games with Bennett. The men pointed at each other, themselves and the picture, Senhor Pompion laughing and Willan with happiness pouring from his eyes. The picture passed back and forward between the two men until Willan realised it was intended as a gift for him; he bowed his gratitude.

The men sat together enjoying their surroundings, as was usual, but Willan felt an increased affinity between them; was it the lack of words that deepened their relationship? He did not know the answer but realised the reason was unimportant; their friendship, however arrived at, was all that mattered. He was at peace with his existence and thought it likely that Senhor Pompion was similarly content.

Willan was the first to leave; he had noticed Senhor Pompion's occasional glances towards two men who were working some distance away and did not wish to detain unduly his friend from his responsibilities. They smiled, embraced and Willan again demonstrated his thanks for the picture.

Back at the Quinta, Willan went straight to the kitchen door and knocked. He needed a translation of the inscription on the painting and hoped Dona Esmeralda was not alone. After a short delay, Jorge opened the door and Willan explained his request.

"You have in your hand," said Jorge, "a fine portrait of yourself and Senhor Pompion, executed by his grandson Afonso, who is now over five years old. He loves to paint and I am also the proud owner of a likeness, although I confess that the rounded stomach and hair to my waist are not quite as I imagined I looked. The paper and brushes are supplied by Sir Roderick, and Dona Esmeralda provides the paints and dyes which she makes from plants and herbs. The words are written by Amalia, Afonso's mother, who is Senhor Pompion's only daughter, and read 'grandfather and friend'. I think Afonso possesses a great talent and has cleverly captured your true character. I can arrange for the work of art to be suitably framed if you wish."

Willan thanked Jorge for his help but declined the offer of framing, stating that only gold could do his appearance justice, and he would seek out the 'frame-maker to the Royal Court' when he returned to London.

Next came the problem of where to site the picture in his room. Willan wandered aimlessly carrying the paper, unable to find a suitable location; laid flat he could not see the picture, propped up the paper curled and he could hardly nail it to the wall. Eventually he put the picture face down on the table; he would re-consider the problem later. Before leaving for the colonnade, hopefully to meet Bennett, Willan took his dose of laudanum, which reminded him that Ashby was to deliver his digitalis; he had much to look forward to.

Bennett was sitting at the table, book in hand, and Willan thought he looked less tired than at soup time; his eyes were definitely brighter. They talked easily about a variety of subjects and Bennett said that when he was very rich and famous, he hoped to be able to commission his portrait, a sure sign that a person had succeeded in life. As Ashby approached carrying his medical bag, Bennett, clearly in good spirits, declared loudly, "Doctor Ashby Smith at our service."

Before sitting down, Ashby placed his bag on the table, opened it and produced a small brown bottle and a tiny measuring spoon made of bone, which he handed to Willan, along with a small envelope. Willan said he would take the items to his room and at Bennett's insistence agreed to bring back his portrait for all to see.

Back in his room he ripped open the envelope, read that the dosage was one measure twice a day and quickly swallowed his first tiny spoonful; it was not as bitter as he had feared. As he returned with the picture, Duarte arrived with the decanter and glasses. Everybody commented on the good likeness and Willan added to the merriment by adopting a straight-limbed pose, as in the picture. The good-natured happiness continued throughout dinner.

Being in the dining room had given Willan the solution to his problem of how best to site his picture. As soon as he was back in his room, he moved his clock from the centre to the left side of the mantle. He then placed a row of books spine outwards along the remainder of the mantle as in the dining room or any library, but with a gap, slightly narrower than the picture, at the centre. The picture fitted in and was held at both sides by the books; Willan and Senhor Pompion looked out with their round smiley faces, supported by the great works of medical science.

32

By Thursday morning Willan had taken six doses of digitalis. He had hoped to have noticed some improvement or at least a change of some description but physically he remained as he was – only his mood had altered. He was a little jittery and becoming impatient, which he attributed to his lack of progress; his constant self-reminders that it was too early to be anxious at the lack of change did little to ease his frustration. Fortunately, he had found that if his nerves were especially on edge he could reduce the restlessness by taking additional doses of laudanum, which also eased his still troublesome cough; he did not think it necessary to note these occasional extra measures in his medical records.

Taking a break from the reorganisation of some of his research papers, Willan took the telescope to the veranda and began a survey of the bay and its surroundings. There were fewer ships than of late so he turned his attention to the terraces and hillsides. He was always drawn to watching the labour of men on the terraces yet felt guilty at doing so. Today was different as by chance he focussed on a group of three men who were leaning against a wall, apparently having a relaxed conversation. Willan assumed they were taking a hard-earned break from their toil and continued to watch their infrequent movements and gestures; strangely he did not consider it wrong to view people not at their work. However, as one of the men parted his clothes and began to take a piss, he removed his eye from the lens and aborted that day's scrutiny of the world beyond the Quinta do Til.

It was too early to take the temperature reading but too short a time until soup to justify resuming his paperwork. Not wishing to return to the veranda but keen to breathe some more fresh air, he headed to the colonnade, from where, despite the closeness, the view was different. Dona Esmeralda was sitting at the table nursing a cup of tea and rose to leave as Willan approached. He gestured for her to remain and politely declined what he assumed to be her offer to bring a cup for him. As they contentedly admired the view, Willan smiled within at how circumstance meant that he now enjoyed some of his finest times sitting alongside a person with whom he could not communicate with words; it was a relaxed feeling for which he was humbly grateful and overjoyed to experience. Even after Dona Esmeralda had returned to the kitchen, Willan could still sense the serenity of her smile and feel the warmth of her character.

Willan continued to float in dreamland and, to the observer, appeared to be admiring the view. In reality he was looking inwards and feeling a calm, pleasurable sense of well-being; his outward-staring eyes belied the truth.

"A penny for your thoughts," said Bennett, which shocked Willan back to the reality of his situation.

"Please excuse me," he replied. "I was enjoying the air and the view, and may have briefly closed my eyes to the surroundings. You have my full attention now."

Bennett thought it better not to mention Willan's trance-like gaze and the talk turned to mundane but polite enquiries as to health and the success or otherwise of their day thus far. Willan gave an attenuated version of his introspective feelings after sitting with Dona Esmeralda, but it was still enough to cause Bennett to comment, "Am I to believe that the clear logical mind of an eminent scientist and physician such as yourself has become blurred by emotion and sentiment?"

Before going indoors for their soup, they visited the til tree, where Willan saw that the temperature was seventy-two degrees as he had predicted. Several lizards held their attention with their darting and positioning as Willan expanded his theory of reptilian movement reflecting age; Bennett pointed out that humans also slow down with the passing of time. They emptied their soup bowls and the gentle good humour continued with Willan leaving the room, his head raised and chin thrust forward, saying that an elderly lizard was retreating to his lair for a rest.

Feeling more tired than usual, Willan decided to rest for a while on his bed and was soundly asleep within 'the blink of a lizard's eye'. He woke an hour later restored and energetic, had a drink of water to untighten his dry mouth and departed his room in the direction of Senhor Pompion and the vegetable terraces. Despite the restorative sleep, by the time Willan was sitting at the second table he was breathing heavily and weak at the knees. He quickly recovered and decided to ensure his return journey was not as rushed as this one must have been.

Composure restored, Willan digested his surroundings; he never tired of the view or the sweet balminess of the earth-fragrant air which cocooned him. He was safe, secure, free from concern and, if in better health, would like nothing more than to lift tools, work on the soil and harvest the fruits and vegetables of his labours. Willan laughed as he realised the over-ambition of this hankering; perhaps he should start with a few herbs in the small courtyard and stable to the rear of his house in Bloomsbury Square.

His smile broadened as he realised his friend was walking towards the table. They shook hands and assumed their usual positions. Willan was the first to attempt a communicative gesture and, after much laughter and confusion, achieved his aim; Willan and Senhor Pompion re-enacted Afonso's picture with rigid postures and the table between them. It was an unfeigned and simple pleasure. Neither man was aware that their actions were being watched by a bemused but smiling Senhora Pompion from just inside the doorway of the second cottage.

The happy encounter ended when Senhor Pompion gently laid his hand on Willan's lower arm to arouse him from his reverie and pointed to an almost-black cloud slightly beyond the hill-top. Willan realised his friend's warning and, after their now-usual embrace, set off on his return to the house. The urgency and uphill gradient combined against Willan and by the time he reached the sanctuary of the enclosed colonnade his chest was thumping and his head reeling. He leant against the balustrade to restore his breathing and then fell into a chair and closed his eyes until the spinning sensation ceased.

"Another penny for another thought," said Bennett.

"Please excuse me again; I can assure you that I do have some periods of consciousness when not in your company. I was merely collecting my thoughts together having raced that cloud from Senhor Pompion's cottage to here with all the speed of a young lizard," said Willan, pointing upwards at a now blue and white innocuous sky.

Bennett, with a wry grin, responded that he was intending a short amble through the grounds himself but that his slow rate of progress would be a hindrance to a lizard-legged athlete such as Willan. He suggested that they re-convene at the table in thirty minutes for a well-deserved pre-dinner glass of 'remedial medicine'. Willan agreed.

He used the half hour to wash quickly and prepare himself, take doses of both tinctures and sit quietly at the table to finally ease his racing heart and return his breathing to gentle normality. He also awarded himself an extra spoonful of laudanum in light of his exertions.

Jorge was with Bennett at the table as Willan returned, so he waved a greeting and sat on a chair which he moved away from the table, enabling the others to continue their strained Portuguese conversation. The confusion of words provided an interesting, if slightly off-key, operatic background to his view of the nautical scene below; the combination of sight and sound under the lowering sun was almost soothing.

Duarte arrived with the decanter and two glasses, and Willan was very pleased as Bennett insisted that he return with two more, and that he and Jorge join them for a pre-Easter toast. Drinks were poured and Bennett proposed they remember all their friends and family, and the sacrifices made by others for all their existences; the glasses were raised and the sentiment repeated. Talk and drink flowed in a free but not disrespectful manner, and centred mainly on Easter-tide traditions. Willan said Quakers did not specifically celebrate Easter, preferring to recall Christ's sacrifice throughout the year, but were completely at ease with the ceremonies and rituals of others. Madeiran celebrations, according to Duarte, centred mainly around the family and food; there was always a cake for every occasion but more so at Easter.

33

Willan was in his room recalling the previous day. Although he had stated quite truthfully that Quakers do not specifically celebrate Easter, he had not explained fully his own feeling that there was a unique poignancy to the day the Christian churches called 'Holy Friday'. It was the most sombre of times and he found it difficult to do anything other than reflect on Christ carrying a cross to his own crucifixion and death. Additionally, and for no logical reason, he was unable to maintain his ongoing daily relationship with God over the final three days of Christ's Passion; he held the curious belief that God was far too occupied with his own works, and it was his obligation to leave his God undisturbed.

His toilet was complete, breakfast eaten, medicines swallowed and the room neat and organised; he was listless and without purpose. It was not a day suited to merriment or self-indulgence but still needed a suitable employment. As he did not think it fitting to leave his room before soup time and chance that he might be a disturbance to others, he took the telescope quietly to the veranda; this might not enhance the welfare of others, but nor would it be of any detriment to his fellow man. He vowed to achieve a day of quiet solitude.

Although perched high above the city and harbour, he could sense a tranquil, muted hush to the day; even the breeze he could see in the trees made no sound. The sun was high yet offered no direct brightness. Was God muting his world as a sign of sorrow and loss?

With his eye to the lens, Willan began a sweep of the ships and other craft in the bay. There was movement but certainly far less animation than usual; he considered that only the most vital or urgent of tasks were being fulfilled. The terraces and hillsides were devoid of any person or activity. Only then did he perceive that there was a noticeable sound: birdsong. A survey of the skies showed sea birds soaring open-beaked, and the bushes were staging posts for the smaller birds' constant chirrupy flights. Willan smiled as he realised that birds and animals were all God's creatures but had no reason to be subdued; they had no sins to confess and needed no forgiveness. He felt uplifted and almost envious of the pure simplicity of life on the wing.

Willan passed the time until soup by needlessly re-arranging his stationery and straightening the edges of files and papers; he hoped to continue his cross-referencing of herpes clusters the following day. Finally, as the hands on his watched mantle clock neared noon, he decided to leave the room and strolled slowly to the til tree to note the temperature was seventy-two degrees, the same as yesterday. He ambled back to the colonnade with his deliberate attempt to appear casual, resulting in a jerked motion more reminiscent of a trot than a walk.

As he sat at the table, he was reminded that, since Duarte had executed his shave and delivered his breakfast, he had not seen any person or heard any sound other than birdsong. This realisation caused him to feel isolated and, to a certain extent, lonely. He tried to disguise this sentiment from the world by looking towards Funchal in a pensive manner with his chin resting on his closed hand. The resultant look, however, was more one of deep discomfort than deep thought.

He was rescued from his unease by the arrival of Bennett who, after general greetings had been exchanged, explained they would shortly be joined by his brother who would be taking his meals with them between now and Sunday. Ashby duly arrived and explained to Willan that Torres had returned to his family home for the Easter weekend and, following other departures, that left only himself and a curmudgeonly, ill-mannered Spanish nobleman of low rank residing at Bachelor's Hall; he had therefore arranged to dine with his brother and hoped he would not be an inconvenience. Willan replied that it was no inconvenience whatsoever, he was always pleased to see him, and that as he was intending to cross-reference vesicular herpes clusters tomorrow, might he be available to assist? Ashby readily agreed and a medical conversation ensued until Bennett intervened, saying that if the unpleasant talk did not cease, he would be unable to swallow his soup.

As if on cue, Duarte arrived and proclaimed that, "Today's soup is ready. It is of fishes and is by Dona Esmeralda for 'Holy Friday'. It is good and you will enjoy. There is also bread with a cross." The soup was indeed delicious and was accompanied by small, salty rounds of bread, each as described by Duarte.

After the meal was over, the men discussed their plans for the afternoon. Ashby was undertaking a long walk in the hills and Bennett intended to rest and finish reading a book on English history. Willan admitted he was not yet decided upon his actions, but he would, in all probability, enjoy a short rest before taking a 'tour of the estate'. They all agreed to meet again on the colonnade before dinner.

Willan decided to repeat his actions of the previous afternoon so, having had an hour's rest, he set off towards Senhor Pompion's cottages. Despite walking slowly, he was still tired by the time he reached the first table which, combined with his thought that if he continued, he might intrude upon a Pompion family occasion, caused him to proceed no further and return to the house. Again tired, and now a little dull in spirit, he settled on the veranda not three hours since his previous visit. Bored with the lack of activity to be seen through the telescope, he dozelled until it was time to take his medicines and return to the colonnade.

Dinner of 'Easter fish' was pleasant and the conversation polite.

34

Saturday had passed quickly for Willan in a complete contrast to the day before. He had worked well with Ashby in the morning, enjoyed his soup, had a rest and now it was nearly time for dinner. They all agreed it seemed strange to be on the colonnade sipping a glass of Madeira wine with the sun still high in the sky; it seemed disreputable in a daring sort of way. Duarte repeatedly apologised for the change of routine and 'troublesomeness', eventually forcing Bennett to joke that if he stopped apologising, he and Dona Esmeralda would be able to depart to their families all the sooner.

It was not long until they were back on the colonnade; the tender lamb followed by sweet cakes had been delightful and they had felt only slightly pressured into eating at an unseemly rate. Jorge arrived at the table, told them everything was going well and he would be back soon; with that he returned inside. The men remained at the table, in silence other than for the occasional idle remark, all of them unsure as to what the rest of the evening held in store.

Some twenty minutes later Jorge re-appeared with a different decanter to the usual one and four glasses. He asked if he could join the party and explained that he thought a glass of good port might 'smooth the throat'. He added, with a smile, that as he was now in sole charge of the entire estate he could pretty much do as he pleased. A fourth chair was pulled up to the table and the drinks poured. Bennett, assuming the role of an underling, picked up the tray and asked Jorge if he might be of service in any way. Jorge replied that Bennett should stand nearby the door and if he was required, he would clap his hands. The table talk was relaxed, interesting and entertaining, and their position on the colonnade and the hour of the day were soon synchronised back to the usual routine.

Willan, although enjoying the evening, began to feel unwell; his face was burning and his cough rasping, causing him to clutch his handkerchief to his mouth. At a pause in the coughing and with his eyes watering he stood up, apologised to the others that he must leave them so soon and headed towards the house. Ashby immediately joined him, took hold of his elbow, collected a chamber stick, opened the doors and guided him back to his room. Only when Willan was sitting on his bed did Ashby speak to enquire of the difficulty and offer his assistance. Willan looked upwards, the redness of his face and eyes matching the bloodspots on his handkerchief, thanked his friend and replied that he could manage quite well and was sure to be recovered by the morning.

With Ashby gone, Willan travelled slowly to his dressing room and with his head over his wash bowl coughed and coughed without restraint, producing a mixture of phlegm, vomit and blood. Only when the last drop of liquid had fallen from his mouth did he raise his head and begin to breathe normally. He remained quite still for some minutes as the heat of his face lessened and he was satisfied that he could walk unaided; he then resumed his seat on the bed. Finally confident that his coughing was finished, Willan returned to the dressing room and emptied and sluiced his wash bowl into the chamber pot. He then undressed, leaving the blood-stained handkerchief, shirt and waistcoat folded neatly on the floor, and vigorously washed his face and neck before climbing into his bed. The deep sleep that followed meant he was unaware of Jorge tiptoeing into the room to blow out the chamber stick and looking in again perhaps an hour later.

35

Willan woke and raised his head. The windows were open, the sun bright and he felt the warm breeze across his face. Some seconds later he saw Jorge busying himself near the table.

"Good morning, Doctor Willan. The long sleep will have done you a great benefit. I tried to waken you as gently as possible. How do you feel this morning? Better, I hope."

Jorge then sat on the chair next to the bed and handed Willan a glass of water, from which he sipped before replying that he was still tired and thanked Jorge for attending to him.

"If I might be so bold as to advise you on your actions," said Jorge, "I suggest that you attend to your toilet whilst I collect the breakfast; there is fresh water and clean clothing. After you have eaten a little, I will scrape the hairs from your chin and we can consider the arrangements for guiding you gently through the day."

Willan, feeling stirrings, nodded his agreement and as soon as Jorge had departed got up and emptied his bowels into the pot. The slurry was not entirely liquid and there was no trace of blood. This cheered Willan. He was further gladdened by his realisation that his dressing room, including his pot, had been cleaned and tidied, fresh clothes laid out and his soiled garments removed; he felt humble and grateful in equal proportion.

Cleaned, dressed and medicated, Willan nibbled at the bread delivered to him and sipped some tea, Jorge having advised that he eat and drink only a little at the present time and that his noon-time soup would be soon enough to start 'building him up again'. His shave was performed efficiently and Willan began to resume some semblance of normality. Jorge suggested Willan go no further than the veranda that morning and that drinking water would help restore his fluid levels. Willan agreed with the proposal and thanked Jorge yet again for his assistance, even shaking his hand just as he departed the room.

Sitting at the table, thoughts raced through Willan's mind. What had caused last night's painful expectoration, and was this an isolated incident or a taste of things to come? Was there still hope he would defeat his illness and make a happy return to England or had a downward decline started? Without reason, his realisation that it was Easter Sunday, the commemorative day of Christ's resurrection, instilled a great optimism in his outlook; he felt quite well within himself and hiccups on the path to recovery were to be expected. Tomorrow Gourlay was intending a visit and God would be available for discussion; he had no cause for worry or fear. He celebrated the positive outcome of his thoughts with a morsel of bread and a sip of water, before stepping onto the veranda.

The day was quiet, not unlike 'Holy Friday', but there was a lighter brightness to the sun and a fresher feel to the breeze; it was a fine day. Foregoing his telescope, Willan sat at the table enjoying the view and basking in the sunshine; his unfortunate memories of the previous evening were diminishing in direct relation to the journey of the sun across the diorama-like scene below. Willan was looking forward; any unpleasantness of the past was fading behind him.

Jorge returned just before noon and informed Willan that the air temperature at the til tree was sixty-nine degrees and he had checked the reading twice. Willan subconsciously paused with his head slightly raised and reckoned the figure to be accurate. It was time for soup and Jorge led the way to the dining room. Bennett and Ashby both rose at Willan's arrival and asked after his health and welfare. He thanked them for their concern and said he felt both restored and hungry. He added that he was far too busy to be wasting his life away in his bed and picked up his spoon as he sat.

At the centre of the table was a large circular bread with white round protuberances. It resembled the eyes of creatures surfacing through a light brown sea. Jorge explained that it was 'folar de pascoa', a bread only served at Easter; the 'eyes' were eggs which had been boiled, and the bread symbolised re-birth. Bennett tore off a wedge complete with an egg, ate it, declared it to be excellent and said that Jorge must praise Dona Esmeralda on her return. Jorge replied that the bread had been freshly baked that morning by a close friend of his and that he would indeed pass on the compliments. The entire bread, and half of a second, were consumed along with the bowls of chicken and vegetable soup, which had been made by Dona Esmeralda. Bennett's suggestion that they were eating a 'mother and child' meal was met with laughter before he was jokingly chastised for his poor taste. Ashby left the table first, intending a long walk; Bennett and Willan returned to their rooms.

Willan, after a short tour of the veranda, removed his waistcoat, lay on his bed and was soon asleep. As he woke, he realised that he had barely moved an inch while he slept and was surprised that two hours had passed; indeed, he felt that were it not for his need to take a piss, he could easily sleep for two hours more. His bladder emptied, he resisted the urge to return to the bed and took himself and the telescope to the veranda, where he began a count of the ships and other craft in the bay. This simple pleasure focussed his attention, without impatience, until it was time for him to prepare for the evening.

Having cleaned and spruced himself, Willan considered his medicine. The digitalis prescribed of late had offered no indication whatsoever of improvement to his health; indeed, yesterday he had suffered an episode of decline. He would discontinue the digitalis and inform Gourlay of his decision tomorrow. By way of compensation, he swallowed a double dose of laudanum, a medicine of which he was confident.

He joined the others on the colonnade and enjoyed a medicinal glass of Madeira wine. The topics of conversation were varied but did not include any matter relating to health, illness or treatment – a polite and sensible way to proceed, thought Willan. Jorge declined their offer to join them, stating he was manfully employed performing miracles in the kitchen and it was not easy 'trying to make a silken repast out of a sow's rear'. Bennett responded that he would gladly assist, but it was well known that 'too many cooks in the kitchen spoil the trough'. Jorge left the colonnade shaking his head.

Dinner was ready shortly afterwards and turned out to be, contrary to Jorge's earlier words, a banquet of delights. The table was covered by meats, pastes, breads, vegetables, chutneys and pickles, sweets, puddings and many items not easily identifiable. Jorge joined the table and helped distribute the food in each and every direction. The meal had the air of a tea party served in a children's nursery and everybody declared it a great success.

36

Unlike yesterday, Willan was feeling impatient. He had slept well and prepared and medicated himself for the day without incident or difficulty but now awaited Gourlay's visit. He was well aware that, understandably, Gourlay would coincide his arrival with that of Dona Esmeralda's soup but he still had in the order of two hours to fill. Eventually he decided that a slight change of scene might suit so he strolled to the colonnade; as ever, his attempt to appear casual would have given any onlooker the opposite impression.

Sitting at the table he was heartened to hear voices, which he knew to be Duarte's and Dona Esmeralda's, coming from the kitchen; there was always security to be found in the familiar. He imagined a military-style inspection was taking place and hoped that Jorge passed muster; the tone of Dona Esmeralda's voice suggested he had indeed passed, but perhaps not with flying colours.

No more than a few minutes after his arrival on the colonnade, Willan was surprised to be joined by Dona Esmeralda and her tea tray, complete with a spare cup. She smiled as she poured the tea and sat alongside him; obviously the state of her kitchen was now satisfactory.

As they sat contentedly, Willan felt he was subject to more of Dona Esmeralda's attention than usual; was this scrutiny her appraisal of his condition? He did not have the answer but knew she maintained the truest of intentions in all she did; he was not alarmed at her interest in his health and well-being.

When Dona Esmeralda collected up her tea things and departed for the kitchen and, presumably, her soup cauldron, Willan beamed the healthiest smile he could summon up before following her at a polite distance along the colonnade towards the house, his gait once more displaying his now familiar ungainliness. He returned to his room hopeful that Gourlay's arrival was imminent but feeling less impatient than earlier. He did not have to wait for long.

"Gourlay of Kincraig at your service!" boomed the doctor as he knocked upon and opened Willan's door. "How are we today?" he enquired in what Willan thought to be a somewhat routine and patronising manner.

Willan replied that he was quite well today and pleased to see him.

They sat at the table and Willan spoke at length; he described all of his symptoms of the last week, his general health and his treatment regime. He missed out nothing, even including his increased laudanum dosage. Gourlay listened attentively and remarked that he had no questions, so complete was his fellow doctor's account.

Gourlay then spoke, carefully and at length. His greatest concern was the hemoptoe; expectorating blood was a sign that the phthisis still raged within the chest. The initial gentle regime and addition of digitalis had, thus far, stabilised but not conquered the disease; a different, stronger approach was needed. He was sure that Willan would have read in his book that he usually treated hemoptoe, quite successfully, with digitalis and blistering; in this case the prescription of digitalis had preceded the expectoration and it was, therefore, correct to cease that treatment, but the application of blisters might still be of benefit.

Willan responded that he had remembered the contents of the book and was generally in agreement with Gourlay but, as a physician specialising in cutaneous complaints, he could not condone deliberately harming the skin; the benefits, if any, were vague and under-researched.

Gourlay accepted the point and outlined his proposal. He advised that no new treatment be given for three days in order that any remaining digitalis could be naturally discharged from the body; laudanum should still be taken, as required. Then he recommended treatment with calomel, a mercurous medicine, and sought Willan's opinion. Willan responded that he had used a paste of calomel to destroy many a suppurating growth or furucle, but he had no experience of the benefits of internal absorption, which he believed to be the intention. Gourlay said calomel was an ancient medicine but was now being increasingly used and was readily available in tablet form; the local pharmacist stocked sweetened pills of varying weights. His suggested prescription would be a pill of about four grains in weight three times a day for the first four days and the dose to be doubled on the days thereafter. He explained that initially the treatment would stimulate and mildly cleanse the system before the increased dosage attacked the phthisis whilst the chest and lungs were purged and sedated.

The planned treatment was agreed and Gourlay said he would forward the calomel and a further supply of laudanum via Ashby tomorrow or Wednesday in order that pill-taking could commence on Thursday morning. He would return in a week's time to check upon progress and improvement, of which he was confident.

Obviously keen for his soup, Gourlay gathered his belongings and left for the dining room. Willan delayed his departure as he checked the room and mentioned to God that he would share his emotions after luncheon; he knew God to be patient and that he would understand the delay.

Arriving in the dining room, Willan was surprised that only Bennett was at the table and Gourlay's loud voice could be heard from the kitchen speaking in Portuguese. This confounded Willan, who had assumed, much as he had done with Jorge, that Gourlay only spoke a single language. Was his health the topic of the conversation? It was no disservice if it were; he held no secrets and was open to any dissection.

Bennett, who had been listening attentively to the now-completed exchange, confessed to Willan that he had not understood any word emanating from the kitchen and hoped the silence heralded the arrival of the soup. Some minutes later Duarte delivered two bowls and said that Gourlay had 'drunk in the kitchen' and was now headed to Funchal. Bennett said they would now be able to sip their soup in a gentlemanly manner without any slurped distraction or the constant vision of the scalp of a lowered pate. The soup was fresh-tasting and delicious.

Returned to his sanctum, Willan gave further thought to the treatment proposed for him. Calomel was a medicine he had used successfully and the plan had logic: strong measures and medicines to obtain a strong result. He was convinced.

Willan was now able to give God his full attention and related all the occurrences, successes and failures of the weekend, resisting the urge to enquire of God as to his. For the first time, however, he sought God's intercession rather than relying on his guidance alone; he asked for restored health in order to complete his work but added the caveat that as he placed his entire life and trust in God's hands, whatever the outcome of this request would be correct and just. He admitted the self-centredness of his entreaty, adding that he hoped all of his friends would be granted good health as well.

37

The problem of when to take his calomel had been resolved; Willan would swallow a pill before breakfast, luncheon and dinner. He would also take a spoonful of laudanum at the same time to maintain a simple routine and avoid any chance of medicinal omission. It was Thursday morning and Willan stood before his two medicine bottles, unsure as to which he should open first. After due consideration, he commenced his new treatment. First the tablet, washed down with half of the poured glass of water, then a spoonful of laudanum and finally the remainder of the water; he was pleased with his decisions and entered a mark against 'calomel' in his newly prepared register.

The day continued well. Duarte was prompt and efficient with his shave and breakfast, and Ashby soon arrived to help Willan transfer papers from folder to folder and heap to pile, as he had done for the previous two days; the assistance proved invaluable. The mantle of Ashby's medical training had passed to Gourlay and would resume next week, leaving Willan to take advantage of Ashby's free hours. Willan was feeling a sense of achievement in his organisation and uniformity, a vital element to worthy research and analysis. Much remained to be done but it was not an unattainable prospect. He happily swallowed his second calomel pill and spoonful of laudanum before collecting the temperature reading.

Following exactly the routine of Tuesday and Wednesday there were three for soup. Ashby then left for Funchal, Bennett returned to his room and his latest book, and Willan slept on his bed for an hour or so. No matter how much sleep he managed he remained almost permanently tired and often exhausted, but never without motivation; he would not surrender to fatigue or adopt lethargy; he enjoyed the exertion of his afternoon walks to the vegetable terraces.

Arriving at the first table nearby the banana plants, Willan felt no more tired than usual but definitely needed to pause his journey. Sitting to ease the tightness in his chest and relax his breathing, the surroundings applied their soothing comfort; he was soon restored. He took a moment to embrace the view and fragrance before resuming his travel.

He was delighted to see Senhor Pompion, who was standing outside his cottage drinking from a very large ceramic tankard. Willan presumed he was quenching his thirst following a hard day's work. Both men waved a greeting and were soon sitting alongside each other at the table, each absorbed in his own thoughts but grateful for the other's presence. For Willan it was always the finest of times; he was drinking God's elixir. As Senhor Pompion rose to leave, Willan felt pleasure and gratitude for their time together, outweighing the disappointment of his friend's departure.

Willan's return journey to the house was made possible by a steady pace with frequent pauses and the stimulus of the extra beat to his heart he always felt after any time in the company of Senhor Pompion. Also, a person cannot be or become a friend without effort, be it physical, emotional or both; his current strain was not an encumbrance.

Bennett was on the colonnade with his book as Willan arrived back at the house so he joined him and pulled up a chair.

"My word!" said Bennett. "Have you been partaking in athletic activity? You appear to be completely drained. Have you exceeded your capabilities?"

Willan, still a little short of breath, replied that he was feeling 'somewhat sapped' and he may have journeyed back from the terraces at an over-optimistic pace. Strangely, as he exchanged pleasantries, not quite tittle-tattle, with Bennett, Willan could feel the blood moving about under the skin of his forehead and cheeks. He was unsure if his features were now beetroot-red or ashen-grey and such was his flustered mind he felt compelled to ask Bennett, who smilingly replied that the jewel on Willan's shoulders was now more of a ruby than a pearl.

Washed and tidied for dinner and with his final dose of medicine on its gastrointestinal journey, Willan decided to sit awhile on the veranda; this would pass the time and prevent any likelihood of unwanted slumber. There was an interesting selection of ships to view and count so he returned for the telescope. However, his normally pleasurable survey was obstructed by an inability to concentrate methodically or to retain figures in his head, a feeling he had never before experienced; the frustration was not unlike a physical nausea. He returned to the room and restored his equilibrium by breathing regularly with his eyes closed, supported by both hands face down on the table. He vowed to himself that he must adopt a more sedentary way of life as his body adjusted to the new medication.

Returning to the colonnade, Willan enquired as to Bennett's health and apologised for not asking earlier. Bennett replied that he felt 'generally well' but always tired and he was relying on his strong will and motivation to see him returned to 'athletic vigour'. Willan said he was of a similar disposition but would settle for a more 'sluggish vigour'; they must, however, persevere with their resolution in order to realise their ambitions. It was not an easy task, but they should both be proud of their strength of mind.

As they sipped their wine the conversation lightened and, by the time they reached the dinner table, was more tittle-tattle than polite; it lifted their spirits and removed any traces of self-pity or bleakness. A fine meal of tuna and vegetables followed by a sweet custard added to their recovery and they both returned to their rooms with satisfied hearts and stomachs.

Walking back to his room, Willan began to feel a tickling hoarseness at the back of his mouth, accompanied by an urge to swallow, although his mouth was empty. He continued to swallow as he created more and more saliva and, by the time he reached his doorway, knew he was about to vomit. No sooner was his head above the pot than his oesophagus relaxed and the entire contents of his stomach cascaded out; he could smell and recognise the fish and vegetables. The evacuation, quick as it was, left Willan not feeling unwell, merely empty; he rinsed his mouth and carried on as usual. It was impossible that Dona Esmeralda's food could be anything other than the freshest available, so he attributed the sickness to his new medication; if anything, he was pleased that changes were taking place inside his body.

38

The lack of any thickness to his morning evacuation of slurry did not perturb Willan. As with the previous night's episode of sickness, it was obviously attributable to the new medication; changes were taking place. His immediate concern was hunger and he greeted Duarte enthusiastically as he arrived with the shaving equipment. He explained the reason for his unusually full pot and sought to re-assure Duarte, whose face showed concern, that a hearty breakfast would soon return him to his regular disposition. After his shave, Willan took his medicine and remained at the table awaiting his food. He was glad the calomel was affecting a change to his constitution and the laudanum was still calming his cough.

Duarte returned soon afterwards with the breakfast tray, surprisingly accompanied by Dona Esmeralda whose eyes never left Willan even when talking to Duarte. The tray held a bowl of porridge, some dry bread and a large pitcher of water.

"Dona Esmeralda informs that you must eat the hot oats first. The bread is for the morning piece by piece with water. Luncheon soup will be thick chicken with vegetables also. Then you will be of good health," said Duarte.

Only when Willan had eaten over half of the porridge did Dona Esmeralda turn her gaze from him and she did not leave the room until he had finished the bowl, although there was never any doubt that Willan would not do as she demanded. Despite his audience, Willan enjoyed every mouthful.

Willan remained listless for the entire morning, nibbling at bread, sipping water and roaming from the room to the veranda and from chair to chair; he made no attempt at desk-work. Eventually his clock signalled that it was near enough to noon for him to commence his soup-time routine. He washed down his pill, slurped his laudanum and playfully tossed the last piece of bread into the air. His casual open-mouthed attempt to catch the falling bread led to an undignified crawl under the table to retrieve the morsel and sweep up the crumbs with his hand.

The thermometer read seventy-four degrees, which surprised Willan as he had thought it a little cooler; nevertheless, he accepted the figure. He relaxed alone on the colonnade for a short while until a chirpy Bennett arrived; he was in good spirits for no particular reason, but stated that he had dismissed melancholia and self-pity from his mind as they could only be a hindrance to his recovery and future. His happy attitude cheered Willan and they enjoyed a gratifying bowl of soup together in an entirely convivial manner.

Duarte's words that he would be 'of good health' after his soup seemed accurate to Willan's mind as he lay resting on his bed. His quiet and un-grumbling stomach was full but not overly so and he felt settled; he was soon asleep. He awoke after his usual hour of slumber eager to visit the grounds and, hopefully, Senhor Pompion; he was soon heading towards the vegetable terraces.

Despite deliberately walking at a slow pace, Willan was already tired by the time he reached the passage through the hedge, but his eager determination carried him to the first table. As he sat attempting to regularise his breathing and with his chest tight and painful, he realised he had reached the end of the day's journey; even if he could struggle to the table nearby the cottages, the return journey would not be possible. As the pain in his chest lessened, so did his disappointment; he was, after all, at the early stage of a rigorous new medication regime and it would not be long until he was hopping and bouncing through the terraces, as before.

Willan was enjoying the scene, despite the absence of his friend, and allowed his mind to drift from place to place, and the past, present and future; he became unaware of his surroundings and lost in his thoughts; his world had softened at the edges. He roused himself with a shake of the head and by closing and re-opening his eyes, took in a last view of his situation and departed the table. An even slower pace than earlier, accompanied by rhythmical breathing and a mind focussed on counting his steps, soon had Willan returned to the colonnade, breathless but content; he was proud of his small victory over languor.

Satisfied he was recovered from his journey, Willan returned to his room and, feeling a tightness in his throat, drank a glass of water. This only served to add to his unease and he was obliged to lean over his pot and self-induce enough retching to bring up the yellow phlegm that was the cause of the discomfort. He immediately felt improved and this, combined with the absence of blood from the phlegm, gave him the reassurance that his treatment was beginning to have a real effect. Greatly cheered, he took his evening medication and sat happily on the veranda enjoying the late afternoon sunshine.

Meeting on the colonnade before dinner, Willan was heartened when Bennett told him that he had a 'healthier look about him' than yesterday and replied that, at present, both of their prospects seemed favourable. This pleasant exchange set the tone for the continuing conversation and the comforting stew of meat and vegetables that followed; the evening was a simple pleasure with no unnatural additions.

39

Saturday began urgently. Willan could feel pangs and twinges in his stomach and bowels even before he had risen to an upright position. Fortunately, although early and before sunrise, there was sufficient light to guide his dash to the dressing room. His evacuation was rapid and, as he expected, completely liquid. This draining start to the day compelled Willan to return to his bed to allow his insides to relax and his breathing to recover. A few minutes of half-sitting, half-lying whilst he related his story to God restored his body's balance and he was able to commence the day.

Having toileted and medicated himself and been shaved, he was pleased when Duarte returned with a breakfast of porridge and bread as the day before. He greedily spooned down the oats and then carefully divided his bread so as to make it last throughout the morning if he ate one piece every fifteen minutes; there was sufficient water for one glass per hour. Having spent half an hour sitting on the veranda looking at nothing in particular, he rewarded himself with two pieces of bread and half a glass of water.

Willan thought Bennett slightly subdued at soup time but said nothing of it. Their talk centred around the serving of baked sweet potatoes as an accompaniment in the place of bread. Willan confessed that the change to his breakfast might be the cause of the altered luncheon. Bennett said that he was very fond of porridge and bread and would enquire if he were important enough also to dine upon such a refined meal. Both men found the sweet potatoes to their liking and Bennett headed to the kitchen after they had eaten to pass on their compliments to Dona Esmeralda in Portuguese.

Although he had slept deeply for over an hour after his soup, Willan felt weary even before he started out on his restorative walk. He persevered at a very slow pace and after several pauses reached the first table beyond the hedge; he was exhausted. His head ached and he was forced to close his eyes, so badly was his vision blurred by the sunlight. All the while his shallow breathing raced, and sweat formed on his brow. He rested his head and arms on the table as he sat, hoping against hope for calm and order to be returned. Gradually his breathing slowed and he was able to lift his head and open his eyes. Only then did he realise that Senhor Pompion was lowered to one knee at his side, resting his right hand on his forearm and offering him a handkerchief with his left. Willan took the cloth to his brow and attempted a smile of gratitude, but the dryness of his lips prevented his intention.

Senhor Pompion, sensing a recovery of sorts was beginning, indicated to Willan that he should not attempt to move and he was leaving him, but only briefly. Willan watched as Senhor Pompion travelled almost at a run to the cottages, his stare remaining focussed on the doorway even after Senhor Pompion had entered. He then watched as he returned carrying a pitcher and a mug accompanied by Senhora Pompion, who did not stop at the table but continued through the hedge towards the house.

As he sipped at the water under Senhor Pompion's gaze it was the first time that shared words could have improved the situation, but each man was reasonably confident of the other's thoughts and worries. Willan's gratitude at his friend's assistance and concern outweighed his embarrassment at being such a hindrance; his wet reddened eyes and thin smile showed his humble thankfulness. The silence between the men contained a tension neither had experienced before; contentment had been replaced by awkwardness at not being able to express true concern or true gratitude.

The silence ended with the return of Senhora Pompion accompanied by Duarte. After a quick conversation with Senhor Pompion, Duarte addressed Willan.

"I believe that you have suffered a turn of illness. You are not to be afraid. Senhor Pompion and I will assist you to the house and care for you. Preparations will be made by Dona Esmeralda. We can leave only when you are ready."

Willan nodded his understanding and assent and began to rise from his chair. Duarte and Senhor Pompion placed themselves either side of Willan and bent slightly to enable him to place his arms and weight on their shoulders. They set off at a gentle pace, sidled through the passage in the hedge and were soon at the house. Senhora Pompion had returned to her cottage. Willan climbed the stairs to the colonnade unaided but with Duarte and Senhor Pompion only one step behind and in deep conversation. As Willan stepped onto the colonnade, Senhor Pompion turned and began his return.

"Senhor Pompion wishes you good health and will give you his prayers," said Duarte.

The door to the house opened and Dona Esmeralda came out. She had an unsmiling face of both purpose and concern but gave Willan the tenderest of looks as he passed through to his room. Duarte and Dona Esmeralda followed and guided Willan to one of the two red leather armchairs which were now placed beside the fireplace.

"Dona Esmeralda says you should not speak or exert yourself. We will care for you. I will assist to prepare you for sleep. We will keep a candle and if nobody is on the chair somebody will come soon. Water is by the bed. There can be food later if needed," said Duarte slowly. As he finished speaking, Dona Esmeralda left the room.

Willan had now recovered most of his faculties and looked about the room. "Thank you, Duarte," he said.

Duarte waited outside the dressing room as Willan sat on his pot for a piss, then helped him to undress and put on a clean nightshirt. As the robe unfurled below his knees, he was reminded of his gavotte with Bennett whilst wearing similar dress. Willan insisted upon taking his evening medication before climbing between the fresh linen sheets; he was soon sleeping but with no sound coming from his open mouth. Duarte closed the drapes and sat on one of the leather armchairs.

*

An urge to cough and the driest of mouths caused Willan to waken slowly and, as he raised himself onto his elbows, he saw there was a person sitting on an armchair illuminated by a small oil lamp; it was Jorge. Fortunately, the episode of coughing was not a lengthy rib-rattling, phlegm-producing one but more of a gentle dust remover and call for water. As his chest relaxed, Willan saw Jorge at his side holding a cup and a handkerchief. He declined the cloth but drank all of the water.

"Thank you, Jorge," said Willan. "But why are you here? I am sure I will manage quite well now."

"A person who is unwell should not be left alone," replied Jorge. "Loneliness and neglect do not aid recovery; care and attention are the requirements."

Jorge then spoke gently and without pause, trying to answer Willan's questions in advance of their asking. He explained that Willan had been asleep for some hours and it was now after ten in the evening. He would remain throughout the night regardless of any protests to the contrary; if he were absent it would never be for longer than a few minutes. Duarte had only recently departed for some rest. Willan should not shy away from making any requests and, if he felt hungry, Dona Esmeralda had left a broth of herbs and vegetables which he could heat for him in a short time. A message had been sent to Doctor Gourlay, who would visit in the morning. Willan thanked Jorge with a thin smile, his red lips contrasting with his ashen complexion, shuffled down the bed and returned to sleep.

40

Willan opened his eyes and stared at the ceiling. He remained perfectly still, gradually realising his situation and remembering the incidents of the previous day. He listened for sounds to indicate if he was not alone but heard nothing, so raised himself to enable a view of the room. Duarte stood up from his armchair and came to the bedside.

"Good morning, Doctor Willan. Let me help you. Do you feel well to get up?" he said.

Willan replied that he needed to go to the dressing room and began to move his legs from beneath the sheets. Duarte helped him to his feet and towards his pot. Willan produced a short stream of diarrhoea almost black in colour; he was unsure if the darkness was the result of bleeding. After helping him to wash, Duarte asked if he wished to return to bed and Willan replied that he would like to attempt as normal a day as possible. It was nearly mid-morning by the time Willan was dressed, shaved and eating his porridge; he had insisted on taking his medication despite Duarte's suggestion that he wait until Gourlay's arrival.

The sun was shining brightly although Willan did not feel especially warm. Nonetheless, he donned his coat and sat at the table on the veranda to assist some fresh air through his lungs. He made only a cursory inspection of the ships in the bay, preferring to concentrate his attention on the birds flitting from shrub to bush to tree and wondering why such small creatures devoted so much energy to short bursts of flight, always trilling and chirping their presence.

Gourlay's arrival was a surprise. He entered without exclamation and reached the table on the veranda, unbeknown to Willan. He sat down, asked exactly what had occurred since his last visit and listened attentively as Willan related the facts. As previously, Willan omitted nothing and even showed Gourlay the contents of his pot which he had asked not to be sluiced until after the doctor's visit; Gourlay opined that the slurry was indeed darkened by blood. They continued their consultation in the room sitting by the fireplace.

Gourlay delivered his prognosis: he was disappointed at Willan's current state of health but considered that the planned strong treatment could yet be effective. He believed Willan's system was now purged and perhaps a little over so. He recommended the calomel be stopped to allow a recovery and sedation of the body, at which point a strong, also mercury-based medicine could be administered to fight the stormy inflammation within the lungs; he would research the most suitable medication. Continuing to take laudanum as and when required would induce relaxation, limit episodes of cough and speed up his initial recovery.

The two doctors discussed the proposed treatment thoroughly. Willan, although he could not offer any alternative to the plan, still needed to satisfy himself of the wisdom of Gourlay's intention. Only when both men were content with the other's thoughts and reasonings did the consultation end; Gourlay would return with a choice of new, fully researched medications on Tuesday. In the meantime, Willan was to rest and continue with his laudanum. Gourlay added that he was only a short ride away and a messenger could be sent for him at any time of the day or night. The men shook hands and Gourlay departed.

No sooner had the door closed behind Gourlay than Duarte appeared. He informed Willan that the temperature at the til tree was seventy degrees, and asked if he would care for some 'soup of vegetables and additions, in about twenty minutes'. Willan replied that indeed he was a little hungry and it would suit him very well.

Returning to the veranda, Willan began to tell God of his situation, hoping for guidance and confirmation of the sense of the decisions. However, his thoughts wavered from their usual logical order and he found himself repeating the hope that he would recover, and seeking God's assistance if possible. Ashamed, he apologised to God and turned his attention to the chirping birds by way of distraction from his selfish entreaties.

Hearing Duarte's voice, Willan returned to the room and swallowed two spoonsful of laudanum before struggling to eat less than half of his bowl of soup; he ate no bread. Very tired, he told Duarte he would take a short rest on his bed but readily accepted his advice that he would rest better undressed and beneath his sheet. Comforted by the soft, clean nightshirt, he was soon asleep.

Willan next woke in near darkness. As he raised himself he saw the glow of a lamp from a small table beside the armchairs; the identity of the chair's occupant could not be ascertained in the faint light. He felt the urge to cough and grabbed a handkerchief from beside the bed just in time to catch a mouthful of phlegm and blood; there was a slight spatter to his sheet and nightshirt. Jorge was now at his side and supported Willan in a sitting position as he finished his retching expectoration then rested back on the pillows, breathing slowly. Jorge replaced the handkerchief and sat quietly next to the bed; he did not speak at first.

After several minutes, Jorge rose, lit several lamps and asked how he could help. Willan replied that he needed to go to the dressing room to tidy himself. Jorge assisted him and listened as Willan vomited and then pissed into his pot. Jorge helped Willan wash and clean himself and change his nightshirt; he then led him to an armchair to sit whilst he changed the upper sheet and blanket on the bed. Willan thanked him for his care and apologised for his unseemly demeanour, to which Jorge replied that he could repay all of his transgressions, if any, when he was returned to good health.

Jorge asked if Willan was hungry as he could easily fetch food. Willan replied he had no desire to eat but would take a large dose of laudanum and drink some water; he was very tired, and rest and sedation offered him the best prospects of recovery.

Willan devoted himself to resting for the remainder of Sunday night and throughout Monday. He was too tired to dress and only left his bed when called by his pot. He drank a little soup, a little water and a bottle and a half of laudanum. He was never left alone but maintained barely any conversation; all his energies were needed to rest and restore his body's functions.

41

Tuesday's sun rose brighter than any sun so far that year although, still being early in the morning, the air remained fresh; the deeper heat would coat the land and the buildings later. Willan was awake, propped on his pillows and looking forward. His gaze, even when his eyes were open, was distanced and un-focussed. Jorge, who had acted as sentinel throughout the night, had been joined by Duarte, and together they arranged cloths, towels, bedding and the like.

Finished with their initial arrangements, Jorge and Duarte eased Willan from his bed; fortunately, he responded to their guidance and nudges. They lowered his brittle body onto the pot and as soon as his yellow-grey skin touched the cold smoothness of the china he spattered out his air and slurry. Then, satisfied that Willan would not fall, Duarte cleaned and washed him whilst Jorge changed the bedding. Together they dressed him in a freshly laundered nightshirt before returning him to sit on the edge of his bed. He was shaved, his hair brushed and he was placed back gently beneath his sheet and blanket. Willan's face had shown no expression or emotion throughout the proceedings and no words had been spoken; his lips had parted only to allow the intake of two spoonsful of laudanum.

213

The day continued. Jorge departed to rest and Duarte assumed his position nearby the fireplace. Willan maintained his steadfast forward gaze. There was no sound whatsoever until some thirty minutes later when the door opened and Senhor Pompion entered. He spoke quietly to Duarte, who then left the room, perhaps a little reluctantly.

Senhor Pompion un-shuttered and opened all three windows and drew back the drapes; sun and a light breeze flooded the room, brightening everything, including Willan's ashen features. Standing beside the bed, he unwrapped an embroidered cloth, revealing a green, shiny, perfectly dimpled anona. He swiftly cut the fruit in half with the folded blade he always kept in his jerkin and scooped a small amount of the velvety, custard-like pulp onto a silver spoon he had also retrieved from his pocket. Willan's mouth opened very slightly as the spoon touched his lips and he swallowed the fruit. Senhor Pompion repeated the action before re-uniting the halves of the anona and wrapping them and the spoon in the cloth; he had already returned his blade to his pocket. There was the faintest change to Willan's countenance, almost a smile.

Having carefully placed his parcel on the foot of the bed, Senhor Pompion turned the bedside chair to face the window and sat alongside his friend as he had done so many times, the opened windows allowing the inflow of the natural world beyond; neither man stirred nor spoke.

After perhaps ten minutes, Senhor Pompion rose to his feet, collected his parcel from the foot of the bed and walked to the fireplace, where he removed from the mantle his grandson's painting of the two men. He rolled the picture carefully and carried it with him as he left the room. He did not glance once at his friend. As he left, he nodded to Bennett, who was outside the door with Jorge and Duarte.

Senhor Pompion returned purposefully to the first cottage. Wiping his eyes as they adjusted to the darker light inside, he went to a window at the rear of the cottage. He placed the picture against the glass and the anona on the already cleared shelf. Using the silver spoon, Senhor Pompion carefully selected and removed six of the black round seeds from within the fruit, carefully checked they were perfect and placed them in a straight line on the shelf; they would be planted next season. Raising an imaginary glass to the window, Senhor Pompion saluted his friend, mouthing the single word 'manga'.

*

As Senhor Pompion left the room, his place next to Willan was taken by Bennett, who turned the chair back to face the bed. As Willan's arm was resting above the blanket, Bennett placed his own hand on that of his friend. No words were spoken.

Willan's memory was returned to the place of his youth. He was walking towards Sedbergh, staring towards the bright sun above the terraced hills beyond the town. The fields to his sides contained row after row of banana plants; he could smell the fruits and the warm soil. He could feel the pull of the sun.

Bennett felt the hand beneath his own tighten and watched as Willan moved his head towards the sun-filled window. Willan opened and closed his eyes before resting back on the pillow.

Doctor Robert Willan was at peace. At peace like a child cradled in its mother's arms. At peace as an adult in the arms of his God.

AFTERWORD

Robert Willan's tombstone in the British Cemetery, Funchal, reads:

SACRED TO THE MEMORY
OF
ROBERT WILLAN. M.D.F.R.S.
OF LONDON
WHO DIED IN THIS ISLAND 7TH
APRIL 1812 AGED 53 YEARS

NEAR THE SAME SPOT ARE
DEPOSITED THE REMAINS
OF HIS FRIEND
THOMAS BENNETT SMITH
JVNIOR
WHO DIED HERE JUNE 1812
AGED 28 YEARS

Ashby Smith graduated doctor of medicine at Edinburgh 1st August 1820.

Robert Willan's entry in the Sedbergh School Register states:

'He was a model of the perfect human character.'

'The best and noblest of mankind.'